DEATH OF A CAR SALESMAN

COLLIN BRANTMEYER

Copyright © 2020 by Collin Brantmeyer

All rights reserved. Published in the United States by Ready Demolition Books.

www.readydemolitionbooks.com

Book design by Asya Blue
Cover design by Alexandria Manson
Edited by Chris Thomas

Library of Congress Control Number: 2020941056

ISBN: 978-1-7352599-0-1 (hardcover)
ISBN: 978-1-7352599-1-8 (paperback)
ISBN: 978-1-7352599-2-5 (ebook)

First Edition

For Jaime

CONTENTS

CONTENTS

THE CAR SALESMAN

1

THE CAR SALESMAN

Big Al Washington

It will get better. It always works out in the end.

Those were the words that echoed in Big Al Washington's mind as he took a morning drive toward his flagship car dealership just a few miles outside of Charlotte, North Carolina. He had been in the car business for nearly half a century, but he had never seen anything like the current economic climate. For the first time in his career, the sellers outnumbered the buyers, and by a wide margin at that. He wasn't entirely confident they could turn it around this time. Perhaps if he were younger, he'd have the resolve. But his bones ached now, and it seemed like he could hardly work for ten minutes without having to take a piss break.

A glance in the rearview mirror was depressing. He sat up a little straighter, as if it would help. Big Al Washington: The man who can sell anyone anything, he attempted to reassure himself. Lately, though, just the thought of his nickname made him wince. It had become a persistent reminder of better days, both professional and personal.

This morning, he debated whether his grandson Luke would be able to steer the dealership through these unprecedented times. Even though Luke was affable and well-educated – schooling for which Big Al had paid handsomely – the kid wasn't much of a salesman. Privately, Big Al had often described Luke thusly: "He's about as charismatic as a day-old loaf of white bread."

Nonetheless, Luke was Big Al's only male kin. In the elder Washington's misogynistic mind, there wasn't much choice in the matter. So, after months of stalling that had become increasingly difficult to explain to his family and financial advisers, Big Al reluctantly planned the first step in officially handing the dealership over to Luke. They'd be filming an expensive TV commercial, announcing the changing of the guard.

3

"What's going on in there, sweetie?" Big Al's latest wife, Eva, tapped the side of his head,   snatching him right off his train of thought. It was just as well.

About a decade ago, they'd met at a charity concert where Eva happened to be the opening act for The Refugees, a local Tom Petty cover band. A native of Iceland, Eva struggled with her grasp of the American accent but could mimic most singers, and in perfect pitch. Her rendition of "I Wanna Be Loved by You" – made famous by Marilyn Monroe in the movie *Some Like It Hot* – was all it took to turn Big Al's head. They married six months later.

Despite an age gap of nearly forty years, Big Al was utterly convinced that Eva was after his heart, not his net worth – which happened to be just north of $212 million at the previous day's market close.

"Nothing much. I just need to stop by and make sure Luke doesn't fuck up the commercial."

Eva scowled.

"But Al – you promised! How long is this going to take?"

"Don't worry. We won't be late for the appointment."

It was clear she didn't believe him. So, Big Al paused, took his eyes off the road just long enough to meet her stern gaze directly, grinned and repeated the one mantra that had served him well over his long life.

"I guarantee it."

She sighed in wordless agreement. Even at eighty-five, Big Al still had it – the charm, the infectious smile. He couldn't have sold more than one million cars without that rare gift for saying just what a person needed to hear. Sometimes, he even meant it.

As they approached the dealership, Big Al admired the fifty-foot digital billboard that proclaimed WASHINGTON FORD. God, how he loved that billboard, far and away the biggest on Independence Boulevard, an arterial thoroughfare lined with every major car dealership in the Charlotte metro area.

The fact that he'd pretty much swindled the City of Charlotte to pay for what most residents would classify as an eyesore tickled Big Al to death. Ever the opportunist, he had made a hat-in-hand appearance before the City Council during the last economic downturn, confiding that he was considering pulling up stakes and finding a more affordable location. They happily handed him what amounted to $600,000 to stay rather than risk losing fifty jobs on their watch.

In reality, Big Al had no intention of leaving – but in an election year, he couldn't resist gigging them and in exchange, they paid for the giant, state-of-the-art digital billboard without too much of a fight. Big Al only had to agree to put the city's name on it somewhere, so the city could write it off as a tourism expense. He made sure that the "Charlotte, NC" was at the very bottom of the billboard, and in an almost illegible font size.

Paying no mind to his designated parking place, he pulled into the dealership lot in his new Ford Expedition and threw it into 'park' right up front, in the well-manicured driveway that led to the main entrance. In forty-six years as the owner of Washington Ford, not once had Big Al ever actually owned a vehicle. Why buy one, he thought, when I can take home a different shiny toy every night?

People who had grown up watching him on TV were always surprised to learn that Big Al had never been a car guy, but he believed this gave him an advantage over his competitors. The average person didn't care about lofty car performance claims or engine terms they didn't understand. Instead of intimidating the customer, Big Al told his salespeople, they should always hone in on, and sell to, that customer's needs.

"A mother doesn't care how fast her Ford Explorer can go from zero to sixty," he'd say, "but she does want to know how safe it is for her children."

As he eased himself out of the driver's seat, the loitering salespeople caught sight of Big Al's lanky frame and famous cowboy getup and quickly began to scatter.

Maybe not quickly enough.

"Get those damn lawn chairs out of my sight!" He slammed the Expedition door.

One brave salesman collected several of the mismatched chairs, avoiding eye contact with the boss in the process.

Big Al plopped his trusty cowboy hat onto his head and headed around to the passenger side of the truck, signaling with a palm out to Eva that he'd be back in five minutes.

With an irritated sense of urgency, he pulled open the large, custom-engraved glass door to enter the climate-controlled headquarters of Washington Ford. The structure measured 5,000 square feet and had been expensively remodeled on three occasions in the past five decades. He strode past a few offices, a conference room and a break room, and entered the main showroom.

It was a well-lit space, with thirty-foot ceilings and marble tile. A dozen open-concept sales desks – an area known as the bullpen – sat to one side of the showroom, which was otherwise jammed with gleaming Ford cars and trucks. Today, a TV production crew was setting up light stands and camera equipment near the reception desk.

Luke was nowhere to be seen. Big Al glanced toward Brenda, his longtime executive assistant, who knew exactly what he was thinking and gave him an animated shrug before turning away and pretending to be busy. So, Big Al aimed his ire at the person who appeared to be in charge of the ragtag TV production crew.

"What are you doing in here? We need exterior shots! I want to see each and every one of my damn cars in these ads, not just the few sitting in here. You understand?"

The woman directing the commercial approached him, opened her mouth to respond. He cut her off.

"Get...out...of...my...showroom. Now!"

"Sir, Mr. Washington told us to set up inside and..."

"Don't you know who I am?"

"Yes, but Mr. Washington said..."

"I AM MR. WASHINGTON! Look around!" Big Al pointed to the massive interior wall of the showroom, on which the commercials he'd made over the years were projected in a video loop of greatest hits. A much younger Big Al could be seen walking through his car lot, clad in the same signature Western wear and holding a monkey's hand.

"It's my face up there! And on that poster! And that sign!"

On the vintage commercial, the announcer was saying brightly, "Here's Big Al Washington – and his dog, Teddy!" For years, Big Al's marketing gimmick was that, if he was too dumb to realize his "dog" wasn't an actual dog, then how could he be smart enough to pull a fast one on car buyers? The reliable schtick was used over and over for years – with a pig, an elephant, a miniature horse, even a tiger playing the role of Teddy.

A popular children's jingle – "If You're Happy and You Know It" – accompanied the ads, with Big Al's lyric changes: "If you want more for your trade, go see Al! For the lowest money down, go see Al!" And in every commercial, the camera panned row after row of vehicles, with their sticker prices plainly visible. "Go see Al, go see Al, go see Al!"

Most importantly, the cars were filmed right on the lot – not driving on some scenic mountain roadway, and sure as hell not sitting in a showroom. The whole idea was to assure people that they could come to Washington Ford, peruse the impressive inventory and drive away on something that day. Something for everyone, with any budget.

Big Al felt his face redden. "My grandson doesn't know jack shit," he told the director. "Now, go outside and set up a proper shot or you're fired. Do you understand?"

"Yes, sir."

The director silently motioned to her crew members, who had been stunned into stone-faced inaction by Big Al's tirade, to pack up the gear and move outside. As they hustled to break down the equipment, Larry Bridges – Washington Ford's senior counsel – appeared in the showroom as if out of nowhere. His expensive suit branded him more than slightly out of place.

Larry ran his hands over a head of thinning grey hair, and spoke quietly.

"We have a problem."

"I would say so, Larry. Where the hell is Luke?"

"It's the finance officer. He's been embezzling money."

"Who, Chad?"

"He's been skimming off the top for years."

"How much?"

"Hundreds of thousands. Maybe more."

Even the attorney's soothing voice and calm demeanor couldn't keep Big Al's blood pressure from spiking. He suddenly felt dizzy. Larry must have noticed, as he reached an arm out. Big Al swiped it away.

"I'm fine. And Luke?"

Just then, a bloodcurdling scream penetrated the showroom. Both men's eyes widened as Big Al realized precisely where Luke was and what he was doing. The production crew members stopped in their tracks, eyeing each other nervously as if to confirm what they just heard. Before anyone could panic, Larry rushed over to escort them into the conference room. There, he would undoubtedly offer them enough money to cause their collective memory to fail and their tongues to go silent, and they would accept it. Larry had become quite proficient at these arrangements over the years.

Big Al, standing alone in the middle of his showroom, reached into an inner jacket pocket for his trusty flask, unscrewed the cap, and took a swig of its contents. Pausing a moment to regain his composure, he let out a deep sigh. He returned his crutch to his jacket, planted his right foot in front of his left, and walked as fast as his achy body would allow him toward the source of the scream.

Now in the hallway, Big Al approached his windowless office nestled at the back of the dealership. Even though he planned to turn over the business to Luke, Big Al had decided he would never give up his office; it meant too much to him. He yanked at the golden handle, but it didn't budge. Unwilling to dig through his pockets for his keycard, Big Al resorted to yelling out his demand.

"Open the door dammit, it's me."

He surveyed the hallway as he waited for the door to open. Finally, Luke peeked his head out, careful not to completely open the door to prevent any onlookers from glimpsing something they shouldn't see. Annoyed with the charade, Big Al threw his right hand up to push the door open. Inside his office, Big Al found Chad lying on the outdated carpet in the middle of the room, beaten to a bloody pulp. He saw Mark Crawford, a floor manager and Luke's friend, standing in the corner by the desk. Mark, uncomfortable with Big Al's silence, broke it by babbling about Chad's long list of misdeeds, but Big Al turned his attention to Luke, who wore a cowboy getup very similar to his own.

He noticed that Luke's knuckles were bruised and there were fresh bloodstains on his white dress shirt.

"What have you done?" Big Al asked, shaking his head.

"What have *I* done? Why don't you ask Chad what *he* did?"

"Listen, Luke, I know what Chad did. But that doesn't mean you can just beat the living shit out of him. The face of the company doesn't get his hands dirty."

"But Grandpa, he stole hundreds of thousands of dollars. He can't get away with that!"

Big Al slowly moved closer to Chad to inspect his condition more thoroughly, taking extreme precautions not to step in the blood pooling on the carpet with his cowboy boots. He knelt, as best as he could for an exasperated eighty-five-year-old, to discover Chad's face was nearly unrecognizable – oozing pus, swelling bruises, and open gashes. And yet, Chad was somehow still breathing. Contemplating his best course of action, Big Al glanced up to see blood had spattered on a framed portrait of himself. He was twenty years younger and in a perfectly fitted grey, western-cut suit, with his arms outstretched as TV cameras filmed in the foreground and dozens of cars filled the background. Big Al swiveled his head to take in the entirety of his office, and appreciate the nearly half-century worth of photos and awards he had collected in his career. A few years ago, he had to start putting them in a storage locker because he'd run out of space in his office.

He exhaled deeply and shook his head in disbelief, knowing full well that his entire legacy could be ruined because of Luke's hot-headed actions that morning.

"Now listen to me, Luke. You need to go home now. Don't worry about the commercial."

"The commercial? This man stole from us, and you're worried about a commercial?"

"See, Luke, this is exactly why you'll never make it. A true leader is proactive, not reactive. You have zero vision, boy. I'm pulling the plug on your big promotion. It's over."

"What? I did this for you. I do everything for you."

"Just go home. I'll have Larry fix it."

With that, Big Al turned his back on Luke and exited the office. In the hallway, Big Al felt a sharp pain in his chest, and grimaced as he attempted to catch his balance. His stumble inadvertently knocked a framed photo off the wall; it was the one of him riding a killer whale at SeaWorld, who doubled as his "dog" Teddy for one of his more popular commercials. But paralyzed by the pain, Big Al didn't even seem to notice the sound of the picture crashing to the floor, or the glass shattering.

Now standing awkwardly against the wall, Big Al closed his eyes and inhaled through his nose to calm his nerves. Instead of a morning spent proudly watching his grandson film a commercial to usher in a new era,

Big Al had to deal with a dying man in his office, a production crew that had heard too much, and the prospect of finding a new successor for his legacy. Just then, Big Al's eyes flared open as if he had received a shot of adrenaline. When he regained his composure, he straightened his bolo tie and set off again toward the main showroom. There, he was immediately intercepted by Larry, who gently held his boss by the arm and escorted him safely outside.

"Are you okay, boss? You don't look so hot."

"I'm fine. Did you take care of the production crew?"

"Of course. And they are setting up the exterior shot as we speak."

"This was supposed to be a monumental day, Larry. Now, look at it."

"I'll clean it up. You and Eva should get out of here."

"Not yet. Luke is a complete disaster. He can't take over for me, Larry. I'm going to shoot the commercial myself."

"Are you sure, boss? I can reschedule."

"I'm sure. It's like riding a bike – or selling a car in my case. You just take care of the Chad situation."

A glint came to Larry's eye as he silently strategized and quickly formulated a plan for what to do with Chad. After confirming again that Big Al felt well enough to continue, Larry darted away to the back office rather than bother Big Al with the details. Even in a moment of chaos, Big Al stopped for a moment to appreciate Larry's unwavering loyalty.

Walking out of the showroom, Big Al felt a rush of blinding light penetrating his cataracts. He squinted to avoid the sunlight, catching a glimpse of his impatient wife sticking her head out the passenger window just fifteen yards in front of him.

Knowing full well he was in for an argument that he'd be too exhausted to take on, he scanned the parking lot for a way out. To his right, he found Madison, the receptionist a few years removed from college, taking a smoke break. Typically, Big Al would chew her out for smoking, since the act repulsed him. But he also knew that Eva would never publicly throw a tantrum as long as other people were nearby.

"Madison."

"Shit. I'm sorry, Mr. Washington; I just needed a smoke."

"No, no. Don't you worry about that. Look, I need a favor. I need you to distract my wife for the next fifteen or twenty minutes. You think you can do that?"

She shrugged. "You're the boss; I'm not sure I have a choice."

"Thatta girl."

To seal the deal, Big Al removed a crisp one-hundred-dollar bill from his pocket and shoved it into Madison's hand. He didn't dare look in Eva's direction, as Madison trudged over to the Explorer and attempted to make small talk, even though the receptionist and the trophy wife had absolutely nothing in common. And, just as he suspected, Eva's look of utter dismay quickly dissolved when Madison offered her a friendly greeting.

With what precious little time he had, Big Al skipped toward the rows of cars, hoping that the production crew had enough time to set up the shot. It was a peculiar sight; Big Al's head bobbing up and down in the never-ending rows of cars searching for the crew. He eventually discovered them lounging under the shade provided by the billboard at the far end of the lot.

"All right! Let's shoot this thing!" Big Al shouted.

"What about the other guy?"

"He's out. It's just me now. Are you ready?"

The director shrugged her shoulders and signaled to her crew to get the camera rolling, as if to say, 'Whatever it takes to finish the shoot from Hell as soon as possible.' Big Al dismissed the makeup artist's attempt to freshen up his face. After a minute of prepping the camera, the operator signaled that he was ready to shoot, prompting the director to yell, "Action!"

"Hey friends, Big Al here! We've got acres and acres and acres, row after row after row of cars and trucks on sale at Washington Ford."

Big Al made a sweeping motion to the cars directly behind him.

"Here's a beautiful Ford Fusion, and here's a top safety rated Ford Escape. Drive it home today with zero money down!"

As Big Al glanced toward the inventory, he discovered that the cars in the shot didn't have sticker prices on them.

"Son of a bitch! Where are the prices?"

"That's a cut. Who has eyes on the sticker prices?"

"Forget it. Just take them from other cars. I don't give a shit."

"Copy that."

A lowly production assistant corralled about ten giant green stickers with different prices on them. Years ago, every single car and truck in Big Al's lot would be guaranteed to display the correct sticker price. Nowadays, the stickers appeared sparsely throughout the lot, assigned to a given vehicle with no apparent rhyme or reason. Out of frustration, Big Al snatched the stack of stickers from the production assistant, quickly sorting through them to find a price that was close enough for each car in the shot.

"Picture's up!"

"And action."

Big Al held up a finger. "Wait a damn minute. I'm not ready yet."

"No worries. Take your time. Whenever you're ready, Mr. Washington."

Big Al shook his head in disbelief, but he was a true professional and had overcome worse shoots before. At least I don't have a snake trying to strangle me this time, he thought. Big Al got into position, took a deep breath, and looked directly into the camera.

"Hey friends, Big Al here, we got rows after acres. No, that's not right."

"No worries. We're still rolling. Go ahead."

"Hey friends, Big Al here, we got acres and acres and acres, rows after rows after rows of Ford trucks and cars."

Just then, Big Al felt a shortness of breath. The morning breeze had vanished, and without a cloud in the sky, the sun seemed relentless. But he felt compelled to continue.

"I ain't going no place, hell, I've been here for forty-six years, so come on down and tell them…tell them Big Al sent you. "

"And cut. Are you feeling all right, Mr. Washington?"

"Yeah, I'm fine. I could use some water, that's all. This damn heatwave is getting to me."

"Can somebody get Mr. Washington some water?"

Big Al opened the door to the nearest car, which happened to be a Ford Escape, and ducked into the driver's seat to catch his breath. A minute or two later, the same production assistant who had hand-delivered the price stickers handed him a bottle of water that had been sitting out in the sun for God knows how long. Big Al took a swig, scowling at the unrefreshing temperature before discarding it under the driver's seat.

Breathing heavily, he loosened his bolo tie and removed his cowboy hat from his head to collect a trail of sweat beneath his thinning hairline. Finally, he stood, unbuttoned the top of his shirt and returned his hat to its rightful home.

"All right. Third time's a charm."

"You heard the man. Roll camera. Roll sound."

"Camera speeds."

"Sound speeds."

The production assistant struck the clapperboard as Big Al stumbled to his mark.

"Washington Ford, take three."

"Whenever you're ready, Mr. Washington."

Big Al paused for a second to admire his lot. Even though it was in some disarray, he was genuinely proud of it. With another deep breath, a thought entered his mind. *It will get better. It always works out in the end.* Big Al grinned at the mantra that he had lived by throughout his career, and fixed his gaze on the camera lens.

"Hey friends, Big Al here and boy, do I have a deal for you..."

At that exact moment, he experienced an agonizing jolt, a pain so violent that it sent shockwaves through his entire body. His towering frame bent at the knees and descended to the unforgiving pavement. Just as he landed, Big Al's head whipped back, striking the hard surface, which caused a stream of blood to gush from his skull.

Big Al Washington died at 11:26 a.m. on July 3, 2028.

THE RENDEZVOUS
IN THE QUEEN CITY

II

THE RENDEZVOUS
IN THE QUEEN CITY

Alice Washington

It was a strange feeling, going back home. For most people, home is their primary identifier, the answer to the single most-asked question when you first meet someone: "So, where are you from?" My working theory is that people ask that question so they can put you into a box that makes sense for them. To the small-minded, for instance, everyone from New York might as well be loud, in your face, and root for the Yankees. *People need their boxes – and you'd better fit into one, or they don't know what to do with you.*

Sitting at the airport bar, I contemplated the gamut of scenarios before formulating my response. My top choice was to ignore the middle-aged man adjacent. Still, I decided tempered politeness would extricate me from the conversation the quickest, with the added benefit of preventing a confrontation.

"Charlotte."

"So, where are you flying to, then?"

"Charlotte. Just got in."

"What are you doing at the bar? The exit is right over there."

The stranger chuckled to himself before taking another swig of his drink.

"I'm not in much of a hurry."

"Charlotte, huh? The city of transplants? You must be the only person actually from here."

"Something like that."

He seemed to have taken the hint, since he abruptly stopped asking questions, but I could tell he was debating whether to say anything more, swirling his drink on the bar's well-worn wooden surface. The ice cubes eddied in the gin and tonic with that perfect clanking sound. My throat felt dry as I pondered my own drink – a lukewarm cup of subpar decaf coffee. I considered swiping through the alcoholic options at my drink station but thought better of it.

My chance convive tilted his glass at a ninety-degree angle and downed the rest of his gin and tonic. In what I believed to be an act of passive aggression, he set his glass on the bar a little too firmly, smacked his gums together and departed for the gate, glaring at me all the while. It must have been a stiff drink – or for him, anyway.

The real question, in fact, the only question people should ask is, "How did you get here?" That question elicits a far more interesting response.

At that point, the news of Big Al's death had spread to media outlets across the country. I noticed the local CBS affiliate, WBTV, was running a special segment about Big Al on one of the TV screens mounted above the bar. I glanced down the length of the bar to see if anyone was watching. They weren't; people were either glued to their phones or checking out the array of baseball games on the other TVs.

The closed captioning allowed me to get a sense of the mood, as the female field reporter stood dutifully, mic in hand, in front of that all-too-familiar car dealership. She was lauding him as the "legendary, wacky car salesman," famous for his over-the-top late-night TV ads, who had sold more than one million cars across the country during his lifetime. The segment then cut to quick, reaction-style interviews of a few locals, all of whom testified to Big Al being a "great guy." It had always astounded me that the public held Big Al in such high regard, never seeming to realize that he made millions upon millions of dollars off them. The news segment ended with a soundbite from my dopey nephew, Luke Washington, in a Halloweenish cowboy costume, mentioning that he would be "carrying on Big Al's legacy" as the new owner and general manager of Washington Ford. This was followed by that awkward pause, ubiquitous in local newscasts, when the reporter "live on the scene," isn't sure whether the video is finished or quite how to sign off and send it "back to Paul and Maureen in the studio."

Unable to endure the newsroom banter about Big Al as an "institution in the city" or the "king of late-night advertising," or whatever platitudes the anchor team could muster, I took one last sip of my uninspiring coffee, gathered my belongings and headed to baggage claim. What I really wondered was why the media continued to give Big Al's misdeeds a pass, even in death. In this particular story, there hadn't been a single mention of the messy affairs, the numerous lawsuits, the fraud allegations. I wasn't surprised, merely disappointed.

No one in my family had the decency to call me, so Larry had been assigned the task. Larry – a.k.a. Larry the Lion – was Big Al's right-hand man for nearly forty years. He always referred to himself as the "Black Tom Hagen," a reference to Robert Duvall's character from *The Godfather* – never officially adopted, but arguably held in higher esteem than the biological Corleone children. Every Thanksgiving, Big Al would retell the story of the day he "found Larry." It went something like this: Larry, accompanied by his mother, went shopping for a used car shortly after graduation from law school. By sheer coincidence, Big Al needed a lawyer to handle his ever-expanding business, and he offered Larry the job, right then and there. He even threw in a gently used Ford Mercury for good measure, albeit with a few bumps and scrapes (cue the big laughs from around the dining table). Personally, I found it more nauseating than those "how they met" couple stories.

For some unknown reason, Larry had told me not to book a return flight just yet. When I pressed him, he muttered that he would talk to me in person "regarding the matter." *Tell me in person?* Was Larry paranoid enough to think someone was listening to the conversation? Or maybe he thought I wouldn't be able to process the news?

Now outside the terminal, on the curb with my roller bag, the North Carolina humidity immediately stifled my senses. One by one, people got into self-driving cars, scanning their phone on the passenger door just beneath the handle. By the time I'd reached the front of the line, I had programmed my destination into the app. When the car stopped in front of me, I held my phone under the barcode scanner, and voilà, I was good to go. It wasn't difficult to see why Washington Ford had been struggling, I thought as I tossed my bags into the seat and climbed in after them. People in cities don't need cars anymore, now that it's become cheaper, more efficient, and safer to be driven around by a computer. *Or who knows – maybe Big Al is right, and it's just a phase?*

I once heard someone describe Charlotte as "the city that always sleeps," and it is mostly true. The city had never had much of a nightlife, since its citizens were tucked away in their suburban homes by seven o'clock. So, the traffic was light as the car made its way around I-485, a seventy-mile loop that circles the city. The infamous highway took nearly thirty years to complete, and shortly after the project finally finished, the city realized it didn't have enough lanes to adequately serve the growing population. An expansion project was outsourced, which resulted in a toll lane. And when that finally wrapped up, autonomous cars were being rolled out and traffic had subsided. The whole process exemplifies Charlotte in a nutshell; never-ending sprawl managed by ineffective leadership.

Larry put me up in a Marriott Courtyard right across the street from a bar, with a flashing 'TOPLESS' sign in red neon. I figured that he didn't want me anywhere near the W. Ranch, Big Al's thousand-acre property on the outskirts of south Charlotte, but I expected something slightly more upscale than a hotel that shared an exit with a strip club.

The hotel's automatic doors opened as I approached and made my way to the check-in counter, where the front desk person appeared to be missing. *Perhaps, they went home for the night?* I checked my phone; it was only 9 p.m. *Maybe hiding in the back room?* I rang the desk bell, but it was a monitor that rose in response, slowly, from beneath the granite countertop. It greeted me with a soothing female voice.

"Hello. Are you checking in?"

"Uh, yes. The reservation is under Washington."

"Terrific. Thank you, Miss Washington. How many keys would you like for your stay?"

"Just one."

After placing my fingerprint on the directed spot, the monitor spat out a keycard along with a printed guide to the layout and amenities of the hotel. I remembered reading about a few hotel chains laying off massive numbers of their guest-facing employees, but I hadn't seen it in person, since technology was always slow to reach Alaska.

"I hope you enjoy your stay with us, and don't forget to take a cookie."

Sure enough, a transparent jar of double chocolate chip cookies appeared through another retractable surface on the countertop. *Do I really trust this cookie? Who could have even made it, and when?* I grabbed two. Still warm. After the first bite, I could confidently call it the best cookie I have ever had.

The room was fairly standard: queen-size bed, desk, office chair, and a mini-fridge. I tossed my bags on the bed. It was a little concerning that the mattress didn't give an inch despite fifty pounds of clothes and shoes testing its durability. I placed both hands on the edge of the bed and pushed down with my full body weight. The mattress still didn't budge. As I unpacked a few things, I couldn't help but notice a persistent, low-frequency hum in the room. Of course – the mini-fridge, its silver key suspended from the lock, taunting me. Daring me to open it. *It's okay if you have one drink. Your father just died. You need to grieve, even if he was a bonafide asshole.*

The blast of chilled air from the fridge was more than welcome on a balmy summer's evening. Inside, there was an assortment of sodas, bottled water, a few snacks – but no alcohol in sight. Atop the fridge, I found a placard that listed the prices of each item. Sure enough, in bold font, it read, "Non-alcoholic Room." *Thanks, Larry, for looking out for me. You prick.*

Realistically, I could have walked across the street to the topless bar to score some oxy or at the very least, a drink, but I figured I would rather be sober than play the 'Who is More Depressing?' game – the single mother of two, trying to make a living, or a forty-year old dirtbag who told his wife he was working late? I'd rather not run into either of them.

So instead, I turned on the TV and took every single item out of the mini-bar, knowing full well that Larry would have to foot the bill. After eating enough chocolate to make my stomach turn, I fell asleep to a local "Breaking News!" report that Charlotte police were investigating the death of Big Al Washington as a possible homicide.

Luke Washington

It was a lot quieter than I had imagined in my head: no extended family, no balloons, and no giant scissors to cut a ribbon like you see at those construction ground-breaking sites. The attendance at the modest ceremony included Lauren, my mom, Larry, and some salespeople. I kept my eyes peeled for a professional photographer, but never saw one. At least my mom took a few photos with her phone. *I'll have to ask for them so I can post them on Instagram and maybe get one framed for the office, too.*

Larry told me that I was officially the youngest car dealership owner in Charlotte, maybe ever? Earlier that morning, he'd been pressing me about expanding our business to sell autonomous cars. Knowing full well how Grandpa felt about them, I quickly dismissed the idea. I was annoyed with Larry but tried not to show it as I struggled to get a read on him, especially not knowing whether he was privy to the conversation between Grandpa and me right before he died. I mean, with my entire future at stake, how could I not be paranoid? *If Grandpa had let Larry in on his knee-jerk decision to go in another direction for his replacement, then Larry is either acting against Grandpa's wishes or actively plotting against me. Assuming Grandpa didn't have time to change his will between our talk and his death, it may not matter. Either way, I'm not going to let Larry take this from me. People might say it's undeserved – a twenty five-year-old, a couple of years removed from a bachelor's degree, running what was once the second-biggest car dealership network in the country. But, you don't build an empire to turn it over to some stranger. You pass it down through the family so your legacy endures. And there was no way Grandpa was going to give it to Alice, the family fuck-up, so it was only right that I take the reins.*

Just as I cut into my single-tier store-bought chocolate cake, complete with a Ford F-150 crudely fashioned in buttercream frosting, a news van pulled into the lot. Larry told me to wait inside Grandpa's office while he escorted my mom to her car and dealt with, as he put it, "the vultures." I grabbed a corner piece anyway, balancing it on my plate through the showroom, past the floor models, through the back hallway, and then into my new office.

Ever since I was a kid, if I was left alone in someone else's space, I took the opportunity to snoop. Whether it was someone's phone carelessly left unattended, a desk drawer, or an employee's search history. *You can learn a lot about someone by going through their stuff. More importantly, it's a hell of a lot harder for them to make a fool out of you when you know a secret about them.* And I've got dirt on just about everybody at Washington Ford. Take Grandpa's longtime executive assistant, Brenda, who just found out she had breast cancer. I went through her search history to find dozens of searches related to cancer: "living with stage IV cancer," "how to tell your family about a cancer diagnosis," and even, "dying with dignity from cancer." That was months ago, and she still hadn't told a soul, which was precisely how I knew that I could trust her.

Grandpa's office is quite the sight. A glass trophy case crammed with awards, a messy montage of certificates, celebrity photos, and even the key to the city of Charlotte decorated the walls. And new carpet, of course – light grey – since the incident with Chad. *Maybe I should go through his desk? Hell, it's technically my desk now.* I sat down, placed my half-eaten piece of chocolate cake safely away from the keyboard and rubbed my hands together to wipe away the crumbs and frosting. The top drawer was filled mostly with office supplies and clutter. From my experience, no matter how clean people appeared to be, they always had a mess hidden just beneath the surface. I yanked the handle of the bottom drawer, but it refused to nudge. I rummaged around the desk for a key but found nothing. Not yet, anyway. Then, just as I started to dig through the trash bin beneath the desk, I heard the office door unlock. As Larry eased into the room, I hoped I didn't look too startled by his sudden appearance. I tried to act matter-of-fact as I sat up straight in the leather chair and slowly slid the trash bin back under the desk with my foot.

I blurted out the first thing that came to mind.

"Are the news vans still out there?"

"I took care of it."

"What did they want?"

"Your comment on your grandfather's death."

"Me? Why?"

"You don't know why?"

"No."

"You're in charge now, Luke. Which is also why the detectives want to ask you some questions."

"Detectives?"

"A Detective Copeland called me this morning. She wants to interview you – well, all of us, but she specifically asked for you."

Interview me? He can't seriously think I was involved somehow. But I could tell, as Larry waited for a reaction, that he was studying me intently.

"I have nothing to hide, but it seems odd that she asked for me, right?"

"Well, in any homicide, detectives naturally suspect the person who had the most to gain by someone's death. And one could reason that person would be you."

"Are you serious? Grandpa already promoted me before his death; it just wasn't official."

"I understand. Well, regardless, as your attorney, I advise you that we shouldn't talk with them right now."

"Okay, whatever you think is best. Say, speaking of the will, what's the timeline on distributing my grandpa's assets?"

"It's complicated."

"What do you mean? Who's getting what?"

There was no one more upset about Grandpa's death than me, but that didn't mean I wasn't also a little excited for my inheritance. To never have to worry about money again? I can't say I hadn't thought about it now and then.

"Well, technically, there's an estate that includes his will. Your grandfather made me the estate executor, which means it is my job to distribute the assets to the inheritors."

"That doesn't sound too complicated."

"Your grandfather made certain stipulations. One being that if he was murdered, then the estate's assets would be frozen until the case is solved. And if any of the beneficiaries are involved, then of course, they would forfeit the right to their share."

"Wait a minute; an investigation could take years. Or worse, what if the case is never solved?"

"Then the money would be good as gone, I'm afraid."

Good as gone? I haven't been working my whole life following in my grandfather's footsteps just to have my inheritance disappear over a technicality. I had dreams. It's not like I wanted to be a car salesman. I did it to make him happy. And for what?

"But you're the executor, right? Can't you just take out that stipulation?"

"No, I'm afraid not. Your grandfather's instructions were unambiguous."

"We should talk to the police then. Get my name cleared so they can find the real killer."

"Listen, Luke. You never talk to the police until you know exactly what they want. It doesn't matter if you're innocent, understand?"

My mind was racing a mile a minute. *How could I be considered a suspect? Who would even want to kill Grandpa? He probably only had a couple years left anyway, so what would be the point? And now, there's a possibility that I might not even get anything? How can I run the business without any money?*

By the time I snapped to, Larry had opened the door to leave. He raised an eyebrow.

"Enjoy your cake. You've earned it."

Was that sarcasm or genuine concern? I can't tell you. Either way, who am I to turn down a perfectly good piece of cake? I picked up the fork and dug back in, careful to get just the right frosting-to-cake ratio. I scooped it into my mouth and scraped the fork clean with my teeth.

I turned on Grandpa's computer. Using his password, one that he once mentioned to me in passing, I typed in a variety of combinations of the phrase 'zero down.' Capital Z and D did the trick.

Grandpa was never fond of computers. He believed that forming a good old-fashioned relationship was the key to selling cars, not technology. Nonetheless, even he had to use a keyboard and mouse once in a while. His desktop background featured a photo of one of his many stunts – this time, strapped to the top of a single-prop plane that doubled as his "dog" Teddy. Navigating through this dinosaur of a desktop wasn't exactly easy, with operating software from at least five years ago. Nearly every time I clicked on something, the Apple wheel of death spun in an accusatory way. But I kept at it and eventually found what I was looking for: the security camera software.

Despite my rank at Washington Ford, I was never granted access to the security footage until Grandpa died – which now might technically be a grey area. Once I finally got the program opened, there appeared to be six cameras in total. Two covered the building's entrance; two cameras inside the showroom; another two in the service department.

Outside the building, the news vans were packing up to leave, just as Larry mentioned. Inside the service department, the guys were busy working on a Ford Fusion. But it was the two showroom cameras that particularly interested me. What exactly could they see? On the first camera, the entryway and reception desk were in view; the other was trained on the floor models of our best-selling cars and trucks. *I'll be damned. there aren't any security cameras watching the conference room, bullpen, offices, or back door.*

I scooped the remaining piece of cake into the trash bin, then picked up the phone and dialed my executive assistant.

"Brenda. I'm going out for the rest of the day. Can you hold my calls?"

"Of course, Mr. Washington."

"One more thing – it's important you don't tell anyone that I'm gone. Let them think I'm swamped with work and can't be disturbed. Understood?"

"You got it, Mr. Washington."

"Thanks, Brenda, I know I can always trust you."

Courtney Washington

T he worst part of my father dying wasn't the grieving; it was dealing with the herd of frauds who offered their condolences. Every few minutes, I got a call or text from a number I didn't recognize telling me how much my father meant to them. There's no way these people had a meaningful relationship with Daddy.

Planning for a funeral – or "celebration of life," as Larry insisted on calling it – was overwhelming. Larry didn't want to have a reading of Daddy's will just yet, calling the situation "complicated." However, he was more than happy to give me every little last detail of what Daddy expected out of his celebration of life.

The event would take place at the Carolinas Aviation Museum against a backdrop of two fighter jets, the same model my father flew in the Vietnam War. Every corner of the museum would be a commemoration of his life. Larry expected one to honor his service in the Navy; in the other three corners, there would be a tribute to Washington Ford, Daddy's famous commercials, and his family.

"Hi, who do I speak to about renting animals for events?"

As I waited on the phone, I flipped through my neglected desk drawers. After some digging, I came across a few of my medals and certificates from my younger days: First Place in the 2001 North Carolina Miss Teen Dream Beauty Pageant, Second Place in 2002 North Carolina Miss Amazing Pageant. I wouldn't say I was bitter about how young and cute I looked, but I couldn't examine the photos for longer than a glance. From what I saw, there wasn't a wrinkle or a bit of flab anywhere on my body; and to think I was self-conscious at the time.

"Hello?"

"Yes, I was wondering if I could rent a monkey for a day and how much that would cost?"

In addition to figuring out the details of primate rental, Larry made it clear that he expected me to contact all of Daddy's family, friends, and employees over the years, to notify each of them of the death and invite them to the celebration of his life. I wasn't sure how exactly I was supposed to track down eighty years' worth of people, although I wouldn't be surprised to see them come out of the woodwork for the slightest chance at his fortune.

"So, $200 an hour with a minimum of two hours, huh? Okay, is he available this Sunday?"

I crossed out "monkey rental" on my notepad with a red marker as I hung up. I figured it was a good sign that Larry asked me to help with the arrangements; I must stand to gain a pretty penny from Daddy's death. He also mentioned that I shouldn't talk to the police if they came around, but what did I care? I had nothing to hide.

I couldn't stand to be in my house for another moment. I had become my worst nightmare: a cat lady afraid to leave her own home. The anxiety was getting worse and worse, but on the bright side, I only had one cat. Eventually, I worked up enough courage to convince myself that I should go over to the manor house – or the 'lake house,' as we called it – on the other side of the property where my father and Eva lived. I needed to start going through his stuff. I imagined there'd be some form of estate sale down the line, and I figured that I might as well take the good jewelry before Eva did. I looked at the clock. *How the hell is it six o'clock already?* I threw on some jeans and a black t-shirt that was only a little stained.

I pushed the start button in the Porsche gifted to me by my father for my fortieth birthday a few years ago. It used to look fabulous, but lately it came off as a neglected old maid, cluttered and in need of a good detailing. Some might call it a common theme. I drove it mostly just to get around the property and the occasional trip into town; not unlike a senior citizen uses a golf cart.

On the short drive to my father's house, I couldn't help but think about how my Luke must be dealing with this whole ordeal. The amount of pressure on him had already reached an absurd level once Daddy announced him as successor to the Washington Ford dealership. It seemed like every day since then saw a new disaster. Luke blamed himself for the failing business and Daddy's death, but if anyone could save it, it would be Luke. And with that MBA he'd been working toward, he should be able to turn the business around in no time. I couldn't be more proud of him.

Just a few acres southeast of the lake house, I passed the remains of my childhood home, lost in a fire years ago. Despite the memories, I wished Daddy would have cleaned up the rubble years ago, but he always said it served as a necessary reminder. I mean, I loved my mom too, but the charred debris had proven to be nothing more than a perpetual eyesore that brought down the property value. *The next time I talk to Larry, I'll make sure to ask him if we can divert some of the estate money to remove it.*

As I pulled up to the circle drive on the lake house, the gardener watering the dogwood flowers waved me through. I quickly discovered that the driveway was blocked by Eva's white Ford Edge and a Tesla with a Charlotte-Mecklenburg Police Department decal. The sight of the autonomous car in the driveway was jarring, since Daddy never allowed anyone in the family to own them. *What was I thinking? I shouldn't have come here. I don't want to have anything to do with Eva, and Larry told me not to speak to the police without him.* I threw my Porsche into reverse – but just as I checked the backup camera on the dash, a loud alarm startled me, and I saw an unfamiliar man blocking my exit. The reverse lights illuminated his face, unveiling a clean-shaven Hispanic man about my age. He flicked his hand toward me in a friendly manner as he smiled into the camera before approaching the driver's side door.

Sweating profusely through a gaudy, Hawaiian button-down shirt, he held his jacket over his left arm. He brought his badge up to my window.

"Hi, Ms. Washington?"

"Yes."

"Now, which one of the daughters are you?"

"Courtney."

"Terrific. Do you mind coming inside? We have a few questions for you."

The detective decided to open the door for me, even though I hadn't given him my answer. *I might as well. Maybe I can find out something more about Daddy's murder.*

In the entryway, the complete chaos of the house struck me as strange. Cardboard boxes littered the wood floors, displaced furniture blocked access to rooms, and I even saw dog shit on one of the expensive Persian rugs – most likely from their yappy little chihuahua, although I hadn't ruled Eva out. The detective steered me to the direction of the kitchen, where through the door frame, I discovered Eva and what looked to be another detective sitting across from each other.

"Sorry to interrupt, but Ms. Courtney Washington decided to join us."

"Terrific! Have a seat, Ms. Washington."

The female detective, wearing a more professional white long-sleeve shirt and blazer, pointed to the chair adjacent to Eva. Just as I looked toward the gaudy chair, Eva lifted her skinny ass three inches off her own chair, then yanked it away from the one I was set to occupy. Eva was in her typical garb, an expensive head-to-toe Lululemon yoga outfit. The female detective took notice and studied our respective reactions. After I sat down, the male detective joined his partner on their side of the table.

"Hi Courtney, my name is Detective Copeland, and you've already met my partner, Detective Garcia."

"Why is she here? It's my house."

"Courtney? That's a fair question."

I cleared my throat and stammered as I tried to think of a response. *Shit. What can I say? 'I came here to rummage through Daddy's jewelry?' That will go over well.*

"I just...I just wanted to check on my daddy's things. Is that a crime?"

"You came to steal my stuff, didn't you?"

I audibly gasped at Eva's accusations, but she was right on the money. The detectives continued to carefully observe our body language from their side of the table. Garcia jotted something down in his pocket notepad.

"That's ridiculous. I mean, look at this place. It's in complete disarray. What's going on? Are you selling his stuff already?"

"That's none of your damn business."

"Gold digging isn't as easy as it used to be, huh? You might actually have to work for once in your life."

"You bitch."

Eva's horrid English accent caused my eyes to twitch involuntarily.

You think she would've waited until the old man was in the ground, at least. In an effort to break the tension, the female detective spoke up.

"Ms. Washington, are you aware that we are treating your father's death as a homicide?"

"Yes, Larry mentioned it."

Larry's name triggered a look between two detectives that I tried to decipher. *What were they so concerned about?*

"Did you know your father's attorney, Mr. Bridges, hired a private pathologist to perform an autopsy? I mean an eighty-five-year-old man keels over, who would bat an eye?"

"That's Larry for you."

"Mr. Bridges claimed it was in accordance with your father's wishes. Do you know anything about that?"

"No."

"Did Mr. Bridges tell you the results of the autopsy?" Detective Copeland asked.

"No."

To get a better look at Eva's face, I carefully stood and worked my way toward the kitchen, still keeping my distance from the table. I settled against the kitchen counter as Detective Copeland continued her interview.

"Well, let me back up, then. When did you become aware of your father's stage IV cancer diagnosis in his liver and bones?"

"What? What are you talking about?"

Both of the detectives paused to study our reactions. My eyes shifted to Eva; her head slumped to her chest as she attempted to turn on the waterworks. *I guess I'm the only one in the room who didn't know.* Eva remained still, unable or unwilling to look Detective Copeland in the eyes.

"How about you, Mrs. Washington?"

"Yes, poor Al found out six months ago. But he's been fighting like hell. That was my Al for you."

Detective Garcia remained silent as he flipped to another page in his notepad. Meanwhile, Eva began full-on sobbing. No one in the room bought her grief, but that didn't stop Eva.

"Mrs. Washington, do you know what type of treatment your husband was taking?"

"Um, what was it called? It started with an 'X.' The side effects of the drug nearly killed him. Xena or Xenigo, maybe?"

"Xofigo?"

"Yes! That's the one."

"How often was he taking it?"

"He went in for an injection about every five days."

"Do you remember the name of the doctor?"

"No. Why? Do you think the doctor has something to do with this?"

"We haven't ruled out any suspects yet, ma'am. Do you know the last time your husband received treatment?"

"No. But, the day he died, we were going to go see his doctor to see how the treatment was going."

Just then, the front door flew open. All four of our heads at the table turned in unison to discover Larry standing in the entryway, out of breath and with his briefcase in hand. Larry didn't even take off his designer sunglasses before he exploded, aiming his wrath at the detectives.

"This conversation is over! Are you kidding me? I told you never to speak to anyone in the family without me present. Was that not clear?"

"We're just having a friendly chat."

"Detectives, you need to leave immediately. Get out!"

Detective Garcia flicked his notepad closed before neatly placing his pen in his shirt pocket. As Larry approached the table, Detective Copeland rose to her feet.

"No problem, Mr. Bridges. I was just informing these ladies that Mr. Washington had decided to forgo his cancer treatment, so it was a little odd when the pathologist found a high concentration of polonium in his blood cells."

"Polonium? What is that?"

"Poison. He was poisoned."

"What do you mean he stopped going to treatment? He went downtown every week to the Levine Institute. He told me so," Eva whimpered.

"That's enough, detective! Thank you."

I shifted my eyes to Larry, hoping for a hint of confirmation of what Detective Copeland had revealed and, judging by how upset he was, it must have been true. Before leaving, Detective Garcia pulled out two business cards from his back pocket and gently placed them on the table before exiting through the front door with his partner.

Larry spoke through clenched teeth.

"You both need to listen to me very carefully. You will never, ever, ever talk to the police without me present again. Is that understood?"

Standing with his fists against the table, he spoke like a disappointed father to two unruly children.

"Why did you let them in?"

"They are the police. What choice did I have?"

"Only one, Eva. Call me. That's all you had to do."

"I got nothing to hide."

"It doesn't matter. The police control the narrative, not you. They are professionals, not you. Is that clear?"

"Yes."

Deciding it was time to leave, I uncrossed my arms and pushed away from the kitchen counter. In the process, I knocked over a phone plugged into the outlet below. The pink sparkle case indicated it might belong to Eva's five-year-old daughter and my half-sister, Margret. The phone sat face down on the hardwood floor. I picked it up to return it to the charging dock, where it lit up to reveal a notification. Before I read it in full, I checked to see if Eva or Larry were watching me. Not a chance – the two remained in a heated discussion near the dining room table, just within earshot. My eyes darted back to the phone, where the screen read, "Confirmation for two first-class tickets, CLT to KEF Monday July 10 at 8 a.m. You may check in 24 hours prior to departure."

Which airport code is KEF? I don't even think that's in the United States. Is Eva going on a trip less than twenty-four hours after Daddy's funeral?

I clicked the side button on the phone to turn the screen off. Reexamining the house from this stunning new vantage point, it was clear that the duffel bags and cardboard boxes were neither the result of neglect nor prepping for an estate sale. Eva was planning to move back to Iceland and take Margret with her.

Alice Washington

Thirty-two hours had passed since my last drink. My head throbbed as I tried to remember the last time I didn't fall asleep without alcohol in my system. Eventually, I pulled my ass out of bed and waddled my way over to my suitcase. I pillaged through my clothes and toiletry bag, hoping I packed some Advil, but no luck. On to the bathroom, where the unflattering fluorescent light immediately caused my dull head-ache to sharpen. I flicked off the vanity light just as quickly as I turned it on. Instead, I used the softer light from my phone to illuminate the bath-room. I noticed a text from Larry telling me to meet him at The Diamond, a local diner closer to uptown Charlotte, at 10 a.m. sharp. It was already 9:45 a.m. I debated blowing Larry off, then figured the sooner I met with him, the sooner I'd be able to get the hell out of here and back to Alaska.

I splashed some water on my face, squinted into the mirror and debated what it would take to be even somewhat presentable within the next few minutes. *Not your most elegant look. Then again, it's just Larry.* I dried my face with a washcloth, threw back the little bottle of Listerine, and returned to my suitcase for a pair of jeans. As I swished the mouth-wash around, I pondered the lengths to which Larry was willing to go. I scampered back to the bathroom, one leg in, one out of my jeans, to check the label on the mouthwash bottle sitting on the sink. It was, of course, non-alcoholic.

On the ride over to The Diamond, I turned the thought over and over in my mind. Big Al – murdered? Undeniably, there was no shortage of people who had their motives. Hell, I wondered how many times I wished him dead myself. As my Lyft approached the restaurant, I compared the building to my memory of it. It looked somewhat familiar with its all-brick exterior, a rarity for a diner but a common aesthetic in North Carolina. In large white letters, "Diamond Restaurant" dwarfed not only the awning they hung above, but the rest of the brick building. I surveyed the nearby buildings for a convenience store that might sell some Advil, but spotted nothing but other restaurants and boutiques.

The bell above the glass door rang as I entered the barren diner and was surprised to be quickly greeted by a real human being, who appeared to be sorting silverware before I interrupted.

"Hi! Welcome. Just one?"

"I'm meeting someone. Thanks."

Walking between the empty tables and chairs, I found Larry sitting at a booth on the far side of the diner. Larry, who looked like he'd barely aged in the past fifteen years, wore his typical ill-fitting suit of a uniform. He read a physical copy of the *Charlotte Observer* as he sipped on his morning coffee; a mini oat-milk creamer pitcher and a used stir stick rested next to the cup. *Where he got a real-life newspaper in 2028, I'll never know.*

"Hello, Larry."

"Alice! Good to see you."

Larry, with his glasses teetering on the tip of his nose, attempted to stand in the booth but was awkwardly blocked by the table and tight quarters. He settled on offering a side hug before exchanging pleasantries. As I sunk into the booth's well-worn cushion, Larry sized me up – to see, no doubt, if I was using. Once he believed he had his answer, Larry clenched his jaw and let out a soft sigh, as if to let me know he was disappointed but wouldn't be bringing it up.

"I wish we were meeting under better circumstances, Alice."

"Do you want to tell me what the hell is going on? I mean – murdered? Seriously?"

"I'm afraid so."

Larry's voice trailed off, almost as if he was paranoid. Before I got a chance to look at the menu, our waitress approached the table, coffee carafe in hand, Larry's fruit plate in the other. She was young, still in college probably, complete with cool tattoos and a slim waist – a stark contrast to the seasoned women with grey hair that used to run every diner across our country.

"Good morning! Would you like some coffee?"

"Please."

"Excuse me, Alice, I have to make a call. Why don't you order something? It's on me."

Larry slid out of the booth, right past the waitress. I wondered if she could sense my discomfort as she poured the coffee into the mug. I fixed my eyes on the table when, about midway through her pour, the steady flow briefly paused. I supposed that she suddenly had tuned in to my jumpy behavior, but my desperation overruled any fear of shame.

"Say, do you think you could make this an Irish coffee?"

"Sorry, ma'am, but we don't serve alcohol here."

"Ok. No problem."

I repeated the word ma'am in my head as I thought about the age difference between us.

"Anything to eat?"

"No, coffee is fine. Thank you."

"The ABC store down the street just opened."

It's too bad Larry didn't choose a chain; an app doesn't pass judgement when you scroll through the alcoholic drinks on a menu. Without another word between us, the waitress finished her pour, leaving me with my cup of regular old coffee.

I sat by myself in the booth, watching Larry pace back and forth outside the front door talking on his phone. I picked up the *Observer* to pass the time, and wouldn't you know it? Big Al made the front page. The headline read, "Legendary Car Salesman's Death Ruled a Homicide." The article didn't mention the details of the investigation, as both the detectives and Larry had declined to comment. I glanced through it, then quickly flipped to the obituary section. Shortly thereafter, Larry slid back into the booth.

"I wanted to include you, Alice, but your dad..."

I skimmed to the bottom of the nearly two-column obituary to find that, of almost a dozen family members who were listed as survivors, my name was not among them.

"He's not my dad." I placed the open newspaper on the table.

"Don't say that. Al loved you...he was just conflicted."

"Conflicted?"

"There's something else, something I shouldn't even be sharing with you since the will is pending due to the investigation, but..."

"What is it?"

Larry leaned back, inhaling deeply as if contemplating how to phrase his next sentence.

"He cut you out of the will."

"Of course he did."

My mind drifted as Larry blabbered on, attempting to save face. *That son of a bitch. All that family talk. It's all bullshit. Big Al looked out for himself, and himself alone. God forbid I was a little different and struggled through life. I guess in the end, I was too much of an embarrassment.*

"I quit."

"What?"

"I'm never stepping foot in the Alaskan dealership again. Do you understand?"

"Now wait a minute, Alice."

"Goodbye, Larry."

Just as I stood to walk out, I caught the gaze of our hipster waitress, staring back at me. I glared at her and darted out the front door. Larry made one last plea to get me back to the table, yelling my name, but I kept facing forward.

Now on the sidewalk, I roamed Central Ave, looking for that aforementioned ABC store. After living in Alaska for so long, I'd forgotten what a pain in the ass it is to be in a state with a self-righteous monopoly on selling liquor. As I walked, I placed my palm against my forehead; the throbbing had worsened. The store was nowhere in sight, so I took my phone out to find it on Maps, which told me the closest ABC store was, in fact, 1.8 miles away. *Just down the street? Fuck.*

Instead of training for a 5k in the rising morning heat, I ordered a Lyft from my phone, simultaneously ignoring Larry's third attempt to call me. The car arrived in about fifteen seconds flat, and I was off to the store. The tranquility inside the vehicle was welcome; no driver making small talk, no radio unless I wanted it, no bullshit.

"You have arrived at your destination."

The car door opened as I gathered my purse and phone. The second after I placed two feet on the ground, the door swung shut and it rushed off to retrieve its next passenger.

The ABC store, with its brick facade and red marquee, was unsurprisingly the fanciest building in the shopping plaza. The sliding glass doors opened as I approached, and an automated bell chime brought the unwanted attention of a cashier, an older man who could likely spot an addict a mile away. I ignored him in my quest to satisfy my craving. I figured I could just get a few mini bottles, to keep in my purse when I wanted a quick taste. Liquor stores usually kept those near the front, as the occasional impulse buy for regular people. I grabbed four mini bottles of Fireball not far from the register.

"Did you find everything all right?"

"Yes. Thank you."

I pulled my ID from my overstuffed wallet and handed it over to the man.

"Oh, right."

The cashier pretended to inspect the photo and birthdate before looking at me and nodding his head. *Terrific acting skills, buddy.* I jammed the bottles into my purse before he got a chance to ask if I'd like a bag. *It's a real shame that he'll be replaced by a computer within a few years once a robot figures out how to pretend to scan the ID of an alcoholic in her forties trying to get her fix.*

On my way out, I kept one hand in my purse, carefully unscrewing the cap from the bottle so I could be ready the second I made it outside the store. The glass doors slid open, the bell chimed, and the liquor slid right down my throat. I closed my eyes, took a deep breath, and exhaled slowly.

"Alice."

When I opened my eyes, Larry was standing five feet in front of me with his arms crossed. I wiped my mouth with the back of my hand. *How the hell does he do it?*

"You didn't give me a chance to finish," Larry announced.

"What's there to talk about? I'm no longer part of this family."

"There's another way."

Refusing to take the bait, I slipped past Larry as he anchored himself to the sidewalk. He sighed as I brushed by him. Only a few minutes passed before he apparently decided to give chase.

"You're the only one I can trust, Alice! The only person who couldn't have killed your father."

Slightly out of breath, I decided I might as well stop and let him catch up with me. We stood among the vacant storefronts of the strip mall.

"I had more of a motive than anyone."

"That's true, but you were four-thousand miles away. You have a rock-solid alibi, with no calls to or from Charlotte in the past few weeks."

"You actually checked?"

"I'm sorry, but I had to do my due diligence."

"You had me come all this way just to tell me I didn't do it?"

"No, no, listen. There's a stipulation in your father's will that in the event of his murder, 10 percent of his estate can be allocated to finding the killer."

"So?"

"So...I'm willing to give you that 10 percent if you help me."

Help Larry find Big Al's killer? This is insane. And it means I would have to stay in Charlotte. How much would 10 percent be, anyway?

"That's $21.2 million, Alice."

"You're going to go against Big Al's wishes?"

"That's not the way I see it."

"And to hand $21.2 million to the family fuck-up?"

Larry turned deadly serious.

"Contingent on your sobriety. I won't give you a dime unless you're clean."

Well, shit. I rubbed the sweat from my forehead and looked around the block.

"Why, though?"

"Like I said, you're the only one I can trust, and I as much as I loved your father, I always thought he gave you a raw deal."

All great salespeople will tell you there is nothing quite like the high when the negotiation has been settled, the deal is done, and you grab the buyer's hand and give it a firm shake. Satisfied with the terms, I stuck my hand out to meet Larry's.

"So...who are the suspects?"

Luke Washington

Grandpa never told me how hot the lights could get or how bright they were — so intense that it penetrated my eyes and scattered my brain. Even worse than the lights, when the words finally did reach my mouth, standing in front of a row of cars, I seemed to forget how to speak correctly. I can't explain it — I never had a problem talking for the past twenty years, but put a stupid camera in my face and I suddenly morph into a stammering fool. It was so embarrassing that even the production assistant, a guy about my age, attempted to hide his giggling by pulling his shirt over his mouth. Nonetheless, the director insisted she would be able to "cut around my flubs."

I never saw Grandpa struggle with shooting a commercial. The moment that he stepped in front of the camera, he truly transformed into Big Al Washington. He made it look effortless, with his Texas charm and infectious smile. I thought if I put Grandpa's signature cowboy outfit on, I'd transition right into the on-screen role, and it would be less jarring for the viewers. Instead, I felt more like a boy drowning in his dad's sport coat. After three hours of this charade, I sent the crew home with a couple hundred bucks each and told them to come back next week for another attempt.

When the crew left, I slowly strolled between the rows of cars and back to the dealership, flanked by Mark, my floor manager. Every time I saw Mark, without fail, one of his hands was jammed into his pockets, playing with change. He might be the only person I knew under age seventy who still carried coins. Big Al never cared much for Mark, and I wasn't sure why — Mark was the kid everyone loved in school; the charismatic magnet for girls and good times. Even though he was more popular and a year older than me, he always considered us a package deal. When he came to me for a job a couple of years ago, there was no way I was going to turn him down.

"How'd the shoot go?"

"Terrible."

"That's all right. You'll figure it out. It's in your blood."

Out of nowhere, Mark yanked me by my bicep to stop me in my tracks.

"Say, I need to talk to you about you-know-who." Mark whispered. "He's gone."

"Gone? What do you mean?"

I jerked my arm from Mark's clutch, took a step back to examine the level of concern on his face. His eyes were wide; his jaw was clenched. I proceeded to cover my mouth with a hand. Mark followed my lead, as if we were a pitcher and catcher discussing strategy in a meeting on the mound.

"When?"

"Last night."

"How?"

"Shoelaces."

"Shoelaces?"

"Shoelaces, dude. I got the whole thing on my Nest camera at home. It's truly unbelievable. Check it out: Chad tied his shoelaces together – while blindfolded, mind you – then pedaled his way through the zip ties like he was in a fuckin' spin class or something. I guess the friction caused the zip tie to break – I don't know, I'm not a scientist. Anyway, just like that, he took off the blindfold and breezed out my sliding glass door."

"You kept him in your townhouse?"

"Where else was I going to take him?"

"What about your neighbors?"

"You're missing the point, Luke. Chad is gone!"

"Shit."

"What are we going to do, man?"

"I should call Larry."

"Larry? Hell no. We don't need to worry him. He's got enough on his plate."

"Then what do you propose we do?"

"I'll drive."

Mark flew down Independence Boulevard, passing car after car in his brand new "Need for Green" Mustang convertible. I still remember when Mark stepped up and bought it, when we were one car shy of our quota a few months back. To me, the whole "Need for Green" color thing was rather pompous, so it suited Mark nicely. One beautiful aspect of the self-driving car revolution was that cops no longer wasted their time writing speeding tickets. I mentioned that line to Grandpa once, and he loved it so much that he had all the salespeople add it to their pitches.

"So...what's the word on Big Al's will? Is my man going to be strip-club rich or sex-party-on-a-yacht rich?"

"Well...it's complicated. The money is frozen until my grandpa's killer is found. And I'm happily married, for the record."

"Frozen? That's some serious bullshit. How does anyone expect you to run the dealership without that money?"

As we pulled off the highway and got closer to Mark's house, I put my hat back on to cover my ruffled hair. The Bruce Springsteen tune on the sound system suddenly blared uncomfortably loud at the modest neighborhood speed limit, so Mark cranked the dial down before glancing toward me.

"You know, there may be a way we can kill two birds with one stone."

"How'd you figure?"

"Well, we could frame Chad."

"Frame Chad? Are you crazy?"

"Now hold on. Think about it – who had more motive to kill Big Al than Chad? We just caught him red-handed stealing a shit ton from Washington Ford. Hell, he may have actually killed Big Al."

We pulled into Mark's driveway. The Plaza Midwood neighborhood was lined with almost identical two-story townhomes on both sides of the street. Every one, painted in a variety of dull colors, featured mostly the same vinyl-siding-clad layout with a single-car garage. The lawns were small and well-manicured. Neither of us unbuckled our seatbelts when Mark turned the car off.

"How much did Larry say you'll get?"

"I can't believe you brought him here. Larry okayed this?"

"How much, Luke?"

"He didn't say, but 200 million, maybe."

"Oh, shit! 200 million?!"

"Well, there could be other beneficiaries."

"Even if you just get a slice of the pie, you'd be set for life – that is, unless this investigation is never wrapped up."

"You have a point."

"I tell you what, you give me just 20 percent of your inheritance if I can successfully pin this on Chad."

"I don't know."

"Or you could get nothing, and Washington Ford will fail. I can see the headlines now, 'Grandson of Famed Car Salesman Sinks Washington Ford.' What do you say, Luke?"

"Ten percent."

"Deal."

After unbuckling his seatbelt, Mark offered his hand to me. I managed a half-hearted smile before returning his handshake. When I looked into his eyes, I practically saw the wheels in his head turning, trying to figure out how much 10 percent of $200 million would be. And the math isn't that tough.

⌒

The stench of piss immediately stung my nostrils as we walked into Mark's place. Surveying the open floor plan, I noticed broken glass, stained carpet, and empty pizza boxes. While Chad's escape must have contributed to some of the disarray, it was quite clear that Mark's newly acquired bachelor status wasn't suiting him well.

"Sorry about the mess. Chad completely trashed the place."

Mark guided me down a couple of steps into his carpeted living room, where I carefully stepped over what appeared to be the glass top of a now-shattered coffee table. Moving on to the spare bedroom, Mark pointed to an empty medium-sized dog crate in the middle of the carpet. I remembered how he said he'd caught Chad's escape on video and searched the room for the camera. Mark pointed to the corner above the door, where I saw it mounted on the wall, red light flashing.

"Want to see the video?"

"No, thanks."

He kept Chad in this thing? A golden retriever wouldn't be comfortable in that size cage, let alone a grown man.

"Danielle took the dog."

I meant to offer Mark a few words of post-divorce encouragement, but the scene in front of me was too damn distracting. I mean, by the looks of it, he'd forced Chad to drink water from a dog bowl. *I know Chad stole money from the dealership – and ultimately, my pockets – but keeping him in a dog a crate felt a little too sadistic.*

"You want a beer?"

Before I had a chance to respond, Mark left the room. I glanced up at the blinking camera one last time. When I reached the kitchen, Mark already had two Olde Mecklenburg bottles in hand.

"Check this shit out."

Mark pointed to his kitchen table as he dug through a drawer for a bottle opener. I couldn't make out everything piled there, but I saw at least three handguns.

"Take whichever one you like."

I got closer to the table, where I noticed a bunch of spy equipment – GPS trackers, cameras, lock-picking tools– in addition to the firearms.

"What is all this?"

"It's all top-of-the-line stuff."

"Whatever you say, Q."

Mark chuckled at the reference. He finally opened the beer bottles, joined me at the table and offered me one. It wasn't even cold.

"If Chad is out there, we'll find him."

"This is all great, but the polonium is the most important thing. That's what my mom said was found in the autopsy. If no polonium is found, the police will never believe it was Chad."

"Don't worry, Luke. I'll get it. In the meantime, you should start carrying a gun."

"No. I don't need that."

Mark, grinning from ear to ear, reached across the table and picked up one of the handguns; if I had to guess, it was a 9 mm.

"Luke, you have 200 million reasons to carry this."

He took a swig of his beer, then rested it on the table. He picked my hand up and placed the gun in my palm. It felt lighter than I thought it would be. A shot of adrenaline rushed through me as I tightened my grip.

"There you go. Nice and easy. Best part is, they're all untraceable. 'Ghost guns,' they call 'em."

I rotated the handle, inspecting the gun more closely. Then, I lifted my eyes to find Mark staring at me, with a slight smile I could only describe as devious enough to make the hair on the back of my neck stand. *How is he so calm?* I put the gun back with the others, stepped back from the table. *I've known Mark for a long time, but he seems completely deranged. I mean, look at this place. He's not an ally, he's a liability.*

I kept my cool.

"No guns."

"What do you mean, 'no guns?'"

"You want your cut? Then find another way."

Then it hit me. *Wouldn't it be easier to set Mark up? At some point, he's even going to have the polonium on him. It would be my word against his. Who would a reasonable person believe? An upstanding, job-creating citizen or a divorced loner with illegal firearms whose life is in shambles? The best part about it is that I wouldn't have to give him 10 percent.*

A FAREWELL TO AL

Courtney Washington

What to wear? What to wear? I couldn't be seen in all black at a "Celebration of Life" – that wasn't fashionable anymore. I took a step back to look in the mirror, and stumbled over a pile of dresses and shoes I had either already tried on or discarded. More clothes than a person could ever need in a lifetime laid on the floor of my walk-in closet. Before I could text the housekeeper to politely ask her to clean up my mess, the doorbell chimed three times.

Still in my robe, I marched through the master bedroom and skipped down the marble staircase to the front door, stopping at the entryway mirror to fix my hair. My bloated face and crow's feet wouldn't let me stare too long.

"Your dad's car is being taken to the museum as we speak. We need to get over there now."

Ben got the words out before I even opened the door wide enough to let him inside. My father's memorial service preparations had gotten so far out of hand that I had to hire a bereavement coordinator. Truth be told, I didn't even know that was a real job until a few days ago.

"Come in. I'm not ready just yet."

"You are the host. You can't be late."

"Just ten minutes. I'm having a crisis here."

Ben, in his tailored suit with a purple skinny tie and a one-corner-fold pocket square, stood firmly on the steps out front. I got the hint, but the daughter of a Washington had certain standards – well, one of the daughters, anyway. I left the door open as I ran back upstairs and put on a more forgiving black dress still hanging in my closet, and paired it with a purple scarf from the pile of clothes to counteract the black. I wound it around my neck and consulted the vanity mirror. *It's not chic, but it'll do*. I put on an abbreviated version of my face, swiftly grabbed my clutch from the counter, shoved it under my armpit, and picked up a pair of black heels by the straps before hurrying back down the stairs.

At the bottom of the staircase, I wrestled my feet into the heels, struggling to keep my balance. One final look into the oval mirror in the entryway. My hair could've been better, but I raked through it with my fingers and told myself to stop worrying about it.

The moment I stepped outside to greet Ben with a side kiss, the sweltering humidity conspired to undo any fashion sense I had managed. I could already feel the sweat bubbling on my lower back. And wearing a scarf – what was I thinking? Like a true gentleman, Ben opened the car door for me as we crawled into the blessedly cool, climate-controlled backseat of the Lyft.

Ben entered our destination into his phone, and the car began its route. Instead of engaging in small talk, Ben stared at his phone, pecking furiously to answer emails and texts as I sat quietly next to him. Aware of the awkward silence, he began to type faster while simultaneously turning his head toward me as he finished. He finally pressed 'send' before raising his eyes to meet mine.

"I'm sorry, dear. There are so many moving parts. How are you holding up?"

"Okay, I guess. Hey, do you mind if we swing by my daddy's house real quick?"

"We're going to be late."

"Please. It's an emergency."

Ben squirmed in his seat, unsure of what to say to someone he knew, under the circumstances, might be emotionally unstable. I knew we were running behind, but something told me that I needed to check in on Eva. Ben reluctantly reprogrammed his phone, causing the car to loop back around the driveway of my house and head north through our property.

The road weaved toward the burnt foundation of our childhood home. Ben did a double-take as the car passed the eyesore. I could tell it piqued his curiosity, but already unsure of what to say, he swallowed his tongue. Now, about one hundred yards from the lake house, two semi-trucks came into view.

"Stop the car."

"What?"

"Stop the car!"

Ben fumbled for his phone for a second before repeatedly tapping the screen to stop the car. Our bodies jolted forward, and seat belts locked as the vehicle stopped on a dime, tires screeching. Two of the movers, straining under an oversized cardboard box, stopped shuffling their feet and contorted their necks in our direction.

"I can't believe it."

"What's going on?"

"She's packing it all up and leaving, can't you see?"

"Who?"

"Eva!"

"Your dad's wife?"

I already had my phone up to my ear to call Larry by the time Ben got out his question. *Pick up, Larry. If that bitch thinks she is taking my family's possessions, she's got another thing coming. Pick up.* I could feel my pulse bouncing through my veins as I waited helplessly.

"Courtney?"

"She has two fucking shipping containers, Larry!"

"Just calm down."

"Calm down? She's taking the entire estate with her to Iceland."

There was a pause on the other end of the phone. I glanced over at Ben, now sitting up straighter; his eyes shifted back and forth between the movers and me as he attempted to discern the situation.

"How did you know about Iceland?"

"Wait, you knew? Were you just going to stand idly by as she takes our family's prized possessions with her across the globe?"

"It's complicated."

"Complicated? You said everything is frozen until the murder was solved. Did you not?"

Another elongated pause. Larry, famously known for his calculated but swift actions appeared to be indecisive for once. It was a common weakness, I suppose, dealing with family.

"Two containers, you say?"

I hung up on him. Larry would be forced to act now. He wouldn't be able to plead ignorance when the bitch disappeared along with everything our family owns. With a gleam in my eye, I scanned the scene carefully, searching for Eva, but to no avail. I would have loved nothing more than to bask in her shock when Larry's muscle showed up, but I couldn't be late for Daddy's service. After all, appearances are everything in the Washington family.

Alice Washington

Even though I expected an over-the-top event, I was taken aback by the scale of Big Al's celebration of life. Perfectly aligned in twenty rows, four-hundred white folding chairs with padded vinyl seats faced a platform stage. The casket, overwhelmed by a massive floral arrangement, sat in the shadow of two full-sized vintage airplanes dangling from above. Despite the immaculate display, I was confident that Big Al would have complained about something.

I sat in the back row, a conscious decision to hide from my relatives. Luckily, the faces in the crowd were unfamiliar. Sitting up a little straighter on the edge of my seat, I gazed toward the front row, where my flesh and blood sat. My sister Courtney, wearing a black dress and purple shawl, sat closest to the aisle and the stage as if to signal that she was the most vital person in Big Al's life. Sitting next to her was Luke, who was being consoled by a young brunette, presumably his girlfriend or wife; I haven't cared enough to keep up with him. Eva, wearing a black pillbox and veil as if she was Jackie fucking Kennedy, was also in the row with her daughter, Margret. A few members of Larry's family filled out the row. I also noted the single empty seat at the far end of the row, with a red sash marked 'reserved' draped over the vinyl backing. Even as a cynic, I had to admit that it was a nice gesture by Larry to do that for me.

Eventually, someone I'd never seen in my life was the first to take the microphone. While I told myself that I wouldn't look at the pamphlet passed out at the entrance, my curiosity got the better of me. It was crumpled, its creases worn from my fidgeting with it. A photo of Big Al's face stared right back at me – a rare picture taken without his big, dumb hat. For how often Big Al smiled, I found it odd that the portrait depicted him with a stern expression, as if he was indicating his disappointment in me one last time. Before I could open it to figure out who was talking, the lights suddenly dimmed and a projector's lights flashed on. The song *Homeward Bound* by Simon and Garfunkel played while images, video recordings, and Big Al's commercials flickered on the screen. I couldn't remember ever seeing him as a boy, but the video began with his early life, as the sixth child in a clan of eight. In the dated photos, he looked unhappy, dressed in hand-me-downs two sizes too big. Next, the video panned and zoomed over images from his days in the Navy as a pilot – whoever had edited this little tribute couldn't stop themselves from overusing the Ken Burns effect. Now out of the Navy, his family fades from focus as Big Al builds his empire. After still photos of the early days of the dealership, the video transitioned into Big Al's commercials with his "dog" Teddy. Then there was a flash; I saw my mother in a home video. She looked about the same age that I was now; she sat on Big Al's lap wearing an apron as Courtney and I opened presents on Christmas morning. *My God, she was gorgeous.* Following the detour, there was more footage of old commercials.

I didn't pay much attention to the remainder of the glorified slide-show. Instead, I tried to place that moment of mom. *A forest green La-Z-Boy with a wooden handle. An oatmeal-colored carpet. My mom scours under the tree, looking for the next present to pass out as Big Al, unshaven and in his robe, sips his coffee. The chair squeaks as it rocks back and forth. A bloody coughing fit. My mom insists that she is okay – flashes of a trip to the hospital. Smiles fade. Illness. Death. A broken family.*

The tribute video ended on a freeze-frame of Big Al and Luke shaking hands in the parking lot of the dealership. The lights switched on again, and an uneasy silence followed; people didn't know whether to clap or remain quiet. *I can't imagine Eva approved that clip of my mother in the tribute.* A single clap finally rang out to break the unbearable dead air. The rest of the room happily followed suit. *It's not like Big Al's second wife Kelly made it into the final cut. Is someone sending me a message?* I kept my head perfectly still as I scanned the audience, careful not to prompt anyone's recognition. Row after row, I searched – but for whom, I wasn't sure. Was anyone looking for me? All I could see was the backs of heads, each indistinguishable from the next.

After the applause died down, Brenda rose from her chair in the second row and dawdled her way up the short steps onto the makeshift stage.

Her head was low as she approached the podium. There was a crack in her voice as she began sharing her deep connection to Big Al (something I certainly never had).

As Brenda babbled through her speech about how the two were practically family, I checked the pamphlet to see how much longer I had to sit through the tortuous ceremony, trying all the while to avoid Big Al's gaze of disappointment. That was when I noticed, at the right side of the fold, a yellow sticky note that read, "Meet me outside. We should talk." Someone with the moniker "E.B." signed at the bottom of the message.

E.B.? Who the hell could that be? I kept my head down as I slid out of my padded seat, careful not to look at anyone. I tried to soften the sound of my heels clicking on the epoxy floor by shuffling my feet. When I finally reached the exit, I awkwardly stumbled into the steel handlebar, which caused the hefty door to crack open. Yet, it wasn't until I threw my entire body weight at it that I managed to make a gap wide enough to slip through. Immediately, the afternoon sun blinded my eyes.

"Shit, I thought you weren't going to show."

A young woman with frizzy hair and a slim black dress leaned against the metal exterior of the museum as she scrolled through her phone. She took one last look at the screen before discarding it in her handbag. After less than ten seconds outside, I could already feel the perspiration forming on my forehead and lower back. Meanwhile, my secret note passer seemed unperturbed by the ungodly heat.

"Did you leave that note for me?"

"Sure did."

The woman smiled at the puzzled look on my face. *Am I supposed to recognize her?* She kicked her left leg off the wall to extend me a proper introduction. *E.B? E.B.?*

"Emily Bridges. Nice to see you again, Alice."

"Emily? You're all grown up."

At that exact moment, I had two revelations. One, that empty chair in the row reserved for family, had been saved for Emily, Larry's daughter, not me. And second, I was being watched – perhaps since the moment that I landed in Charlotte.

"What's it been, ten, fifteen years?"

"Have you been following me?"

Emily smiled. She had a naturally beautiful one, one that didn't require braces as a child or bleach as an adult. Instead of looking away while she thought of a rebuttal, Emily maintained eye contact until her smile receded into her response.

"Yes."

"Why?"

"I'm a private investigator now."

"Aren't you a little young to be a PI?"

"Just because I'm not the stereotypical retired cop means I can't be a PI?"

"Who hired you?"

"It's not important. What *is* important – "

"Who?"

Emily cleared her throat. She no doubt wanted to avoid disclosing her employer, but I could tell the idea of skirting the truth made her uneasy. *She would make a terrible car salesperson.*

"My father."

Larry? What's his angle in all of this? Is Larry just pandering to his daughter, or does he actually believe there is a conspiracy afoot?

"I know what you're thinking."

"What's that?"

"I only got the job due to nepotism."

"I wasn't thinking that. But that's a good point. A spoiled girl, fresh out of college with no job prospects, who listened to one too many true crime podcasts and thought, hell, I could do that."

"Couldn't something similar be said about you? What would your career look like without Big Al? Even if it means you ended up in Alaska."

Lacking a retort, I remained tight-lipped as a last-ditch effort to win the bout. The beads of sweat on my forehead began to trickle down toward my eyebrows. Emily's confidence was striking for such a young woman. I was nothing like her at that age.

"Look. I'm on your side. I think it's total bullshit that you got cut out."

"So what?"

A desperation bluff; one last attempt to get her to show me her cards. *Of course, I want to see this through. There are millions of reasons to see it through.*

"Not worth the effort? Do you really want to go back to living in desolate Alaska, working sixty hours a week as a sales manager at a dying car dealership? Hell, you might even be out of a job before the end of the year. Then what?"

Smart too. Emily smiled again, a grin that I would characterize as cocky, by a person who thought they had everything figured out.

"Just how cold does it get in Alaska, Alice?"

I tried to formulate a response, but the words never came. Big Al once said the worst thing you could do as a car salesman was to play defense. But, if you embraced the truth, you could flip the tables on the buyer and learn their real motive.

"You're right. So, what's in it for Emily Bridges then?"

"Same as you: money, honey."

I can get behind that.

"Fuck it. You're hired."

Another beautiful smile. Emily's hand was soft, well moisturized. Even though I had just given her a reason to confirm her vexing confidence, I was going to need all the help I could get.

Emily insisted that we return to the memorial service separately. She told me she would contact me within a couple of days. It could have been my boredom with Charlotte or my lack of a sense of purpose, but for the first time since I arrived in my hometown, I had something to look forward to – it was as if we were spies in a low-stakes James Bond movie.

Emily returned to the museum through the back door, which left me all alone in the sweltering heat. I completed a quick sniff test of my pits and undershirt. *Good, not great.* I then checked my phone to kill a couple of minutes. No texts. A few dozen work emails to ignore. Promo emails from Alaska Airlines and Amazon. *Didn't I unsubscribe?*

Finally, I figured enough time had passed to avoid suspicion and slipped back into the hangar. The "canned speech" portion of the service appeared to be over as guests mingled throughout the open space. Frozen by anxiety, I stood motionless in front of the door I just entered, observing the crowd. A group of five or six senior citizens, near Big Al's age, admired Vietnam war memorabilia in the corner designated for his military career. The majority of the attendees were either waiting in line at the buffet or the makeshift bar. *I could use a drink. Hell, I deserve a drink. If a woman can't drink at her father's funeral, when can she?*

Two men stood between me and a much-needed drink. They seemed close – not in an intimate way – more like old friends who were excited to reminisce despite the circumstance. The first guy asked whether the bartender had any single-malt scotch after the first option, which I didn't hear, was turned down. Apparently there wasn't any scotch either, because he begrudgingly ordered a Jack and Coke. The second gentleman, shorter and plumper than his friend, quickly ordered a Miller Lite. When he spoke, I immediately recognized his voice. It was my nephew Luke. Although I'd already seen him on TV, he didn't turn out how I imagined he would, and never had outgrown that baby face. I briefly considered bailing to avoid talking with him, but the lure of alcohol was too strong. I doubted he would recognize me, anyway.

Luke and his friend didn't bother with the tip jar; instead, they concentrated on guzzling their free drinks. As the bartender overtly motioned that it was my turn to order, both men dutifully stepped to the far side of the bar, close enough to quickly hop back in line. The bartender then asked what I'd like as he tidied up his serving area.

"Gin and tonic. Please."

He nodded, uninterested in looking at my ID, while trying to figure out which of the ten bottles in front of him was the Tanqueray. Just then, a finger tapped twice on my left shoulder. I knew who it was before I turned around.

"Alice. Didn't we talk about this?"

"Can't a girl drink at her own father's funeral?"

Larry's look of contempt was unyielding. He brushed past me, reached behind the bar – to the bartender's surprise – and grabbed a plastic water bottle. As Larry turned back around, he glanced toward Luke and his friend, drinking near the end of the bar. His eyes darted back and forth between them and me.

"Luke."

The two men pivoted toward Larry. Luke's friend stood up a little straighter once he realized Larry's presence.

"Hey, Larry."

Luke didn't appear nearly as intimidated. He was almost defiant in tone and posture.

"Luke, do you remember your Aunt Alice?"

Luke immediately sized me up. I could only imagine the stories that Big Al and his mother had fed him over the past fifteen years.

"The infamous Alice."

"Holy shit. Look at you, all grown up. How are you, Puke?"

Luke rubbed his tongue along his front teeth, plainly ignoring my question before he took a swig of his Miller Lite, then wiped the side of his mouth with the right sleeve of his white dress shirt. I could hear his audible gulp, even over the country-western band playing in the background. Finally, he glared at Larry for just a split second before turning his attention back to me.

"This is a family matter, do you mind?"

No, I do not. I yanked the plastic water bottle from Larry before brushing by him. *I should just go. You made an appearance; if I can't drink, there's no need to stick around.* I was about twenty feet from the exit when I heard a loud thud, followed by gasps. I turned to see people gathering around the bar. Concerned, I quickly changed course to return to the bar, pushing past some onlookers, including a woman on the phone with 9-1-1. All I could make out were the toes on a pair of black wingtips, swaying back and forth on the floor. I struggled my way past a few more onlookers to find Larry attempting CPR on Luke.

Luke Washington

O
n Thursday nights, they offered a buffet in the atrium. The spread
wasn't anything special – veggies and dips, fruit platter, and deli
sandwiches. More times than not, the dessert was a cookie tray
– chocolate chip, oatmeal raisin, double chocolate chip, and macadamia
nut. However, on the last Wednesday of the month, we were treated to a
full ice cream sundae bar.

The line already started to form – *I should've sat closer to the door*. By
the time I was out of the lecture hall, there were about twenty people in
front of me. At the end of the buffet was a caterer, most likely an undergrad
working for beer money, watching over the sundae bar. After about ten of
my classmates made their way through the double-sided buffet, the caterer
finally got his first taker. He offered an option of two different ice cream
flavors – I couldn't make out the flavors just yet, but I prayed that it wasn't
just chocolate and vanilla, like last month. After I filled my plate with the
standard buffet fare, I finally approached the promised land.

"Care for a sundae?"

"Hmmm...I probably shouldn't."

"Okay. Care for a sundae, miss?" The caterer asked the woman behind
me in line.

"On second thought, I'll take one."

"Great. Vanilla or chocolate?"

Ugh. Vanilla and chocolate again? I asked the caterer if he could do
a mixture of both. He obliged and scooped one of each flavor into a paper
cup. As he reached out his hand to offer the sundae to me, I gave him a
blank stare until he figured out he should add an additional scoop of each
flavor. I did notice a hint of judgment when he finally handed the cup over
to me, but I let it go. *If only he knew who I was.*

Now the fun part: chopped peanuts, shredded coconut, crumbled Oreos, walnuts, pecans, M&M's, some round chocolate things with tiny colored sprinkles that I didn't even know the name of, and finally the caramel and fudge. As I juggled my dinner plate and ice cream sundae, I looked for an unoccupied highboy table so I could enjoy some much-needed alone time. Table after table featured at least one classmate of mine. I could have gone back to the lecture hall and sat in my seat, but that would have been too depressing. I ended up picking a table with a girl eating by herself.

"Mind if I join you?"

"Please."

My impromptu dinner date didn't even get a sub sandwich, just a mixed green salad. It wasn't like they didn't have veggie subs available. My sundae started melting before I was even midway through my turkey and swiss sub. Meanwhile, she was down to the final few bites of her rabbit food. I didn't recognize her from the lecture, which was odd because she's pretty cute, and my eyes tended to wander.

"Eighty thousand dollars for a few lousy dinners and a piece of paper."

"You're not wrong. Hi, I'm Kate."

"Luke."

"Wait a minute – Luke Washington? I didn't recognize you."

"Have we met?"

"No. I meant I didn't recognize you without your hat."

"Oh, yeah?"

"The commercials are so good. Big Al would be proud."

That was how the conversation could've gone had I said anything. Instead, I stuffed my face with the ice cream sundae as Kate collected her trash and walked away after my second heaping spoonful.

I only needed eighteen more credits. Two night classes a semester at three credits each, and I would be done in three semesters, or a year-and-a-half. Then again, the ever-so-appealing alternative was just to drop out. It wasn't like Grandpa would hold me accountable anymore. *I'm in charge now – who cares if I have an MBA or not?*

I told Mark that I'd meet him at the Legion Brewing Co. in Plaza Midwood after class. Lauren didn't put up too much of a fuss like she usually would. *You have to play the sympathy card while you can.* It didn't take me long to get there from campus. Only a handful of people were scattered throughout the taproom, so I quickly spotted Mark sitting at a table by himself, halfway through his beer. He stood and eagerly waved before the door even closed behind me. Instead of joining him, I beelined straight to the bar. Legion Brewing Co. was the type of place that felt the need to name every one of their beers after a pun, but I loved them anyway. After glancing at the tap list on a chalkboard behind the bar, I ordered an oatmeal stout.

"*Path to The Dark Side*? You got it."

I paid the bill with cash, took a sip of the stout, and finally joined Mark at the table. He and I were the only patrons at a table; everyone else was belly up to the bar. He drank a lighter beer – maybe a pilsner or wheat. I think I saw it listed as *Wheating Rainbow* on the chalkboard.

"Cheers."

"What shall we drink to?"

"To justice."

As our glasses clinked together, Mark smiled and winked at me. His smile grew wider and he began chuckling to himself. His uneven teeth poked out of his mouth as he raised his beer and finished it in one large gulp.

"What is it?"

Mark played coy. He looked at the time on his phone, then over to the bar. The legs of his chair squealed loudly against the hardwood floor as he rose abruptly from the table and practically skipped to the bar. He motioned two fingers to the bartender, who swiftly produced two beers. As he waited, Mark glanced back at me, as if to see if I'd taken the bait. To be honest, my interest was piqued. I barely had two sips of my beer before he put a cold glass of *Wheating Rainbow* in front of me. Mark sipped his fresh beer as he plopped back into his chair. His lower lip curled over his upper lip as he soaked up the foamy head. Unable to take the suspense any longer, I moved in close enough to whisper.

"So...what is it?"

"The plan is coming together beautifully."

"You found Chad?"

"No. That's phase two."

"What's phase one?"

"The polonium! You seriously don't remember?"

It took all of my might not to sigh audibly. *This plan is fucked. Mark is never going to find Chad. And even if he did, there are a million ways for him to screw it up.*

"Okay, but how do we find Chad?"

"Chad? Why are you fixated on Chad? It's better for us that he left, it makes it even more suspicious. But we don't have much time. We have to act now, or else the timeline won't make any sense."

"Fine. What were you saying about polonium?"

"I found a guy."

"You found a guy with polonium?"

Mark's sly grin returned as he nodded his head slowly. He went on to explain that he knew a biology professor from the university who had access to the stuff. When I asked why the professor would offer his help and potentially jeopardize his career in the process, Mark dismissed my concern and told me I should be more appreciative of the "measures he had taken to secure our future." He leaned back in his chair, clearly frustrated that I wasn't sharing his enthusiasm. *You need to let him believe that you're behind him if you're going to screw him over later.*

"I'm sorry – it's just been a stressful time. Thank you for putting this together."

"That's my guy."

The color seemed to return to Mark's face as he downed the rest of his beer. Hovering over his wooden chair, he pulled it closer to the table to once again talk logistics.

"If we do this, we have to do it tonight."

"Tonight?"

"I told the guy that we'd meet him at ten. You have to decide right now, Luke. Are we doing this or not?"

"Fuck it."

Mark took the liberty of pouring half of the beer he bought for me into his own glass. His eyes glazed over as we held our pints in the air and finished them with ease.

The humid night air actually felt comforting as we walked outside. *There's something about a summer night in Charlotte: quiet – no mosquitoes, no people, and most importantly, no blazing sun.* When Mark stumbled on the stairs, I insisted I should drive to the meeting. He didn't put up much of a fight. Once we were inside the car, he explained that we'd be meeting the professor at the Waffle House down the street from the dealership, so we could go plant the polonium in Chad's desk afterward. *When was the last time I was in a Waffle House? Maybe in high school, since it was one of the few establishments to be open late and allowed underagers.*

At this hour, a single cook manned the nearly empty restaurant. Wanting a premier vantage point, we sat in a booth with an unobstructed view of the front door. I made the first move for the point-of-sale menu, sitting in front of the stack of condiments. The touchscreen, as presumably all Waffle House tablets on the planet, was encrusted with drops of dried maple syrup. *Why do I bother? I'm at a Waffle House – what else would I have?* But Mark continued to study the menu by the time the cook showed up with my coffee.

"The waffles will be up in a few minutes."

After I had mixed the creamer into my cup, Mark finally went with my exact order.

I checked my phone for the time. A message from Lauren; she was going to bed, and she loved me. It was 10:14 p.m., and no sign of our mysterious supplier. Just as the cook brought over Mark's coffee, the table began to vibrate. It didn't take long to notice Mark's right leg, bouncing up and down so fast that even the silverware was shaking on the table.

"You good, Mark?"

"Yeah, why wouldn't I be?"

My eyes drifted from the vibrating silverware to Mark's blank stare. He abruptly brought his restless leg to a stop when he saw my sight line. At least he had the sense to ask the cook, who had already turned his back on us, for a cup of decaf instead.

"How did you get this guy to agree to give you the poison anyway?"

"I've been meaning to talk to you about that."

"Is that right?"

"I thought you could put up the money as, eh, sort of an advance?"

"Oh, did you now?"

"Well, you know, I'm in the middle of a divorce, and you stand to gain the most...financially."

"How much?"

"Ten grand."

"Ten grand? I don't have that kind of money on me."

"There's an ATM around here somewhere."

"Are you crazy? You can't just withdraw ten grand from an ATM."

The moment I took my first sip of coffee, I heard the bell above the door ring behind me. Mark, with a clear view of the door, gave a gentle wave in that direction. I turned around to see a man I presumed to be our professor. He wore blue jeans, a plaid shirt with a vest, and a baseball cap that mostly shadowed his face. He slid into our booth, on the same side as Mark. The cook also approached, flopping the plates of waffles in front of Mark and me. The professor kept his head low, careful to conceal his face from the cook. Despite his skin color, the professor didn't speak with a hint of any accent.

"Luke. Nice to meet you. Want to order anything?"

"Dr. Chakrabarti. Do you have the money?"

"Hold on now, professor. Dinner first, sex later," Mark interjected.

"Whatever. I'll just have some tea then."

Obliging the man, I clicked on the tablet to order a tea. Meanwhile, Dr. Chakrabarti and Mark continued their dance, and the professor got angrier each time Mark dismissed his concerns. As the two bickered, I cut into my waffle. It seemed like every other establishment had transitioned to the Belgian waffle, but Waffle House had stuck to their guns, with the classic thin waffles cooked with butter-flavored, non-stick cooking spray. *An amateur might dump the syrup on the entire surface area of the waffle before cutting it into pieces, but not me. If you do it that way, the part of the waffle you don't immediately eat quickly becomes soggy. Instead, I cut the entire waffle at once, into about a dozen bite-sized pieces. Then, I stack the pieces on one side of the plate and pour the syrup into a pool on the unoccupied side. This way, I can pick up each piece and drag it through the pool of syrup. The result is a perfect waffle-to-syrup ratio, and most importantly, it's never soggy.* This waffle tasted even better than I remembered.

"We had an agreement. Ten thousand dollars or I walk."

"Luke, tell him we're good for it."

"Yeah, we'll make it right," I said in the middle of a delicious bite of waffle.

"Are you serious? This isn't how it works. I'm not risking my life for some...handshake deal."

"Where are we supposed to get ten grand this late at night?"

"I don't fucking know. Maybe you should've figured that out before-hand."

The cook brought Dr. Chakrabarti's cup of tea to the table, and Mark told me to close out our tab, which I thought was odd since we'd just gotten our food. As I returned to the tablet, the professor reached across Mark for some sugar and cream. The table was silent except for the sound of his spoon on the edges of the porcelain cup. Mark snatched the spoon from the professor.

"Now, you listen good, Doc. We are going to get up as a group and walk out the front door. Then, we're going to casually stroll to your car, where you will hand over the polonium. And finally, you will drive home – all without saying a single word. Nod if you understand."

Dr. Chakrabarti remained perfectly still, gaze fixed on the tea. Then I heard it: a click. The hammer of a gun being cocked. *Fuck.*

"Nod if you understand."

"I understand, but..."

"I said, 'Not a single word.'"

"But I took a Lyft over. I don't have a car."

"Well, where the fuck is it then?"

"I hid it behind the dumpster before I came in."

"Fine. We will calmly walk out of here together, and over to the dumpster, where you will hand over the polonium and then call a Lyft home – all without saying a single word. Okay?"

The professor reluctantly nodded. Mark pointed at the tablet and looked to me as if to say, "You got this, right?" I reached for my wallet. *What the hell is Mark doing? First Chad. Now, he's fucked this up.*

I opened my wallet to find only plastic. *Shit. I must've used the last of my cash at Legion.* I inspected every crevice, hoping to find a folded up twenty somewhere. It was a rare occurrence for me to carry cash anymore, but it still had the benefit of being untraceable, which was precisely why I'd gotten a few twenties from the ATM yesterday.

"What's wrong?"

"Nothing."

I inserted a credit card into the point-of-sale tablet, knowing the risk. Impatient as ever, Mark stood from the table and pushed the professor out of the booth. Apparently, Mark didn't seem worried about the clearly visible outline of the gun tucked under his shirt and into his waistband. I gave the cook the standard 20 percent tip, so as not to jog his memory for being either too cheap or too generous.

By the time I got outside, Mark and Dr. Chakrabarti had already disappeared. Behind the Waffle House, the glow from the streetlight was strong enough to block the view of the stars, but too dim for full visibility. Mark used the flashlight on his phone to help the professor search near the dumpster. As Dr. Chakrabarti, belly down on the pavement, scrounged underneath it, I ensured no one was watching us. After a few moments, he offered a brown Harris Teeter grocery bag that was clearly too large for its contents. Mark snatched it from the professor before he was able to get back on his feet. Finally, Mark rushed toward me, opened the bag, stuck his phone inside to illuminate, and confirmed that we had the goods.

～

Ten seconds was usually plenty of time. However, when the dealership was only partially lit and the pressure was on, ten seconds was going to prove challenging. Mark had decided that I would unlock the door while he rushed past me to disarm the alarm.

"What's the code again?"

"12-28."

"Then press one to disarm. Or is it two?"

"One to arm. Two to disarm."

"So it's 12-28, then two?"

"Yeah. Ready?"

Mark gave me a nod, and I turned the key to the back door. The beeping started the second that I yanked the door open. Mark darted past me toward the alarm just a few feet down the hall. The flashlight from his phone bobbed up and down as he ran. As I walked through the back door toward the offices, I heard the five keypad strokes followed by the resounding chime.

The paper bag was light, as if nothing was inside. I unfolded the top to take a look for myself. Inside was a small amber-colored glass vial, accompanied by a syringe needle in a plastic top. I clamped the bag shut right before Mark caught up to me at the door to The Box; that's what we call the finance office. When a customer went into The Box, there was already a handshake deal in place, and it was Chad's job to iron out those details and get them on paper. In that respect, The Box was the "most pressurized" room in the building, where deals could die an instant. That night, however, the office was quiet, lifeless. I had never been one to get to work either early or late enough to be the only person at the dealership, so it was a strange feeling seeing the place empty.

"All right, there's Chad's desk. Go ahead."

Chad didn't have much on his desk; no family photos or stray papers, just a nameplate, a calculator, and a Washington Ford mug with a few pens sitting inside.

"Here's Big Al Washington and his dog Teddy," an ominous voice bellowed.

What the fuck is that? A life-sized cardboard cutout of Grandpa appeared in front of me. Mark laughed his ass off at his attempt to scare me. He was so pleased with himself that he twisted the standee around and started dancing with it.

"Stop dicking around. C'mon."

"All right, fine."

Mark finished his dance by pantomiming a curtsey to my grandpa. After returning the standee to its home, Mark met me back at Chad's desk. His fully stocked desk drawer contained any office supply a person might need, and all shockingly organized. I opened the bag for Mark to pull out the polonium. Using the sleeve of his shirt, Mark planted the vial and syringe on top of a stack of sticky notes.

"Let's get out of here, shall we?" Mark said.

Mark turned away from me. The drawer remained open. *It's now or never.* I took one last look at Mark to ensure he wasn't watching me. Using my thumb, I gently flicked the orange plastic cap off the syringe and then injected it into the vial. I didn't take much of the poison, maybe a few millimeters. Satisfied, I returned the safety cap onto the needle. I shoved the capped needle into my left sleeve, grabbed the vile tightly in my right hand, and closed the drawer.

Now exiting The Box, I yelled to Mark, already on his way to the back door, that I left my phone charger at my old desk in the bullpen, and I was going to quickly grab it. He Told me to hurry, joking that he didn't want to be here any longer than he had to when he was off the clock.

Hustling to the bullpen where Mark's desk also was located, I jammed the syringe farther up my sleeve, using the button at the cuff to secure it. I figured Mark would most certainly look back once he's at the alarm panel to check on me, so seeing as he was currently thirty feet away from it, I gave myself about ten seconds.

With my sleeve covering the vile, I simultaneously tried to wipe away my fingerprints and open Mark's desk drawer. His drawer, unlike Chad's, was a complete mess, filled with assorted scrap paper, receipts, and even used tissues. I carefully positioned the poison behind a container of paper clips, so Mark would never notice it, but someone with a search warrant would. I gently closed the desk drawer so it wouldn't make a sound before rushing over to get my phone charger.

The exact moment that I looked up, I saw Mark's outline at the alarm. He raised both arms to indicate frustration at my slow pace. The distance between us was too great to offer an explanation, so I just gave him a thumbs-up as three millimeters of deadly poison shifted from side to side in the sleeve of my shirt.

⌒

Being forced to stand in a room with your grandfather's lifeless body as strangers offered condolences could only be described as excruciating. Lauren was kind enough to stand next to me, and stepped in whenever I became too emotional. Meanwhile, I bit my tongue as every single attendee showed up in a driverless car. They might as well have spat on Grandpa's grave as they said their goodbyes. I could guarantee that he would have been shit-talking every last one of them, and not behind their backs like me – he would have called them out straight to their faces. They each voiced it a little differently, but people's overall sentiments were that they were sorry for my loss and wished me luck on taking over. *As if luck will be the only reason I succeed.* The theme for my mom was a nondescript plea of sympathy; some included a tidbit on how Grandpa affected their lives; others focused on her well-being during "this difficult time." No one questioned Larry's placement at the end of the receiving line. In fact, it seemed like every attendee devoted most of their time and condolences to him. About halfway through the allotted time, the line to see Larry backed up so much that an employee of the museum felt bad enough to direct my mom and me to an adjacent space.

Larry held all the cards as the executor of the estate. *No one has dared to question him about this murder clause. And since no one has seen the will, how do we even know for sure that it exists? I'm not saying the murder was bullshit, but Larry is well connected enough with the media to plant any story he wants. But today is the day where the narrative will change, and most importantly, I will be able to control it.*

I had it all figured out. *After the memorial service, when everyone will be socializing and drinking on the family's tab, I will poison myself. It's a significant risk, but a necessary one to clear the investigation and receive my rightful inheritance. My intake has to be enough to cause a reaction, but not enough to kill me.* As far as dosage went, I couldn't exactly reach out to a medical professional. And there were always stories of investigators looking into Google searches – like that Casey Anthony case years back – so I settled on four drops from the syringe, and if need be, I could make it look worse than it feels. The next obstacle was the syringe itself. I couldn't just inject myself, so I thought I might be able to release it into my beer after the service – the only problem I foresaw was the presence of the syringe. The best solution I came up with – and I did think it was rather ingenious – was to inject the polonium into a beer at home and bring it with me to the service. That was precisely why a lukewarm Miller Lite bottle was tucked inside my left jacket pocket. Knowing I would be receiving sympathetic hugs at the service, I purposefully draped my jacket over my forearm from the moment I walked into the building. With the typical North Carolina summer in full swing, no one would even question why I'd shed the jacket.

Larry asked me to say a few words, but I couldn't do it. I wasn't even able to get through a pre-taped commercial, let alone an emotional speech about how much Grandpa meant to me. What if I flubbed a line? Or worse, what if I completely froze in front of the crowd? I'd be branded a fraud, the undeserving heir to my grandfather's business without a shred of his glibness or charm. Instead, I figured it would be best to sit in the front row and play the sympathy card. Lauren even played her part to console me when I became emotional. No one was the wiser.

I t was almost time. I'd been playing out every scenario in my head since the night of my rendezvous with Mark. *The ceremony will end, and then I'll shake a few hands before going to the bar. I won't immediately order a Miller Lite; it will be a spontaneous order, as if I can't decide on a drink, so I'll just go with a staple.* At some point, I would covertly switch to the bottle inside my coat – and then eventually, wake up in the hospital with a fortune to my name. But first, there was the memorial service. I had to sit through the story I'd heard a million times before – about how Grandpa gave Larry, a kid right out of law school, a chance when he didn't have to, at a time when no white North Carolina businessman would hire a Black man for a lawyer. My mother spoke next.

I played her remarks over and over in my head. Because, while I planned on following through, there was always a chance I might have backed down. Or at least, I might have taken a step back to realize that consuming a poison I knew almost nothing about was a risk probably not worth taking. Instead, it became my affirmation that I was doing the right thing. It was also the last thing I could remember.

Courtney Washington

The moment I walked through the automatic doors the A/C stopped my sweat in its tracks. Perhaps they froze the entire hospital to keep the dead bodies cold – Including Luke's? The thought of his naked corpse laid out on a steel drawer in some compartment sent a chill down my spine.

Rubbing my exposed arms for warmth, I realized I was still wearing the dress from the memorial service, in stark contrast to the t-shirts and sweats of others in the waiting room. Suddenly self-conscious, I pulled the scarf tighter around my shoulders and breasts. Before I could think of someone to call to bring me a change of clothes, Larry came rushing through the automatic doors and headed straight for the reception desk. Still wearing his black mourning suit sans jacket, he'd soon find out exactly what the staff told me, which was that the doctors were working tirelessly on Luke and that they'd update us as soon as they knew anything. Despite his best efforts, even Larry the Lion couldn't talk his way in to see Luke. Dejected, he hung his head and meandered into the waiting room, where he eventually spotted me amongst the commoners.

"I'm so sorry, Courtney."

"Thanks, Larry."

"Have you heard anything?"

"No."

Larry settled into the second chair to my left. Still pissed at him from earlier in the day, I refused to engage any further. Taking the hint, he bit his tongue as he furiously texted on his phone. *It's no secret, Larry is a fixer for our family. Sure, people on the outside might see him as the lawyer for the dealership, but what other lawyer do you know who'd stepped foot into a courtroom only twice in the last forty years? Regardless of Larry's track* record with our family, my patience and trust wore thin. I could forgive him for missing my father's murder – *I mean, who tries to kill a man knocking on death's door?* But, what I couldn't forgive was the attempt on my son. *Either he's getting too old, or he's complicit.*

N o one else helped set up beside the funeral coordinator, caterers, and me. Once again, Larry had designated me as the only family member to help with the memorial service. How was I supposed to look presentable after running around to make sure a damn monkey dressed in a cowboy costume was happy? Nonetheless, I powered through without one complaint. I tracked down Daddy's war photos, home videos, and Washington Ford commercials, all within seventy-two hours. *Do you think Eva would've been able to do that? Hell, no. She's too busy packing her shit so she can catch the first flight out of the country.* One silver lining to the estate being frozen was the thought of the dumbfounded look on her face when Larry sent the group email to update us. On one accidental 'reply all,' Eva had threatened legal action and rambled about how it was her money, because Big Al told her she was going to get all of it to raise their daughter Margret "properly."

"Excuse me, ma'am. Would you care to see him?"

A giant man, well over six-feet tall, with a goatee, suddenly stood before me. I guess I'd been staring down, because his khaki pant legs, which engulfed his shoes, drew my attention first. I raised my eyes up... and up...the pants were properly creased, but the rest of his suit was a mess and his belly flopped out over his belt, which prevented him from buttoning up his jacket. One would think a man who practically lived in a suit would know how to wear one.

I finally lifted my chin to meet his eyes before offering a controlled nod. He slowly folded his left arm away from his chest, pointing to an off-shoot room. I followed him, leaving two paces between us. *How miserable must this poor guy's life be? He has to be somber at all times. I bet the guy probably hasn't been able to laugh since high school.*

The giant with the goatee ultimately led me into what must normally be an office, but doubled as the visitation room for the day. A mahogany casket with gold handles sat at the far end of the room.

"Would you like me to open it?"

Suddenly, the room seemed smaller. A memory flashed. *My mom is hooked up to wires as a machine beeps every few seconds. She is in a hospital bed, almost unrecognizable and so slight that you can see her bones; in place of her hair, a bandana covers her head. Then there is a casket, much like the one that sits in front of me. My father shakes hands with people, while Alice and I sit quietly in a corner on leather armchairs. I'm not sure why my sister is crying. Mom will get better; everything will be fine.*

"Miss Washington?"

I snapped back to. The funeral director looked at me with sympathetic eyes that he had most definitely perfected over the years. He didn't even bother to ask if I wanted to be left alone, he just informed me that he was going to open the casket and give me a few minutes to say goodbye. Before he left, he warned me that Daddy might look a little different than I remembered, but said it was because his "soul has left his body." He then proceeded to tell me how his world-class makeup and stylist team had attempted to recreate what Daddy looked like, and he believed I would be pleased with the result. The casket opened to reveal a withered body. It had only been a few days since Daddy passed away, but he was already deteriorating. A fear passed through me that if I looked directly at him for too long, I would forget what he truly had looked like. His ghostly paleness and skin sagging past his cheeks made me question whether it was him or not. The door clicked shut. I wandered around the room, fragmented memories attempting to make their way into my stream of consciousness. When I tried to focus on a singular recollection, images faded away before I could safeguard them. As my emotions overwhelmed me, all I could think of was why I didn't have anyone here to console me. *Both of my parents are dead; I don't speak to my sister; my son is too consumed with his new wife and responsibilities to care about his aging mother.* I was completely alone.

After what seemed like hours, Larry and Luke joined me in the visitation room just as the guests began to arrive. I greeted Luke with a big hug, holding onto him for a few moments longer than usual. I could see he struggled to hold back tears, but he put on a stoic face for the guests that came through to offer their condolences.

I didn't notice anything at first, but it became abundantly clear that the guests prioritized speaking with Larry over Luke and me. People would generally offer a brief condolence to Luke and me, but would then speak ad nauseum with Larry as if he was the new patriarch of the family. It got to the point where the funeral director took us out of the room, so people didn't feel awkward making small talk with us while they waited to speak to Larry. I tried to imagine what Luke was feeling at that moment. Those people should have been waiting to see Luke at the end of the line, not Larry. *Who the hell does Larry think he is?*

⌣

I hated to admit it, but Larry knew how to captivate an audience. Half of the bloodsuckers had heard the story of the day Larry and Daddy met at least ten times, yet they still hung on every word. Some people just had a gift for public speaking; even though I could pinpoint everything Larry did right, I could never command the crowd like him. *Is that why he went before me, just to make a fool out of me?* My palms started to clam up.

"'Now, let's think about that. Big Al put his trust in a twenty-five-year-old Black kid fresh out of law school. Who does that? I'll tell you who, a man with integrity and strong principles. That was Big Al above all else, and I'm going to miss him dearly."

Funny how a man that preaches loyalty has the gall to hold his so-called family hostage.

"Next to the stage is the woman who not only helped bring this celebration of life together, but was able to experience the other side of Big Al, that of the family man. Please welcome Big Al's daughter, Courtney Washington."

Just speak from the heart. You'll be fine. I wiped my hands on the sides of my dress as I walked to the podium. *Avoid shaking anyone's hand. Give them three quick minutes that no one will remember within a week.* Larry waited for me at the podium. Before I had the chance to offer a hug, he grabbed both of my hands, held them tightly between us, and offered a look of compassion – the one where a person looked right into your eyes, flattened out their frown, and softly nodded their head a few times. Larry's expression swiftly transformed into confusion – and then discomfort – at my sweaty palms. I slid my hands away as quickly as possible, but it was too late: his shock was my embarrassment. I looked away as I adjusted the microphone. *Three minutes, then it's over.*

"Hello. First, thank you all for coming out today to celebrate the life of my father or 'Big Al,' as you might know him. It's odd growing up when your father is a celebrity. You don't really notice anything different until you're older, because you don't know any better. People would come up to him when we were out for dinner or at a parent-teacher conference to take a photo, or just to say 'hi.' Everyone would always tell me how lucky I was that I got to be the daughter of the famous car salesman, Big Al Washington. But, I never saw it that way. He was just my daddy. We had a special relationship, him and me. After my mother died – "

For the first time since standing at the podium, I glanced down to the surface I was leaning against. Among the various notes, I saw a piece of paper labeled 'Courtney.' It appeared to contain talking points for me, as well as topics to avoid. The first topic to avoid was Daddy's murder, followed by his estate. *Seriously Larry? You really had to spell that out for me?*

Larry, now sitting back down in his assigned seat, squinted at me, perhaps to make sure that I'd received the message. *Who the fuck does he think he is? This is my father's funeral!* A throat cleared in the audience.

"I'm sorry, but I can't just stand up here and act like everything is okay. My father was murdered. No one can tell me who did it or why. An eighty-five-year-old man with one foot in the grave was murdered. The detectives have no leads; instead, they insist on relentlessly interrogating my family, when they could be spending their time tracking down the real killer. Meanwhile, I'm expected to put on a fake smile and act like everything is okay. But I refuse to be silent in the face of a conspiracy against my family."

Now I have their attention.

"As I grieve over the loss of my father, did you know that the oh-so-eloquent man who was at this podium just before me is holding my family by the balls? I'm sorry to put it so bluntly – but Larry Bridges has frozen our rightful inheritance because of a technicality. That's what he says anyway, because he won't let any of us actually look at the will. Speaking of leeches..."

A gasp from the crowd interrupted my pause. In my speech class at community college, the professor hammered into us that selective pauses were among the most effective tools for any orator. The murmurs began to build as Larry stood from his seat. My time was running short.

"For those of you who don't know, Eva Washington, my quote, unquote stepmother – who is practically my same age, by the way – has purchased first-class tickets back to her home country of Iceland, for herself and my half-sister for tomorrow morning. My father's body isn't even cold yet, and this gold-digger plans to take all his valuables and never come back. You could've at least waited a week to pretend that you were grieving, Eva."

Suddenly, two hands grabbed my shoulders; the grip was firm, but not strong enough to hurt. My voice faded from the speakers, despite the volume of my reproach remaining steady. I turned my head to see the Reverend, with a look of kind concern, pulling me away from the podium.

A TALE OF
TWO BRIDGES

VI

A TALE OF
TWO BRIDGES

Larry Bridges

No matter how many times I watched the video, it didn't seem real. The footage itself was surprisingly clear, but my brain didn't seem to want to comprehend that he was gone – or that I was watching his last moments on Earth.

"Do you want to watch it again?"

"Just play it until I tell you to stop."

"Yes, sir."

Javy, an ambitious young mechanic who sometimes doubled as our IT guy, clicked the mouse to rewind the video. After about three viewings, Javy purposefully distracted himself with his surroundings instead of watching the footage. I wouldn't describe it as an enjoyable task to watch a man die over and over, but if I wanted to find out who killed Al, it was a necessary one.

"I need to clear my head for a minute. You keep watching. Tell me if you see anything."

"If you say so."

"You need some coffee?"

Javy shook his head no. When I stood, my legs felt heavy with the sheer number of hours I had been putting in lately. When I grabbed the handle to exit the office, I heard a deep sigh and the click of the mouse.

The dealership was busier than it had been in years, which I suspected was a direct result of the media frenzy surrounding Big Al's death. The salespeople had no idea what to make of all the "ducks on the pond," as the sales managers often refer to customers who wander the lot. The problem was that the onlookers would rather talk to the hovering news reporters than to our salespeople.

For the first time since I could remember, the kitchen was markedly empty. Unfortunately for me, so was the coffee pot. As I went through the motions to refill it, I finally had a minute to myself, just to think.

Who had a motive? I could identify at least three groups of people. I grabbed an extra coffee filter out of the box to jot down my thoughts.

In the first group, there was anyone that could have financially benefited from his death. In the will, Big Al listed five beneficiaries: Eva, Margret, Courtney, Luke, and myself. Margret was far too young to have concocted such a devious plan, and I knew I had nothing to do with the murder. That left Eva, Courtney, and Luke as possible suspects in group one.

In the second group, I put anyone who incorrectly assumed they would financially benefit from Big Al's death: Alice and his second wife, Kelly. However, they both seemed unlikely culprits to me, as Alice had been halfway around the globe in Alaska, and Kelly had received her divorce settlement already.

In the third group, there was anyone with a personal vendetta against Big Al. Realistically, this would be by far the most arduous group to dissect. The suspects ranged from a slighted worker to any number of the dissatisfied customers over forty-six years.

There also was one outlier to consider, who didn't fall into any of these groups: Chad. Clearly, his motive was to avoid detection. Chad's first instinct would undoubtedly be self-preservation – and he was at the scene of the crime on the day in question.

The hot water slowly dripped through the coffee grounds and into the glass carafe. The sink, littered with used coffee mugs and dirty dishes, radiated an overpowering stench that I didn't notice until catching sight of it. I decided to wait out the coffeemaker at the kitchen table, as far away as possible from the sink.

At the table, I discovered a stack of Detective Copeland's business cards fanned out among the old magazines and crumbs. Without hesitating, I scooped all seven cards into my suit jacket pocket along with my list of suspects. I could understand why Detective Copeland insisted that we should be working together on the case; after all, we did want the same thing – to find Big Al's murderer. It was just everything else that I couldn't allow her to uncover that made collaboration impossible.

⌒

The steering wheel felt hot to the touch; the stagnant air, suffocating. After I turned the engine over, I dialed up the A/C to full blast and rolled the windows down to dispel the trapped heat. Sweat formed on the back of my neck for at least the third time that day as I adjusted the settings on the seat and mirrors. *There's nothing quite like a summer evening in Charlotte. Despite the resting sun, the humidity decides to work overtime. Your sweat glands, confused by the source of the heat, secrete moisture through every pore of your skin. Showers become a nightly necessity. Air conditioners get pushed to their limits.* I took note of the odometer, but doubted anyone would notice a discrepancy of eighty miles, give or take. It wasn't as if anyone had ever noticed before.

I never understood Al's obsession with living in the country. Personally, I couldn't stand it; give me a penthouse in a high rise over a hundred acres in the middle of nowhere – and with God-knows-what roaming around just outside the door – any day of the week. But first, I needed to make a stop.

The car's navigation took me to a lower-middle-class neighborhood where the two-story houses all looked the same. After a couple of turns, I ended up at a poorly lit cul-de-sac where I saw Javy, visible from his phone's glow, sitting outside on the front porch, only his face and hair protruding from his black hoodie. *How the fuck can he be wearing a hoodie on a night like tonight?* It took Javy a minute to realize the truck heading toward his house was me, but when he did, he quickly turned inside the house for a moment where, if he was following my earlier instructions, he would be leaving his phone behind.

After I turned off my headlights, I backed the truck into his driveway and watched him go to work in the backup camera. First, Javy removed the wooden blocks from the boat trailer's wheels. Then, he lugged the receiver to my 2027 Ford Super Duty. After some troubleshooting and loud grunting, Javy finally managed to attach the trailer hitch to the truck. Still somewhat unfamiliar with my loaner, I searched for the button to unlock the door as he tapped on the glass and waved enthusiastically. I thought about stalling for a few seconds when I eventually found the button, in hopes he might calm down before our journey, but figured I couldn't allow him to make any more noise.

"Hey, Mr. Bridges."

"Javy."

"I don't think I've ever seen you without a suit. Still had to tuck that shirt in though, huh?"

"Hmm. Are we all set back there?"

"Yes, sir. Had a little trouble with the hitch. I've only done it a couple of times, but I figured it out."

"Good."

"Did you leave your phone?"

"Of course."

I put the truck into drive before Javy had time to put his seat belt on. I kept it under the speed limit and waited until we got out of the cul-de-sac before turning my lights back on. *Wait a minute –*

"Just a couple of times? Is it new?"

"No, sir. My dad has had it for as long as I can remember."

"Your dad?"

"Yeah, it's his."

"His? I distinctly remember you saying, 'I have a fishing boat we could use.'"

"Well, technically he doesn't know about it. But you said it would only take a couple of hours. He'll still be asleep when we get back."

"Still be asleep? You mean that isn't your house, either?"

"No, it's my parent's place."

"Aren't you too old to be living at home?"

"You are aware of how much you pay me, right?"

I pulled a sharp turn out of the quiet neighborhood onto the main drag. Somehow, the trailer didn't flip over. Javy took notice of my test.

"It's secure, Mr. Bridges. Don't worry."

His confidence failed to ease my concerns. If we got caught, my credibility would be blemished forever. As Warren Buffett once said, it takes twenty years to build a reputation and five minutes to ruin it. Javy wasn't exactly my first choice, but he was around and willing. What Javy lacked in experience, he made up for in his work ethic. And he might be on the fast track for a managerial position if he could pass this crucial test.

"Mr. Bridges, please don't take this the wrong way, but why can't we just go through the front gate? You must have the code, right?"

"Yes, I have the code. However, there is a log generated every time someone comes and goes on the property. Couple that with a security camera, and we'd be dead to rights."

"That's why you're the boss. I didn't even think of that. It's like you're playing chess while I'm still trying to double-jump motherfuckers in checkers."

The perfectly paved road quickly transitioned to a pothole-riddled one just as we crossed the border into South Carolina. Signs for half-priced fireworks littered both sides of the road for the next couple of miles. The signs made me recall a memory I hadn't thought about in years. It was maybe twenty-five years ago, when I ran down to the border to get about a thousand dollars worth of very illegal fireworks for a Washington Ford Fourth of July commercial. We were having a "blowout" sale for the holiday weekend, so Big Al had the idea to film a commercial with his "dog" Teddy being a box of mortars, artillery shells, fountains, roman candles, and bottle rockets. When the night for the commercial shoot came, we placed three cars at ridiculously low prices in the background of the frame with an oversized box of fireworks in front of each of them.

"Action."

"Hey, folks. Big Al Washington here. This fourth of July, we are having a blowout sale at Washington Ford. A 2003 Ford F-150 is now ten thousand dollars off the sticker price! Can you believe that, Teddy?"

Big Al proceeded to pull a long-reach butane lighter out of his pocket, twirled it around his finger then flicked on the flame. The fuse, now lit, raced toward the first box of fireworks. Big Al stepped back from the fireworks with a shit-eating grin on his face just as a series of fireballs exploded, resulting in a cloud of gunpowder engulfing him. Big Al later told me he almost shit his pants when an artillery shell shot right past his head, but you would have never guessed from his on-screen savviness. The famous Washington Ford theme music kicked in right as he reappeared through a cloud of smoke, lighter still in hand. The second and third boxes of fireworks were just as boisterous as the first one. It might not have made logical sense that the fireworks doubled as his "dog" Teddy, but the commercial was a huge hit. The dealership had record sales that weekend, and the cops were only a little pissed at us.

"Between you and me, Mr. Bridges, who do you think did it?"

"Did what?"

"Come on! Quit playin'. You know what I'm talking about. Who killed the old man?"

"I truly don't know."

"It's got to be the trophy wife, right? She couldn't go another day of having sex with that old, limp dick and saggy balls, so she just went ahead and knocked him off."

Javy cleared his throat when he realized I did not share his enthusiasm for theorizing about Big Al's love life.

"She's gotta be a suspect though, right?"

"Anyone who stands to gain millions from Big Al's death is a suspect in my mind. So yes, she is one of them."

"Millions, huh?"

I'd said too much. Before I even looked over at the passenger seat, the glint in Javy's eye was blinding.

The cicadas grew louder as the street lights dimmed. We passed a desolate Carowinds, the 400-acre shared amusement park of the Carolinas, eventually turning onto a back road that spilled out onto one of the many Lake Wylie boat ramps. It wasn't the closest boat ramp to the W. Ranch by any stretch, but I knew for a fact that it didn't have any cameras.

On the ramp, the only sources of illumination were the truck's taillights and a distant dock light. After a non-verbal nudge, Javy climbed out of the vehicle to guide my truck down the ramp. Within a couple of minutes, Javy had the boat into the lake and gave me the thumbs up to drive away. Careful not to be noticed, I parked the truck about a quarter-mile away. By the time I got back to the water, Javy was standing in the shallow water, waiting to load me in.

"Equipment check."

"It's all here."

"It's all here until we drive three miles across the lake, and all of a sudden it's not there. Equipment check."

I pulled out a single yellow sticky note from my shirt pocket.

"You got it, boss."

"An LED tactical flashlight."

"Check."

"One pair of night vision binoculars for me."

"Got it."

"Two walkie talkies with headsets."

"Check."

"See, now we know."

"You forgot the gun."

"Gun? No guns."

"Says the guy who will be on the boat while I'm out on the front lines."

"No, says the guy who makes sure you get paid. Put the fucking gun back in the truck. Do you understand?"

I shot Javy a look of disgust as he clung to the bow of the boat, a dumbass smile on his face. Without a word, he loosened his grip and trudged through the shallow water. Lacking any urgency, Javy made the quarter-mile trek back to the vehicle. *A gun? Javy is quickly disappointing me.* His decision gave me no choice; I was forced to enact my insurance plan. Taking advantage of Javy's short absence, I placed a tiny night-vision camera, the size of an ant, on the front strap of his backpack.

When Javy eventually trudged back to the boat, I sat ready on the handle of the motor. The moment he threw his leg over the side, I punched it. The boat launched across the water. Javy stumbled to the bench, struggling to find his balance as I sped through the no-wake zone. I flicked the button on for the masthead light; I didn't know the lake well enough to go without it, even if it did give away our position.

The breeze wasn't exactly refreshing, but it beat the unbearably humid July air. A stray mortar whizzed across the dark sky, eventually producing a thunderous boom and glow bright enough to brighten the lake for a few moments. As we approached the W. Ranch, Javy remained quiet, perhaps harboring his anger after the stunt that I pulled. *I'd better play nice; he is committing a first-degree trespassing felony on my behalf, after all.*

"We good?"

"Yeah."

"Look, I appreciate your help with this thing. With the initiative you're showing, you're due for a nice raise, you know."

Javy remained seated, hands clasped, his back facing me. I gave Javy a minute to think over my proposal. *I said what I needed to say. By the time we arrive at the W. Ranch dock, Javy will be so thrilled with the idea of a raise that he'd forget all about our misunderstanding.* I switched off the masthead light as we approached the dock. The intermediate fireworks provided enough lighting for me to drift in the rest of the way.

"One million."

"Excuse me?"

"My raise."

"One million dollars? You are just getting a fireproof box from inside of a closet."

"I'm committing a crime. Also, you're forgetting about the old lady."

"What about her?"

"She could shoot me and claim self-defense."

"Al didn't believe guns. There's nothing to worry about."

"One million dollars."

The balls on this kid. If I wasn't in a pinch, I might've tossed him overboard at that very moment. But there we were. I had to hand it to him, he seized his moment at the most opportune time.

"Twenty large. And I'll double your wage. Take it or leave it."

Javy took a moment to do the math in his head. Truthfully, I didn't even know what the kid earned, but it couldn't be more than a few bucks over minimum wage. Javy appeared to have tallied the numbers, yet he still hesitated, before finally turning to face me.

"Do I have your word?"

"What else is there?"

"All right, deal."

Javy stood to gather a few items in his arms while I tied us off from the dock.

"Here, take these."

Javy, with his eyes nervously scanning the property's edge, handed over the walkie talkie and the night vision binoculars. I clipped the walkie talkie to my belt and strung the earpiece under my shirt before jamming it into my ear. By the time I got situated, Javy had already climbed onto the dock with his backpack full of gear.

"Check, check. Do you copy?"

"I can hear you," Javy snidely remarked.

"Use the walkie, so I know it works."

Javy pressed down the button on his earpiece, with a sigh and a blatant eye roll.

"I copy."

"Thank you. Shall we go over the plan one last time?"

"Do I have a choice?"

"Nope. You will go around the house through the woods, avoiding the floodlights and the guard down the road. Once you reach the house, you will enter the side door with the key that I've provided you. The basement will be the second door on your right. Once downstairs, you'll find Big Al's desk and a closet. In that closet, you will find a locked fireproof briefcase under some banker boxes filled with files and whatnot. Finally, you'll grab the key to the briefcase, which should be in the top drawer on the left-hand side of the desk."

"Got it."

"If you do get caught, it should go without saying, but I'm going to say it anyway: you will not utter my name from your mouth. I'm not your boss. I'm not your lawyer. We both coincidentally work at Washington Ford, but for all intents and purposes, I don't know you. Understood?"

"Copy that."

The walkie talkie buzzed in my ear. *Smart ass.* I was quickly regretting our partnership, but the job should be so damned easy, even Javy wouldn't be able to screw it up. After handing over the house key, I untied the boat from the dock, letting the tide slowly take me out to the middle of the lake as Javy ventured onto the W. Ranch property.

⌣

The fireworks continued to light up the night sky every couple of minutes. *Hopefully, the patrol boat doesn't come by to find the source. God, what would my excuse be for drifting in the middle of the lake damn near close to midnight?*

It had been a couple of minutes since I left Javy on the dock. Growing impatient, I reached for the binoculars, next to a paddle at my feet, to locate him, but the shoreline didn't offer any insights to his whereabouts.

"How are we looking, Javy? Over."

Radio silence. *That little prick. Well, I gave him a chance.* I fired up the handheld video monitor with a feed of the hidden camera that I planted on his backpack strap. While it didn't have any sound, the image was crystal clear.

"Javy? Can you hear me? Over."

The video hesitated for just a second before continuing up the path to the main house. He could positively hear me.

"Javy, where the fuck are you?"

"I'm right here. Chill."

"Javy. Don't test me right now."

"All right, damn. I'm almost at the house."

"I'd recommend staying off the main path. Over."

Another hesitation. Perhaps Javy had just realized the possibility that I could be watching him. Nonetheless, the kid took my advice and veered off the path. As I scrutinized his approach to the house, a boat entered my peripheral vision. It was far enough off in the distance where the driver wouldn't see me, but with one ill-timed firework, I would have yet another headache to deal with for the week. By the looks of it, the watercraft had the outline of a speedboat, but I couldn't be certain if it was patrol or not.

On the monitor, Javy inched closer to the perfectly manicured driveway of the lake house. Starting a quarter-mile from the front door, hundreds of pine trees lined both sides of the driveway. Big Al had them planted after a trip to Hawaii, where a tour guide told him that Hawaiian royalty would use the practice to display their power for everyone on the island. Just as the camera caught sight of Eva's Ford Edge, the floodlights turned on to expose Javy, apparently scaring him enough that he dashed for cover behind one of the pine trees. The camera pulsated on Javy's chest as he gathered his composure. After a few moments, he picked himself up off the lawn and darted toward the side of the house.

Now on the wrap-around porch, Javy dug the key out of his pants pocket and clutched it firmly, careful not to make a noise as he opened the side door. Once inside, Javy's steps became slower, more deliberate. Just as I instructed him, he entered the second door on the right, leading down to the basement. Instead of turning on the lights, Javy wisely pulled the flashlight from the backpack and used it to guide himself down the stairs.

Big Al's home office set up was similar to his dealership office, in the sense that framed photos and accolades lined the walls. Javy pulled the sleeve of his sweatshirt over his left hand to prevent the transfer of his fingerprints as he opened the closet door behind the desk. I couldn't help but shake my head – our mastermind thief just now realized this evidence might be a problem? Never mind everything else he had already touched.

Continuing his search, Javy scanned the closet's shelves for any signs of the fireproof briefcase. *Add poor listening skills to the list of Javy's faults.* After scouring three of the four shelves in the closet, he whispered a request for a reminder of its whereabouts.

"Under the banker boxes on the floor. Over."

Adhering to my direction, Javy got on all fours, where he eventually uncovered the briefcase exactly where I said it would be. Without cleaning up the mess he created, Javy grabbed the prize and shut the closet door behind him. The kid apparently remembered that the key was in the upper left-hand drawer of the desk. The moment that Javy got hold of the key, he inserted it into the briefcase lock and unlatched it. *Nosey little prick.*

Inside, there were many important papers, such as Big Al's birth certificate and social security card, but none was more valuable than Big Al's will. Well, technically, wills – as in plural – since he'd made a few over the years, some more favorable to particular family members than others. If someone ever discovered these wills, it would give credence to a challenge of Big Al's true wishes. As the executor of his estate, I simply could not allow that to happen.

Javy twisted the knob on the desk lamp to better examine the brief-case contents. Whether or not he understood the significance of those contents, I couldn't be certain. But, one thing I knew was that Javy made yet another poor decision when he took out his phone to take photos of the papers inside the briefcase. Not only had I specifically instructed him to leave his phone at home before I picked him up, but I distinctly remember asking him about it before we left his parent's house. Due to his selfish disregard, the cops could now track Javy's cell phone to the W. Ranch, officially putting my secret operation – and who knows what else – in jeopardy.

I should just fucking leave him. I entertained the idea for a moment before thinking better of it – because if Javy got caught, he would undoubt-edly squeal to the cops, and where would that leave me? I could be disbarred or worse yet, be compelled to tell that detective all the dirty secrets about Washington Ford. *You've made a grave mistake and now you need to fix it. What would get him out of there as soon as possible?* Then it came to me. The lake house had an alarm system that I deactivated for our mission, but Javy didn't know that.

"Javy, listen to me, son. You've tripped the silent alarm. You have one minute to get the fuck out of the house and meet me at the dock! Do you understand?"

Javy nearly jumped out of his dumbass shoes; the ones those punk kids wear with loose shoelaces to slip in and out of them easily. Once Javy processed the threat, he threw the papers back into the briefcase and slammed it shut.

Another roaring boom echoed through the lake, illuminating the area where I saw that speed boat trolling around – nothing in sight. I yanked the cord twice on the engine before she rattled to a start.

With one hand on the motor and the other on the video monitor, I watched as Javy frantically scampered up the lengthy steps to the main level. Without slowing down, he held onto the door frame with his left hand as he turned the corner toward the side door. Then, he made an abrupt stop.

Javy remained frozen for a few moments. *Why did he stop?* A second later, I saw exactly why on the bottom of the frame: Margret's head. I kicked the motor into top speed.

Due to my limited view and lack of audio, I struggled to decipher the developing situation. That was until Javy's right arm reached across his body to pull a gun from either his sweatshirt or pants.

"Javy, listen to me very carefully. Don't do anything stupid. Do you understand?"

Radio silence. If Javy had any doubt that I was watching him, it had now ceased. Neither Javy nor Margret appeared to move. The gun remained fixated on Margret.

"Javy, walk away right now, and you'll get your million. You so much as touch her, you'll get nothing, and I'll leave you for the cops."

"Do I have your word?"

"What else is there?"

Javy lowered the gun and brushed past Margret toward the side door.

Meanwhile, I angled the skiff into the dock as carefully as I could, but still nicked the starboard against the wood in the process. Out on the W. Ranch, Javy opted to take the shorter, more direct path through the backyard, moving as fast as his chubby legs allowed down the wooded slope.

Now in position for a speedy escape, a jarring noise pierced my ears. It sounded like a hammer repeatedly hitting a nail into a piece of wood. Seeking the source, I looked over my shoulder to discover Javy racing across the dock. His strides were violent, uncontrolled. As I watched his arms frantically flailing through the air, a bright light struck my eyes. Instinctively, I raised my palm to block the irritant before thinking better of it when I realized it was Eva. I doubted that she could see my face, but just the color of my skin might raise the wrong question, so I turned my face away from the shoreline in hopes that would be enough to conceal my identity for the next few seconds.

The moment that Javy and the briefcase landed in the boat, I twisted the throttle to its limit. The engine roared as the boat's weight shifted toward the motor, and the bow lifted into the air. It took a few moments for Javy to gather himself, but I was more concerned about our surroundings. The ear-piercing sound of the engine took away one of my senses, so I relied on my aging vision. Back at the W. Ranch, the flashlight disappeared as Eva most likely retreated to the lake house to assess the damage and wait for the police to show.

Meanwhile, on the lake, I scanned across the water for the slightest of movements. With our masthead light off, our only hope was that no other boat was nearby. Just as we had enough distance between us and the dock, I let off the throttle to slow down. The quick deceleration jolted both Javy and me forward, but we stabilized ourselves by holding on to the gunwale. That's when a shimmer of light caught the corner of my eye. By the time I turned my head, the firework had exploded and lit up the lake. I let go of the throttle entirely to kill the engine.

"Why'd we stop?"

Still disgusted with Javy, I refused to answer; instead, I lifted my eyes to the previous whereabouts of the patrol boat. I immediately spotted it making its way toward the dock at the W. Ranch. *Do I turn the masthead light on to make us less suspicious? No, if I do that, then they will definitely see us and track us down in their much faster boat. Maintain stillness, and hope to God they don't spot us.*

Eventually, Javy turned his head around to see the patrol boat just as the firework fizzled out. The light from the patrol boat remained focused on the dock, giving us a brief window to escape. I was hesitant to restart the motor, however, perceiving the risk to be too high.

"So, when are you going to pay me my money?"

Saying nothing, I stretched for the paddle resting on the cold shell next to my feet. Holding it by its shaft, I offered it to Javy, the grip side closest to him.

"When do I get the money, Larry?"

Javy, shaking his head in disbelief, brushed away the paddle and reached into his hooded sweatshirt to grab his gun. With his finger on the trigger, he rested the weapon on his thigh, business end pointing at me.

"My money, old man."

"The job ain't finished yet."

I offered Javy the paddle once again.

"I don't think so, abuelo. The way I see it, one of us has a gun, and the other has a paddle."

Even with limited visibility, I could make out Javy's smile, missing molars and all. I shoved the tip of the paddle into the glassy lake and began a forward stroke toward the truck. Satisfied with himself, Javy flipped his long dark hair back as he chuckled in my misery. Another firework shrieked across the sky, catching his undivided attention. While he was distracted, I jerked the paddle from the water, wound up with all my might and struck the side of his head. Disoriented and breathing heavily, Javy dropped the gun at his feet. He tried to speak but struggled to form a word as blood trickled down his face. Using my shoe, I dragged the firearm away from Javy and toward my side of the boat.

"You fucked up, kid. Hand me your phone."

"Fuck! What the hell, man. That shit hurts."

"Shut your mouth and give me your phone."

Javy touched his hand to his forehead to assess the damage. When he saw the blood, he pulled up the hood of his sweatshirt to apply pressure to the wound. Using his free hand, he dug into his jeans for his phone before tossing it over to me.

"Face ID, please."

I tossed the phone back to Javy before he begrudgingly unlocked it. That's when I learned that the Face ID still works even if there was blood streaming down a person's face. Before he handed the phone back to me, a flash of light blinded my eyes – *that motherfucker*. I snatched the phone from his hands as fast as I could. *Did anyone see that?* I nervously surveyed the water as Javy had an old-fashioned belly laugh.

"Shut the fuck up," I ordered under my breath.

Remarkably, he appeared to instantly listen to me for the first time that evening. With no one seemingly alarmed at our presence, I returned to Javy's unlocked phone to find the illicit images. All in all, he took eleven pictures of various documents from the briefcase, including one of Big Al's most recent will. I could forgive that betrayal, but as I stared at the last photo taken seconds ago, featuring me holding a gun. He left me no choice. I promptly deleted all of the images and then threw his phone and handgun in the lake.

"What the fuck, man?"

Without saying a word, I wound up the paddle again and smacked Javy in damn near the same spot on his head, causing him to fall over the side of the boat. Stunned by the blunt force, he was unable to tread water or cry out for help. Just then, a colorful blast flashed on the surface of the lake. However, unlike a mirror, the reflection was warped by the ever-so-subtle ripple caused by Javy's body sinking into the lake.

Emily Bridges

"You may begin."

In unison, everyone in the gymnasium opened their test booklets to the first page – everyone but me. Instead, I observed. The space was anything but glamorous. On the basketball court, there must have been forty or fifty heavy-duty white plastic folding tables. Each table had two uncomfortably hard metal chairs at opposite ends where each test-taker sat.

The woman sitting across from me – a Millennial, mid-forties maybe – sported a black blazer and matching skirt. The bags under her eyes told me she was a mother of two, who worked an unfulfilling full-time job for shit pay while simultaneously going to night school the past five years for a better life. *How is she so fit? I can barely find the time to shower once every few days.*

As she turned the page of her test booklet, I got a look at her left hand: no wedding ring. The woman was a superhero; there was simply no other explanation.

I finally unsealed my own test booklet. After skimming the instructions, I read a verbose passage about a case with a married couple named Hank and Wendy, who had a tumultuous relationship with complicated business dealings. I didn't bother with the rest of the question. Instead, I thumbed through the pages until I found an empty one. *This will do.*

Over the next few hours, I sketched out a comic of "The Lovely Lawyer," an ass-kicking prosecutor who sought justice in and out of the courtroom. She closely resembled my deskmate, whom I had named Agatha Walker, a cross between my two favorite authors: Agatha Christie and Alice Walker. Her costume took a couple of drafts to perfect. At first, I gave her a cape and mask, but it felt trite – so instead, I gave her a leotard that could fit comfortably under her inconspicuous pantsuit. To cover her face and subsequently her identity, she wore a buff over her nose and mouth. The front of her leotard featured two red L's overlapping within a white circle. Finally, I gave her a pair of Chuck Taylors because, well, fuck heels.

In the first strip, Agatha Walker was preparing to prosecute the degenerate wife-beater, Hank Robinson. But there was a problem: Agatha's star witness – Hank's wife, Wendy – decided not to testify out of fear of retribution. Despite Agatha's best efforts to convince Wendy that she would be able to protect her, Wendy was adamant that she could no longer help the prosecution. Even with mounting physical evidence and five different recorded 9-1-1 calls, in which Wendy was on the phone crying to operators, the District Attorney implored Agatha to drop the case. With no other trump cards, Agatha reluctantly agreed.

But that wasn't the end of the story. There was no way Agatha Walker could just let a scumbag like Hank get off only for him to continue his abuse. The next time Hank's anger boiled over, there wouldn't be any 9-1-1 calls or photos of the bruises on Wendy's body. Wendy would undoubtedly be dead. But, Agatha Walker had a commitment, a commitment to...justice.

Agatha plotted her next move; using the Robinson's home address from court documents, she held a stakeout of the suburban home. With a solid plan in hand, Agatha tailed Hank to his work at some ubiquitous office building. There, she learned an employee keycard proved necessary to access the parking garage and subsequently, his office. Forced to improvise, Agatha walked into the shadows behind a dumpster in the alleyway as a beaten-down ADA and came out the other side as an ass-kicking superhero. The Lovely Lawyer didn't wait around twiddling her thumbs for the wife-beater to come out at the end of the day. Using her wits, she slipped into the parking garage through a gap between a steel railing and the precast concrete. She then crept up to the security booth, slipped her hand through the crack of a window, and nabbed a keycard for the office building. Riding the elevator to the fifth floor, our heroine strutted directly into the office of Hank the lowlife and showed him up in front of his boss and coworkers. By the time the Lovely Lawyer had finished with Hank, he laid helplessly on his back, crying out for help, much like his victim. While the entire office looked on in horror, the Lovely Lawyer casually sauntered to the copy machine. There, she pulled out a folded photo of

Wendy's face beaten to a pulp from one of her Chuck Taylors. After making dozens of copies, the Lovely Lawyer flung them throughout the office as she returned to the elevator.

I don't think The Lovely Lawyer is destined to be the next iconic comic book franchise – there's no origin story, and I focused too much on the details of her changing outfits – but it has some potential. More importantly, it kept me occupied.

"Time's up. Pencils down."

Ignoring the proctor's demand, my deskmate scribbled away furiously in her test booklet well after the allotted time. Thirty seconds later, Agatha slyly placed her pencil down before looking around to see if anyone saw her egregious crime. Like all great protagonists, Agatha was flawed.

❧

My dad insisted on driving me to and from the bar exam, even though he'd lent me a dealership car for the summer. I had never seen him so proud of me as he was on the ride over to the testing site that morning. Unprompted, My dad lovingly recalled his bar exam experience and offered some last-minute tips. He had always been a decent father, even though it was clear that he coveted his standing in the Washington family more than his own. My mother had gotten used to his absence; I believed she eventually preferred it.

"So...how'd you do? I bet you aced it, didn't you?"

"Yeah, I hope – "

"You definitely aced it. I mean, with your grades, there's no way you didn't pass."

I can already envision the expression on his face when he finds the letter in the mail – he'll open it right away, even though the envelope will be addressed to me – and then his excitement will quickly turn into confusion. I had been avoiding the conversation with him for almost a decade now. My dad, while always supportive of my individuality, had consistently steered me away from my dream of being a detective or private investigator. He would argue that his profession was basically that of a detective – in the sense that you solved a different puzzle for every case – but lawyers get paid better. After a while, I stopped fighting and just went along with his plan, knowing full well that I could never be a lawyer.

"Listen, I have to run an errand, do you want me to drop you off at home?"

"Can we get some food first?"

My dad nodded, as if he suddenly remembered that he was hungry. The car swerved into the left-turn lane, where he waited for a few cars to pass before pulling a u-turn. As the car swung around, I tried to remember the last time that just the two of us had gone on an adventure. We used to see movies together; it was our thing. My mom hated it – mainly because it was always on Sundays, his one day off every week. I could still vividly recall talking about the latest releases on Saturday mornings as he guzzled his morning coffee and pancakes before taking off for the day. He even saved the Friday newspapers, with all the reviews from the local critics, and had it laid out waiting for me at my seat at the breakfast table.

Hell, I remembered the last movie we saw together: *Creed*. My dad absolutely loved the *Rocky* series. He would always be watching the reruns on AMC in the background as he worked late into the night – and as a young girl desperate for a common bond with her mostly absent father, I too fell in love with the *Rocky* series. So when *Creed* came out, my dad and I were so pumped. I mean, a Black character was now the lead in the franchise that we loved. The story, the fight sequences, even an older Sylvester Stallone were all incredible. *You know a movie is great when you regurgitate the scenes after the credits roll.*

The day after I saw it, I told my friends in homeroom that they had to see *Creed* – and it didn't hurt that Michael B. Jordan was the star of it. I told them all about how my dad and I loved the entire series, but the latest entry easily surpassed its predecessors. Instead of sharing my enthusiasm, they couldn't believe that I willingly went to see a movie with my dad. *Middle schoolers are a particularly cruel group of people.*

The next Saturday, when my dad had the newspaper reviews laid out in front of me, I was purposefully noncommittal about seeing any movies the next day. He probably figured I just wasn't interested in any of the new releases that week. Then came the next week, and the next – until finally, he gave up. My apathy confused him in the beginning, but he eventually realized that our outings were abruptly over, and I'm sure he had no idea why.

Sitting in the car at the South 21 Drive-in, a restaurant that had been a mainstay in Charlotte since the fifties, my dad washed down a bite of his veggie burger with an ice water while I nibbled at my pulled pork sandwich. Realizing the uncomfortable silence between us, I reached over for a piece of roasted cauliflower out of his basket. He even lifted the basket of food toward me so I could dip the cauliflower in his vegan bleu cheese sauce.

"So tell me, what's going on with the investigation?"

"What do you mean?"

"Any leads?"

"It's still early."

"C'mon. You can tell me, Dad."

As he paused to decide how much to divulge, he rolled his tongue around his teeth to collect any leftover scraps from his veggie burger.

"Follow the money. Who benefits from Al dying now – as opposed to say, a year from now?"

"Okay. So, someone in the family then?"

"Possibly. But I truly don't know."

"Don't give me that shit, Dad."

"Language, Em."

I could feel my eyes rolling back as the silence between us grew again. For some reason, whenever I was around my parents, I felt as if I was sixteen again, and in a struggle for my independence. Even my body reverted to its former self; I caught myself slouching in the car seat, and I became suddenly insecure about my appearance.

"Why are you so interested, anyway?"

"Interested in a murder mystery? Whoa, that doesn't sound like me."

My dad bellowed a chuckle, one of those rare, authentic parent laughs. Only this time, his amusement abruptly transitioned into audible discomfort. When I looked over at him, he held his chest as he fought through his pain. Unsure of what to do, I offered the cup of water to him, but he waved it away.

"You all right?"

"I'm fine."

"Dad...what's going on with you?"

"The doctor said it was nothing to worry about."

"*You* went to the doctor?"

A pause. My dad realized he slipped. Not only had he been eating significantly healthier, but the man who'd sworn off going to see a doctor his entire life? It must be pretty bad if he actually went. Maybe Big Al's death really spooked him.

"The doctor said it was coronary heart disease."

"Dad, did you have a heart attack?"

"She said it's manageable with some lifestyle changes and stress management."

"I can't believe you had a heart attack."

"It wasn't a heart attack, all right? It's heart *disease*. And I can manage it."

I narrowed my eyes as I absorbed the bomb he'd just dropped on me.

"It's just between Al's death, running the business, and this estate thing. You thought our family was crazy? The Washingtons take the cake."

"You're doing too much, Dad. I mean, most guys your age are retired."

"Confucius once said, 'We have two lives, and the second begins when we realize we only have one.' And my second life just started."

"Well, maybe you could use some help."

"Don't worry about your old man. With my new diet and exercise routine, I'll be fine."

"That's not what I meant. I can help you with the investigation into who killed Big Al."

My dad took the final bite of veggie burger, crunched the wrapper into a ball and tossed it onto the tray outside his window as he mulled on my not-so-subtle suggestion.

"All I'm saying is that you could use the help. And it's going to take a month before the bar results come back anyway."

My dad pressed the start button on the car's dash, clicked his seatbelt into place, and shifted the car into reverse. Before my dad took his foot off the brake, he shrugged his shoulders.

"Okay."

AN INSPECTOR TEXTS

Alice Washington

I woke up with a dry mouth and a pool of sweat underneath me. While I couldn't see a thing, I knew the air conditioner wasn't running. The room felt like a balmy eighty degrees or more. Still facing into my pillow, I patted the damp sheets and pillows, looking for my phone. Eventually, I found it under the pillow, but in the process made my headache considerably worse. The throbbing intensified once my retinas interacted with the bright screen. My phone said 7:09; I assumed that meant morning, but the closed curtains wouldn't allow me to be positive. *Of all the hotel rooms, I get the one with the busted air conditioner.* By the time I eased my way out of the bed and into the bathroom, my head was spinning to the point that I had no choice but to force myself to throw up.

For the next hour or so, I passed the time lying on the shower mat in what turned out to be a futile effort to sober up. I eventually gave up trying to piece together what had happened the previous night once I realized my head got angrier with each attempt. After downing three ibuprofens, I managed to draw a cold bath with the hope of stopping my sweat glands or, better yet, the puking. Sitting in the cold tub, I could finally open my eyes for more than a few seconds without getting the spins. *Get your shit together, Alice. This is what happens when you drink – you're an addict who has no self-control. You have to stop drinking. What the hell did you do last night, anyway?*

Perhaps my phone would offer some clues. I dried my right hand on the shower mat before grabbing it off the bathroom tile. There was a text from a number with a Charlotte-area code that I didn't recognize.

"Hey, it's Emily Bridges. Meet me in the lobby at 8 a.m. I have a lead."

A real go-getter that one. Who meets at 8 a.m.? Get the fuck out of here. At any rate, I checked the time – it was a quarter after eight.

Back to trying to figure out what happened last night. I scrolled through the text messages, only to find unhelpful texts from Larry from the previous few days. My Lyft rides, however, provided at least a general outline of the day: a ride to the aviation museum around noon, followed by a trip to the hospital at three, and then I returned to the Country Inn Suites at 1:30 a.m. from what must have been a classy bar by the name of Angry Ale's. There was a sizable chunk of missing time between the obligatory hospital visit and the trip back to my hotel. *Perhaps I went to dinner with someone from the hospital, an old friend or distant cousin I haven't seen in forever?* I picked one of the washcloths stacked neatly above my head, dunked it in cold water, then folded it across my eyes and leaned back in the tub.

Just as the soothing, wet rag began to soothe my eyelids, my phone buzzed. While I did like Emily, there was no chance in hell that I agreed to meet her at an ungodly hour. *She'll undoubtedly call a couple more times, leave an angry voicemail and then, maybe a scathing 200-word text about how disappointed she is in me. She might even call me an 'unreliable alcoholic.' But then, she will leave me alone.* Meanwhile, I could attempt to sober up and recharge the batteries – *maybe even figure out how to stop drinking forever.*

Just as expected, my phone blew up a few more times, until I was left with that sweet sound of silence. *Exhale.*

"Why is it so damn hot in here?" I thought I heard a voice say.

Right as I lifted the washcloth off my eyes to check if I'd imagined things, the bathroom door flew open. I instinctively attempted to cover my lady parts and yanked the shower curtain shut as if it were my mother barging in to complain about how long I was taking in the bathroom. Before I closed the curtain, though, I was able to catch a quick glimpse of my intruder.

"What the fuck," I yelped. "Emily?"

"Your air conditioner is broken. Are you aware of that?"

"Mystery solved. I guess you can leave now."

While the curtain between us blocked my sight, I could visualize her disappointment as she rifled through my stuff on the vanity.

"I don't think you understand the situation here, Alice. With every passing hour, we are less likely to find out what the hell happened to your father. Don't you want answers?"

"I don't care about him."

"Do you care about the money? Because you won't see a dime otherwise."

Emily took my stillness as a yes and told me to get dressed and meet her in the lobby in fifteen minutes, then slammed the bathroom door shut behind her. A few seconds passed before I poked my head out from behind the shower curtain, and fruitlessly cried out to ask her how she got into my room. *Maybe I could use a drink if I'm going to make it through this day.*

⤳

Despite my body actively plotting against me, I somehow pulled myself together and presented myself in the lobby, only a few minutes past Emily's arbitrary deadline. When I pressed her about how she was able to gain entry into my room, she masterfully changed the subject.

"I reported your broken air conditioner. It'll be fixed by the time we get back."

As our Lyft wove in and out of morning traffic, Emily offered me a cup of coffee and a banana she'd grabbed from the continental breakfast while she was waiting. I politely declined, preoccupied with doing everything in my power not to throw up. I had to admire Emily's unflappable attitude. Even with the setback I'd caused earlier, she exuded all the bright eagerness of a recent college grad before the real world had beaten her down. I tried to think back to when I was her age, ready to take on anything that stood in my way, nothing to impede my lofty dreams of becoming an entrepreneur, just like my father. I chuckled audibly at the thought of how naïve I was all those years ago. Emily, taking my laugh as a sign of me coming back to life, proceeded to ask my questions about my family tree and any rifts that might have led to a murder. I understood that she was only trying to help, but between my hangover and sincere, general disdain for my family, I was reluctant to share anything of substance. Undeterred by my laconic answers, Emily continued pushing me.

"So let me get this straight. Big Al had three wives, correct?"

"Yeah."

"The first, your mom Elizabeth, Al's high school sweetheart from Texas who, uh, tragically passed away in the nineties from breast cancer, is that right?"

Refusing to offer a comment, I stared blankly ahead at Charlotte's skyline. Emily cleared her throat, recognizing the sensitive subject, and forged ahead without a confirmation.

"Then, according to my source, his second wife, Kelly, was married to Big Al a few years in the early aughts, ending in a messy divorce. Is that right?"

"Source? Why are you asking me then? It sounds like you know everything."

"Not everything. What happened with the house fire?"

"Kelly was sauteeing mushrooms, didn't you hear?"

Emily took her eyes off the surrounding area to study my facial expression.

"So, what actually happened?"

"Kelly caught him red-handed with the beverage cart girl at the country club's annual charity golf tournament, giving the term "nineteenth hole" a new meaning. But because of the prenup – on your father's advice – her only recourse was to burn the house to the fucking ground."

"No shit?"

"It wasn't a bad move, really. Kelly received a hefty payday to sign an NDA after the Charlotte Observer got wind that there might be a story."

"What happened to her after that?"

"Not sure. The last I heard she enjoys drinking away the money at a nice beach house somewhere on the coast."

"Do you think she could have killed Big Al?"

"Anything is possible, I guess."

"And then in the early twenty-twenties, Al met Eva, an Icelander, quickly married, and had your half-sister Margret shortly after, right?"

"Yeah."

"Do you know of any strife between Eva and your dad?"

"No. We didn't talk much."

"That's right, when did you relocate to Alaska?"

"Relocate?" I laughed.

"Is that not what happened, or– ?"

"He sold it to me as a prerequisite for succeeding him one day. I worked my ass off for him. I made a dealership in fucking Alaska the most profitable in his portfolio. But it didn't matter how well I performed. Sad to say, it took me more time than I care to admit to realize the farce."

"So why did you stay?"

"I'm an addict – a functioning one, but an addict nonetheless. We lie to ourselves constantly. I made good money; I learned how to successfully run a business. But truth be told, I thought my father would eventually come around to accepting me. I wanted nothing more than that bastard to wrap his arms around me and tell me how proud he was of me. I guess that's not going to happen now, huh?"

Emily nodded. She didn't ask anything more, and I didn't blame her – even a licensed therapist wouldn't know how to respond appropriately. Instead, she checked her phone repeatedly, carefully studying the screen and then the road as if she was trying to figure out our whereabouts. Although I welcomed the peace and quiet at first, curiosity eventually got the best of me.

"So, are you going to tell me where we're going?"

"To tell you the truth, I don't know exactly."

"How's that?"

Emily released a deep sigh while simultaneously closing her eyes.

"If we're going to find the killer, we're going to have to trust each other completely."

"Okay?"

"For me to trust you, I need certain assurances."

"Like what?"

"Everything must remain between us. There are some rules we'll need to bend to discover the truth. You good with that?"

I quickly realized that I had misjudged Emily. She wasn't as innocent as I previously thought.

"You got it."

Emily, still on high alert, looked directly into my eyes for one last confirmation. Even with our aligned interest, it was clear she was hesitant to trust me, no matter what I said or did. *She is her father's daughter, all right.*

In what I would call a reluctant necessity, Emily finally divulged her plan. She apparently had placed trackers on the cars of Courtney, Eva, and Luke – since in her mind, the prime suspects would be within the family. As the Lyft pulled into a barren strip mall, Emily highlighted the irony of how in an automated world, everyone worried about their privacy, yet, it was easier to track someone who used an antiquated mode of transportation.

In the sea of idling Lyfts and Ubers waiting for their rides was a white Ford Edge that stood out like a sore thumb. It turned out that Eva had parked outside a seedy pawnshop. In front of the doors, the sidewalk overflowed with both riding and push lawnmowers. Our Lyft questioned us through the sound system, if we wanted to continue our ride or not. Emily tapped her phone, prompting the system to leave us alone. Just then, a familiar face exited the pawnshop.

Eva zigzagged her way toward her vehicle, past the lawnmowers that were crudely tied together with a steel cable and padlocks. It didn't appear that she was carrying anything other than a medium-sized purse, which swung underneath her left forearm as she walked.

"The place must have just damn near opened," I said.

"And she must be in a hurry."

Emily and I calmly debated whether to follow her or see which family jewel she just sold off. After I pointed out that we could easily find Eva with the tracker, Emily agreed to check out the pawnshop once Eva was out of sight.

We exited the Lyft and ventured past the field of lawnmowers to the front door. As we went inside, Emily told me to play it cool and follow her lead. Immediately, my eyes settled on the store clerk, a tall, overweight man with an unsettling number of guns mounted on the wall behind him. He appeared to be occupied with his store-opening tasks.

Emily and I mulled around the nearly empty store for a minute, whispering back and forth and pretending to be interested in the flat-screen TVs and power tools. After working up enough courage, Emily made her move.

"Excuse me, sir?"

The burly clerk paused and turned his attention to Emily as I lurked awkwardly behind her.

"Yes?"

"I'm looking for an item or items, maybe a family heirloom of some kind that was sold recently at your fine establishment."

"You don't say? Can you describe the item?"

"Well, that's just it, I'm not sure what exactly she sold; however, I can tell you who sold it – a blonde woman, middle-aged, with a European accent. You seem like a smart man. I'll bet you know the one."

The clerk, unmoved by Emily's flattery, offered a blank stare in return. Just as he was about to return to his morning duties, Emily interjected once again.

"Maybe we can work out some kind of deal."

"Is that so?"

"Yes – you see, my friend here would be happy to offer you a little something for your trouble," Emily said.

What now? The clerk leaned his head to the right to get a better look at me. Once Emily saw the change in my demeanor, she gave me a nod as if to say everything was going according to plan, and it was time to pay up.

"What? I don't have any cash on me. Who carries cash anymore?"

"Are you serious, Alice?"

Emily let out an exaggerated sigh of frustration. Her jaw moved from one side to another as she considered her next move.

"Okay, how about this – we buy an item in exchange for some information. Say twenty dollars worth?" Emily asked.

No answer.

"Fifty?"

No answer.

"One hundred?"

The clerk turned his back to us, meandering down the aisle to a case located on the back wall that required a key from his belt to unlock. Emily, now realizing that the clerk was taking advantage of her persistence, swiveled her head toward me long enough to give me a hubristic wink.

The clerk stretched his arm above his head to get the mystery item out of the case, hiking up his ratty-looking T-shirt high enough to reveal a disturbingly hairy lower back. I tried to distract myself, taking note of other items in the store until I heard a loud thud on the glass display case closest to us.

"All right, take it or leave it."

Sitting on top of the case, right in front of the clerk, was a bright red, twenty-pound fire extinguisher. The clerk's shit-eating grin told me that he already knew we would bite.

"A fire extinguisher?" Emily asked.

"Not just any fire extinguisher, it's the fire extinguisher that Kyle Busch used for his entire 2019 Monster Energy NASCAR Cup Series Championship. He even signed it. Right there."

The clerk pointed to some scribble in black Sharpie.

"Are we supposed to be impressed by that?"

"Not at all. But, for some dumb reason, I paid five hundred dollars for it, and it has been collecting dust for a year now."

"You want five hundred dollars for this?"

"No, no. I want eight hundred, and then I'll tell you everything you want to know about that woman who was just here before y'all."

Now that Emily had her confirmation that the clerk had the information we needed, she shrugged her shoulders and agreed to the purchase without consulting me.

"Hold on now, Emily. I'm not paying eight hundred dollars for a useless fucking fire extinguisher," I pleaded.

"Useless? That's what everyone says until they need one."

"I don't even live in Charlotte. What am I supposed to do, put it in my carry-on back to Alaska?"

Emily smiled playfully at the clerk, asking for a moment to talk me off the ledge. She whispered that the expense would be a tiny blip on the radar after they found the killer, and I got paid out. When I remained stone-faced, she offered to pay for half if we didn't find out who killed Big Al. I couldn't imagine that an opportunistic pawnshop clerk held the clue to a big break in the case, but Emily's brimming confidence won me over.

"Okay," I muttered.

"Fantastic," the clerk said with an extraordinarily punchable smile on his face.

The clerk rang up the door stopper and angled the credit card machine toward me. I scrounged through my handbag for a credit card so I could pay for this one-of-a-kind collectible. Meanwhile, Emily could no longer contain her curiosity.

"So, are you going to tell us what that woman sold earlier, or what?"

The clerk, breathing heavily through his hairy nostrils, motioned again to the credit card machine. I finally found the one card that had the best chance of not being declined and paid for the stupid thing. The moment I signed my name, Emily asked again.

"Congratulations on your purchase, miss."

"Hello, we paid for the stupid thing. What did she sell?"

"Nothing."

"Excuse me?"

"Would you like a bag for this, miss?"

"Are you fucking kidding me?"

To her credit, Emily knew how to have someone's back. Now, while I was certainly upset, she was ready to burn the place to the ground. If that was the case, perhaps I could at least sell the fire extinguisher back to him and get my money back – or hell, maybe even make a profit.

"She did try to buy a gun, though. But, I couldn't sell it to her, since she didn't have any of the proper credentials."

⌒

The next stop on Emily's wild ride brought us to none other than Washington Ford. Now midday, the traffic was lighter as we passed idling Lyfts and Ubers in parking lots waiting for the end-of-day rush hour. On the ride over, Emily attempted to engage me in conversation about Eva's motive for buying a gun, but I was too preoccupied with the dreadful thought of returning to the dealership where I'd practically grown up. Just as fast as the partial, indistinct memories flooded my thoughts, I ran from them. *Is there a bar near the dealership? I can't remember. I think there used to be a Chili's nearby; they might serve at this hour.*

Emily, annoyed that I wasn't entertaining one of her theories, snapped her fingers in front of my face. I politely apologized and made an effort to maintain eye contact for the remainder of the ride, still too distracted to retain any of the information.

As our Lyft approached the quiet Washington Ford lot, typical of a weekday afternoon, I became entranced. For all intents and purposes, it was exactly how I remembered it.

"Do you think I should go in? People may recognize me."

"You're my second set of eyes now. Get over yourself."

The car came to a slow halt ten yards from the front door. For a moment, I seriously considered leaving my newly acquired "collectible" in the back seat, but ultimately decided to lug it with me instead. Not a single salesman greeted us as we exited the car. I couldn't say I was surprised: even in desolate Alaska, it was standard practice for salespeople to ignore anyone that arrived in a driverless car. We figured if they know how to use one, we had already lost them as a customer.

Walking toward the main entrance, it was as if I'd been transported back to the late eighties when the dealership was in its heyday. The coat on the building had changed, but the foundation remained. We let ourselves in the front door where we were greeted with a friendly hello from Brenda, Big Al's longtime executive assistant. She may have been a fixture there for over thirty years but failed to recognize me as she passed us on her way to the parking lot. She did, however, manage a puzzled look at the oversized fire extinguisher. Truthfully, I couldn't blame her for not recognizing me; years of substance abuse takes a toll on the body. Eventually, the receptionist – a young platinum blonde who introduced herself as Madison – welcomed us and offered her help. As Emily explained our presence, I took in the showroom. The place doubled as a shrine to Big Al; I saw his face plastered in every spot imaginable – posters, cardboard cutouts, you name it. I found it oddly reassuring to know that Big Al would live on only as a caricature of himself.

"Is there a room we can set up in?"

"Yes, Mr. Bridges has permitted you exclusive use of the conference room for the foreseeable future."

Madison pulled two keycards attached to a lanyard from her desk drawer. She informed us that the keycards granted access to the main door, conference room, and break room. Any additional access, like personal offices or the service department, would need authorization from Larry or Luke. Madison also handed over a pile of documents that might help in our investigation: work schedules for employees, sales numbers, and payroll.

The conference room sat against the back wall of the showroom. The three sides facing the showroom had full-length glass windows equipped with roller shades; the fourth side featured a series of still shots, framed highlights from Big Al's commercials, mounted on a light grey wall. And, like any standard conference room, it wouldn't be complete without an oversized table in the middle. The boat-shaped table, most likely custom, was stained with a dark coat and surrounded by a dozen black, excessively padded office chairs. If I had to use one word to describe the room's overall vibe, it would be 'dated.'

Emily threw her purse, along with our newly acquired paperwork, on the table. Without taking a moment to relax or compose herself, she laid the documents out across the table. Before I knew it, she had pulled a highlighter from her purse and started to mark up the first document.

Meanwhile, I caught a few of the salespeople rubbernecking us from the bullpen. Quickly examining the room, I found the metal linked cord for the roller shade. The shade's weight and the cord's short loop combined to require a comical amount of time to lower it.

"What are you doing?" Emily asked.

"Giving us some privacy. They're all out there watching us."

"Stop. Let them watch. The more visible we are, the more likely someone comes forward with some information – or better yet, someone panics and exposes themself as our perpetrator."

"Or we're just providing them with ammunition for gossip and in turn, stoking the fires of misinformation."

"Believe me, the only thing they're gossiping about is why a woman is dragging around a giant fire extinguisher."

Emily smiled from ear to ear. *She's got jokes.* I couldn't help but let out a chuckle at the absurdity of it all. Giving in to her persuasive argument, I pulled the metal chain again, returning the roller shade to its fully open perch at the top of the window. Then I found a seat at the oversized table, setting the fire extinguisher in the chair between us.

"So, do you have an extra highlighter for me or what?"

Courtney Washington

A flat-screen television mounted on the wall in the waiting room played *The Price is Right* with closed captioning. The sounds of the hospital filled the silence – announcements over the loudspeaker, footsteps in the hallways, people talking too loudly on their phones. I couldn't hear myself think. As the day wore on, a handful of friends and family stopped by to offer their surface-level support and, without fail, repeated the same trite line over and over again, "Let me know if there's anything I can do." *Can you make Luke better? Because, if not, then you can fuck right off with your empty offer.*

To her credit, Luke's wife Lauren started intercepting the visitors when my frustrations visibly escalated. Larry, like Lauren, stayed at the hospital through the night. Workaholic that he was, he cordoned off a table in the cafeteria so he could perform his duties, for the family and Washington Ford.

"Care for a cup of coffee?"

Larry carried one of those brown compostable drink trays with a few medium-sized coffee cups and an assortment of cream and sugar packets in the middle. His attempt at offering an olive branch? Both Lauren and I welcomed a cup, but we couldn't let him go before peppering him with questions.

"He's still in critical condition."

"That's what they said hours ago," Lauren whimpered.

"Recoveries take time. Luke is in great hands," Larry assured her.

"That's all they said?"

Larry's eyes pivoted to me as I poured a second creamer into my coffee. He cleared his throat, motioned for both of us to come closer, and lowered his voice to a whisper.

"No, the doctors ran some tests, and uh, Luke was poisoned."

Lauren looked dumbstruck.

"Are you serious? Poisoned?"

"I'm afraid so."

My head felt light. The taste of coffee only made my stomach feel worse. Larry continued to answer Lauren's questions in an indistinct murmur before he realized my face had turned white.

"Are you okay, Courtney?"

⌒

Outside the window, news vans had gathered in the west parking lot. Larry had either arranged or paid, probably the latter, the hospital to give Lauren and me a private room to avoid the circus forming outside. They had to have been tipped off.

Lauren was always my favorite of all of Luke's girlfriends – not that he had too many he brought home for me to meet. Lauren made my Luke focused, driven to become something – unlike me, drifting my way through life without a passion or purpose. I couldn't blame her for not caring too much for me. Usually, it was the other way around for mothers-in-law.

The private room included an empty hospital bed that neither Lauren nor I felt comfortable resting in, although we were encouraged to do so. Much like the public waiting room, there was a flat-screen TV mounted on the wall. Lauren, looking for a way to end the uncomfortable silence, grabbed the remote and started flipping through the channels. Eventually, she landed on our local news station – WSOC-TV, Charlotte's ABC affiliate – broadcasting its midday half-hour of news.

"Coming up, the saga of the Washington family, of Washington Ford notoriety, takes a dark turn as the grandson of the murdered patriarch is in critical condition after a suspected poisoning. But first, Steve Udelson has your weekend weather forecast."

Lauren slumped into one of the uncomfortable armchairs on the perimeter of the room as meteorologist Steve Udelson delivered more bad news: the weekend's temperatures would most likely reach record highs. Even though I felt light-headed, my anxiety prevented me from sitting still.

A knock at the door. It was Larry. The two detectives from Daddy's case were behind him. Larry instructed them to wait outside for a few moments while he conferred with Lauren and me. After entering the room, Larry carefully closed the door and then put his ear against it to check if it was soundproof.

"How's the room treating you both, better?"

"What are they doing here, Larry?" I asked.

Lauren's ears perked up. Confused as to who I referred to, Lauren sought clarification. Larry explained to Lauren that two detectives that were right outside had questions regarding Luke's poisoning.

"Normally, I would never advise anyone in the family to talk with the police. However, seeing as we have more men poisoned than we have leads, I think it might be time. Also, they may have information we're not privy to at this moment. Thoughts? Concerns?"

"Fine with me," Lauren said.

"Sure," I added.

Before Larry permitted the detectives to enter the room, he emphasized that we didn't have to answer any questions, and if at any time either one of us wanted to end the interview for whatever reason, just signal by coughing twice. Lauren and I both told Larry we understood, but he insisted on pounding it home.

"Just be mindful, these detectives are highly trained in the art of interrogation. They can and will lie as they see fit. But desperate times call for desperate measures."

And with that, Larry opened the door to allow the detectives into the room. Lauren remained seated while I leaned against the window. No one offered a handshake, but the detectives did introduce themselves to Lauren as Detective Garcia and Copeland. Before Detective Copeland launched into her line of questioning, she offered her deepest sympathies on behalf of the Charlotte-Mecklenburg Police Department for, as she put it, "the tragedy surrounding" our family.

"I just want to get some background on the family so I can make sure I have everything straight. Mrs. Washington, how long have you been married to Mr. Washington?"

"Two years next month."

"And how long were you dating before that?"

"Off and on since our Freshman year in college."

"Off and on?"

"Yes, we were in college."

"Okay. You were both young, didn't know what you wanted. Or perhaps it was something more?"

"More?"

"Perhaps a big argument – or maybe someone cheated on someone else?"

"You don't have to answer that," Larry interjected.

"No, nothing like that."

Lauren appeared to be genuine in her answers. Meanwhile, Larry remained on high alert, as if poised to shut down the questioning at any moment.

"Mrs. Washington, did your husband Luke have anyone that would want to cause him harm?"

"No, not that I know of."

"Did you notice any unusual activity by your husband in the days leading up to or following Big Al's death?"

"I don't know."

"Anything might be of help."

"He mainly just went to work and school."

"School?"

"Yeah, he goes to night school at UNC-Charlotte on Tuesdays and Thursdays. He's working toward his MBA."

Detective Garcia, who had up until now only been scribbling Lauren's answers in his notepad, chimed in, "Why did you say mainly?"

"Excuse me?"

"You said quote, he *mainly* just went to work and school, unquote. Where else did he go?"

"He did some errands: dry cleaners, grocery store, that sort of thing. And got a drink with Mark one night, to watch a game or something."

Detective Copeland cleared her throat, presumably to remind her partner that she was in charge. Taking the hint, Detective Garcia reluctantly buried his chin into his chest, refocusing on his note-taking.

"Who is Mark?"

"Mark? He's a longtime friend of Luke's – from middle school, I think. He works at Washington Ford, too."

Larry, jaw clenched, looked on anxiously, wrestling with the notion of intervening.

"And Mark's last name and job title?"

"Mark Crawford. He's a floor manager." Larry answered.

Apparently sensing that her line of questioning with Lauren was headed to a dead end, Detective Copeland turned her attention to me.

"Okay. And Miss Washington, Luke is your only child, correct?"

"Correct."

"Is the father in the picture?"

"No."

"What's his story?"

"He moved away, I haven't heard from him in years."

"When was that?"

"I think he sent Luke a high school graduation card. Maybe seven years ago, I want to say."

"When did y'all split?"

"We were never really together, I guess."

"Mind if I ask, why you and – uh, what did you say his name was?"

"Jake Johnson, but people called him JJ."

"And the reason why you and Mr. Johnson split?"

"You don't have to answer any questions you don't want to," Larry reminded me.

"We were young, just graduated high school. Jake didn't want to be a dad."

Memories of Jake interrupted my thoughts; the good and the bad. Mostly the bad.

"You never got into the family business?"

"It was my sister's thing."

"Alice, right? Why wasn't she the heir to the Washington Ford dynasty? I mean, she was the firstborn and has worked in the business much longer than your son."

"I guess Daddy didn't want her to fuck up his legacy."

"How so?"

"Let's just say I don't know what's higher: the number of cars Alice has sold or the number of rehab stints."

Detective Copeland paused a moment to reference her notes in her manila folder, giving time for Detective Garcia to play catch-up on my answers.

"Okay then, are either of you familiar with one Chad Baker or Javier – a.k.a. Javy – Perez?"

"No. Why?" Lauren answered and asked.

"Mr. Bridges, do you want to tell them, or should I?"

Larry held his tongue, presumably fishing to see precisely what the detectives knew.

"Chad Baker is the finance officer at Washington Ford – or was, anyway. And Javy Perez is a mechanic at Washington Ford – or was, anyway. I suppose the past tense is more accurate, don't you think, Mr. Bridges?"

All the eyes in the room turned to Larry, who remained silent, poker-faced.

"Chad Baker was officially reported missing on Thursday by his ex-wife. And Javy Perez's body was found floating in Lake Wylie early Saturday morning. Do you happen to know which day they worked last, Mr. Bridges?"

"I'm not involved in the day-to-day operations."

"Oh, that's right, you're the dealership's fixer."

"Senior counsel, detective. And watch your tone."

"So, let me get this straight, Mr. Bridges. Two people from Washington Ford – one being your longtime boss – have been murdered. Another is missing, and a fourth is currently in critical condition – all in what, the past week? And the ever-loyal fixer – excuse me, senior counsel – knows nothing about any of it?"

"This interview is over," Larry asserted.

"And when you say senior counsel, don't you really mean president of Washington Ford, since the poisoning of your two predecessors left you in charge?"

Before Detective Copeland had finished her rhetorical question, Larry had the door to the hallway open. His face fuming red, he informed the detectives once again that the interview had concluded, and they would need to see themselves out. Detective Garcia closed his spiral notepad, clicked his pen, and deposited both objects into his shirt pocket.

"There is a young man in this hospital that is counting on you to find out who put him here. Instead, you have concocted a baseless narrative, wasting precious time, to destroy this family even further," Larry lectured.

"Thank you for your time. We'll be in touch," Detective Copeland replied.

Both detectives, Detective Garcia in the front and Detective Copeland in the back, walked toward Larry, who held the heavy metal door open for them. Just as Detective Copeland reached the door, she paused and turned directly to me.

"Miss Washington, are you aware there was a break-in at the W. Ranch a couple of nights ago?"

"No," I replied.

"Hmm...one would think Mr. Bridges might share that information with someone who lives on that property."

"It's time to go," Larry reiterated.

Larry all but pushed the detectives out of the room. The moment they were free of the door frame, Larry attempted to slam the door shut, but the automatic steel door closer prevented a timely fastening. Instead, Larry struggled to hasten the process, even using his shoulder to throw his body weight into the door. Meanwhile, Detective Garcia, visible through the vertical slot of glass on the door, grinned ear to ear.

"Is that true, Larry?"

The door finally clicked shut. Now out of breath, Larry looked to turn the deadbolt on the door, but couldn't find one.

"Yes, there was a break-in at the lake house."

"Why didn't you tell me?"

"I didn't want to worry you with yet another thing."

"What did they take?"

"I don't know."

For the first time since I had known him, Larry looked overmatched, a broken old man who had overestimated his experience and wisdom. He calmly walked to the chair next to Lauren and sat down to rest, embarrassed to realize that he was the one being interrogated, not us.

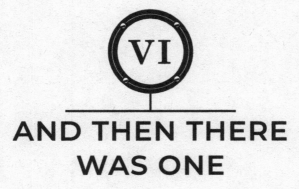

AND THEN THERE
WAS ONE

IV

AND THEN THERE
WAS ONE

Larry Bridges

Located on the outskirts of uptown Charlotte in the gentrified community Plaza Midwood, Mark's townhouse sat in a relatively quiet neighborhood away from the main drag. Still, the authorities' response time would no doubt be swift. Mark's neighbors were practically right on top of him. I drove around the neighborhood, doing exactly the speed limit so as not to attract any attention until I found the alley behind Mark's backyard. As I patiently waited inside a borrowed car from the dealership, engine on, I watched for the slightest sign of a nosy neighbor or dog walker. After a few minutes of inactivity, I put on a pair of latex gloves and quietly exited the car with a folded IKEA-sized bag in tow. With sweat already dripping inside my shirt and pants legs, I carefully walked downhill toward the wrought iron gate of the backyard fence.

The key to the backdoor proved to be under a bright red, Christmas-themed doormat featuring a tree atop a blue sedan and the phrase, "Oh, what fun!" in cursive lettering. Careful not to aggravate my bad back, I bent at the knees, keeping my head forward and back upright. I slowly stood and turned the lock open.

It can be easy to criticize the tidiness of someone else's home, but my God, Mark's place is a fucking pigsty. Avoiding the shards of broken glass or pools of dried blood became an obstacle course as I wandered into the living room. Mark hadn't bothered to clean up his bong, let alone any of the evidence, even though Chad escaped more than forty hours ago. *You got lucky that Luke told you about this before he was poisoned; otherwise, someone would've discovered this disaster sooner rather than later.*

Tip-toeing my way through the house, I collected a few framed photos of Mark's family sitting on window sills, every piece of mail from the countertop, and anything in the drawers with any semblance of a connection to

125

Mark into my sturdy bag. Once satisfied that I had done a proper sweep of the place, I exited from the same door through which I'd arrived.

Once again, I kept my eyes peeled for any cars or neighbors on the uphill walk back to the car. The street was quiet, except for the humming of the air conditioners on overdrive. I threw the bag stuffed with Mark's mementos into the trunk of the Expedition. Moving to the rear doors, I gave one last hard look for any potential witness or visible street sign. Satisfied, I opened the door.

"Okay, you can remove your blindfolds now."

Maria and Bianca hesitated a moment before slowly exiting the car. I reassured them that everything was fine and thanked them for their discretion. Still reluctant, but unsure what else to do, Bianca gathered the cleaning products in her arms, while Maria collected the larger items like a mop and vacuum.

Before heading toward Mark's townhouse, I politely advised them to be quiet, even though they hadn't spoken more than a few words since we left Washington Ford. Sensing we were taking too long, I helped Maria with the vacuum as we made the short trek down the hill and to the back door.

Once inside, I instructed the women to clean every inch of the house thoroughly and that I would be back in a few hours with some lunch. Most importantly, I told them they were not to leave the house, emphasizing that they would not receive the second half of their $10,000 payment if they did so. The women expressed neither shock nor disgust at their first glimpse of the unkempt and bloody space. Instead, they took in their surroundings and strategized with each other in Spanish on how to most effectively clean it in a timely fashion. Well, that's what I think they said. My Spanish wasn't what it used to be. By the time I reached the door to leave, the two women had already put on their blue rubber gloves and started their deep clean.

⁓

Chad Baker had been officially missing for three days. Employed at Washington Ford for just shy of nine years, there was no way of telling just how much Chad had swindled from us. However, I was confident of one thing: when someone gets caught stealing money, it was never their first time. From my experience, a thief gets caught only when their greed outweighs their guilt. And for Chad to have the audacity to try and steal over a hundred thousand dollars in one fell swoop, I knew for a fact it wasn't his first go at it. If I had to ballpark it, I'd wager he had stolen at least a million dollars from Washington Ford during his tenure.

The way I saw it, Chad had only two hands he could play at that point in time: One, take the money and run, assuming he could access it, which couldn't be easy for any embezzler on short notice, let alone someone who had been declared missing. Second, Chad could go to the cops, admit to his embezzlement in exchange for leniency and, in turn, offer his cooperation in the murder case – or perhaps some other sort of probe into the dealings of Washington Ford? The first option seemed more likely for a weasel like Chad, but either way, I wouldn't sleep well as long as Chad was on the run with our money. *Where are you hiding, Chad?*

With the cops actively searching for a missing person, I figured I wouldn't be able to get close to Chad's house, but neither would he. What little I knew about him, gleaned from the past nine years of a mostly cordial working relationship, was that he was divorced with a kid, a common theme amongst car salesmen. Even though hiding out with his ex-wife seemed like a longshot, I did my due diligence, only to find out she had remarried and moved to the D.C. area.

From Chad's personnel file, I located one Logan Riley, an ex-girlfriend, whom he listed as his emergency contact at the time he was hired. I'll admit I might have misrepresented myself by telling her that I was a P.I. hired by Chad's family to find him, but I figured she wouldn't ever have talked with me otherwise. I met Logan at a coffee shop about thirty miles outside of Charlotte, near the North Carolina side of the border, in a quaint town called Waxhaw. Much like every other small Carolina town, a train ran right through the middle of the "historic downtown," and due to the fruitful clay soil, all the buildings were 100 percent brick, sitting two or three stories high.

When I arrived five minutes early, I found Logan already settled into a booth with a frappé coffee in front of her. She wore a turquoise sundress and expensive-looking, ankle-strapped sandals. She was cordial enough, but I wouldn't say she was genuinely concerned about Chad's wellbeing. I opened with a few innocuous questions like how they met – "high school"; the length of their relationship – "three years"; the last time she saw him – "2020"; and the last time they spoke or texted – "six or eight years ago, maybe."

Satisfied with her willingness to talk – albeit with concise responses – I decided the time had come to press Logan further.

"If you don't mind me asking, why did you and Chad break up?"

She paused for a moment, presumably to sift through the memories from the relationship. Her face expressed conflict, leading me to infer she still had feelings for him. She took a deep breath before finally answering.

"You know, it's funny, I can't point to or remember a specific reason. Chad was a decent guy, maybe it was the late nights and always having to work on the weekends. We had a good run, but it just didn't work out."

"So, you ended it then?"

Logan's eyes began to well. Perhaps embarrassed or upset at the dredging up of old memories, her tone changed, and rather quickly.

"What does any of this have to do with Chad being missing?"

"I'm just tracking down any possible leads."

"Who did you say hired you again?"

"Chad's parents."

"Is that so? What are their first names then?"

"I just know them as Mr. and Mrs. Baker," I told her without skipping a beat.

"I think we're done here."

Logan took one final taste of her frappé before rising to her feet to collect the purse draped over an adjacent chair.

"Did you know he was embezzling money from Washington Ford?"

Logan paused for a half-second before throwing her purse strap firmly over her right shoulder. Without a word, she quietly but briskly exited through the front door. I waited a moment to follow her so as to not raise any unwanted attention. By the time I reached the door, Logan had already made it across the street to the other side of the railroad tracks. She didn't bother to look back at me. Despite not being able to see her face, I could tell she was flustered, possibly panicked, as she dug through her purse for the keys to the Ford Fusion parked in front of her. *A woman under the age of fifty who doesn't use Uber/Lyft and drives a Ford. There are coincidences, and then there is Logan Riley.* As she drove away, I studied the license plate on the rear of the car: CJT-4768 with a Washington Ford license plate frame around it.

⌒

C had could have easily told Logan to ignore my calls for any number of reasons. Instead, Chad had given away his position, forcing himself to run again. This time, however, he failed to possess a serviceable plan. With the odds stacked against him, I had absolutely no reason to follow or track him down – my energy would be better spent pinning Big Al's murder on him. If I were Chad, I would've taken off not ten minutes after Logan informed him of our meeting. But also, if I were Chad, I would have never embezzled that money in the first place.

Once everything goes according to plan, I believe the week will unfold something like this: tomorrow, with a little help, Alice and Em will discover an indelible break in the case that points to Chad as a person of interest. Then, the detectives will finally be brought into the fold. Search warrant or no search warrant, we will allow the detectives to search Chad's office. There, they will discover a vial of poison, which will be sitting in Chad's desk drawer. This piece of evidence, coupled with the fact that Chad is currently a missing person, will ultimately make him the prime suspect in the case. The detectives will eventually track Chad down, now that he is on the run, without a plan, face plastered across the news. Once he's caught, Chad will, of course, deny everything, and say that Mark and Luke kidnapped him.

"Sure, I stole a little money," he'll say, "but I had nothing to do with the murder, you have to believe me. I'm the victim here. Just go to Mark Crawford's house. You'll see."

Detectives Copeland and Garcia, being the thorough detectives that they are, will oblige. Mark will kindly let the detectives search his residence. There the detectives will find an empty pizza box, a few beers in the fridge, but overall a perfectly clean, stereotypical townhouse of a responsible, divorced father who is in the process of putting the pieces of his life back together. With all indicators pointing to Chad, the detectives will quickly recommend the District Attorney – who so happens to be an old friend of mine from law school – to bring charges against Chad for first-degree murder, or as the law defines it, "intentional murder that is willful and premeditated with malice aforethought." After learning of the evidence presented against him, and the press all but telling the public that he is guilty of murdering a local hero, Chad will have no choice but to take a plea to avoid life in prison. After a few months of headlines, Washington Ford will go back to normal, Big Al's estate shall be dispersed appropriately, and Chad, the thieving bastard, will be rotting in a prison, the fate he deserves.

Emily Bridges

Two people were dead; Another lying in a hospital bed, poisoned; a
fourth was missing. All these events occurred within a week, and
Washington Ford was at the center of it. No matter how Alice and I
looked at these facts, it was clear that coincidence was not the explanation.
After failing to identify a primary suspect, we decided that focusing our
attention on any possible links between the events would be the obvious
next direction in our investigation.

Alice rolled the whiteboard from the corner of the room closer to the
conference table. Written in red ink were the top salespeople for June. The
sales numbers were low, just thirty-three cars sold for the month, or a little
over one per day. All the salespeople and their target goals were listed;
not one apparently had been able to hit their lofty numbers. Alice wiped
away the sales stats with a dry-eraser, leaving messy red and black streaks
across the whiteboard after every shift in direction. Any attempt to clear
the stains using the eraser proved to be futile. Alice, not to be defeated,
spit into her hand to test her saliva against the almighty streaks, which
helped some, but left her hand covered in an oily red polymer. Content
with how clean it was going to get, Alice drew a thick horizontal green
line across the width of the whiteboard. Switching to a black marker, she
denoted Big Al's death on the left side of the line – Monday, July 3.

"Okay, what happened next?"

"Chad Baker is reported missing on the 5th."

"Right, Chad goes missing…"

Alice simultaneously repeated the information while noting it on the
timeline under the date 'July 5.' Her penmanship was pristine, meticu-
lously ensuring perfection with every stroke of the marker.

"Then what?"

"Your father's death is ruled a homicide on July 7th. Then, that evening – or early morning July 8th – Javy Perez and an unidentified accomplice broke into the lake house on the W. Ranch. Javy is later found dead floating in Lake Wylie around 8 a.m. on the morning of the 8th."

"July 7th/8th: Javy 'B&E', found dead in the lake. What else?"

"July 9th, at your dad's, uh, celebration of life, Luke was poisoned, and rushed to the hospital where he was put into a medically induced coma.'

"July 9th: Big Al's funeral, Luke poisoned, coma. All right."

"Hmm...what about Eva? According to Courtney, she was supposed to leave the country with Margret on the 10th, remember?"

"Yes, but then we found her trying to buy a gun today instead."

Alice noted Eva's attempt to buy a gun under 'July 10' on the timeline.

"Does anything stand out to you?" I asked.

"Eva's behavior doesn't add up."

"It is odd. My dad mentioned that she got spooked from the murder and break-in at her house, but I would be curious to know when exactly she bought that one-way plane ticket."

"And why she didn't end up going."

Alice paced back and forth, tapping the closed end of the marker against her flushed cheek. I was happy to see her motivated, having a purpose. Until now, my memory of Alice had been clashing with her current, listless state. When I was younger, I looked up to Alice. She was the only kid allowed to sit at the grown-up's table – and by allowed, I mean it was expected at every holiday. Alice could hold her own in just about any topic at the dinner table: politics, business, you name it, she would have an interesting take that would impress every single one of the adults, even if they disagreed with her. With or without a male heir to the throne, it seemed all but inevitable that Alice would take over for Big Al when the time came. But then, things changed. I couldn't recall precisely when Alice was shipped off to Alaska, maybe fifteen years ago? But the rumors immediately swirled – everything from Alice being pregnant, or going to rehab, to killing someone. Years later, my mom made an offhand comment to my dad about Alice being pushed out of the family business for being gay. I assumed it to be true when my father told my mother to be quiet rather than correct her.

"What about Javy?"

"What about him?"

"Of all the dead, missing, or hospitalized, he's the outlier."

"How so?"

"Think about it: As of a week ago, Big Al, Luke, and Chad were three of the top brass in the company. But, Javy was a mechanic, a low-level employee."

"Okay, so?"

"That tells us that Javy is either the most important piece to this puzzle, or a common thief who saw an opportunity and had nothing to do with the three others."

"The fact that Javy was seen leaving the W. Ranch by boat, but ended up dying from blunt force trauma, all but guarantees that someone else is involved?"

"It could have been our missing person, Chad."

"By all indications, Javy made it all the way inside the lake house, but nothing appeared to be stolen. So, what does that tell us?"

"Either he took something no one knew was there, or he didn't get anything at all."

"At the very least, Javy and his accomplice must have thought something valuable was there," Alice retorted.

"Well, Eva lives there, she might know something about it. Do you think you could get her to talk to us?"

Alice initially dismissed the idea, but shrugged her shoulders after thinking about the request for a moment.

"Eva and I have never had much of a relationship," Alice sighed, "I suppose It doesn't hurt to ask, though."

"Good. Meanwhile, I say we shake the hornet's nest and see what comes loose."

⌐

"Tell us what you know about Javy."

The service lift lowered a car down to the ground, making it a challenge to hear. I turned my head ever so slightly outside the bay doors to breathe anything other than the overwhelming stench of oil and gas that flooded my nostrils.

"¿Que?"

"Javy. ¿Que sabes?"

"No sé. Era ambicioso. Trabajador duro."

Alice asked Miguel, a mechanic wearing the stereotypical blue coveralls with a sewn oval name patch in red cursive lettering, a series of general questions about Javy. Miguel eventually handed us off to another mechanic, who handed us off to the supervisor on duty. The supervisor, frustrated that we were slowing down his guys on one of the few busy days of late, politely asked us to come back another time.

"Does he have a locker or anything we can look at?" I asked.

The supervisor looked at the clock on the wall before shrugging his shoulders.

"All right, but this is only happening because of your father. Hey Eric, get the bolt cutters, would ya?"

The supervisor yelled across the shop to a tall Black man holding a clipboard in one hand and a thermos in another. The man, presumably named Eric, set the thermos on the closest workbench before removing his earplugs.

"You talking to me?"

"Yes! Bolt cutters. Now please."

Eric and the supervisor yelled back and forth across the shop in what could best be described as an attempt at communication. It was only when the supervisor pantomimed the use of bolt cutters that Eric finally understood his task. The supervisor muttered a series of profanities under his breath as Eric searched through a rolling tool cabinet. Once located, Eric lumbered across the shop's floor, careful not to get in the way of the other mechanics working.

"Hurry up, would ya?"

"Here you go, boss."

Eric held out the bolt cutters, but the supervisor quickly pushed them back, instructing Eric to take us to the break room and cut off Javy's combination lock. The supervisor added that Eric should clear any clothing from the locker so it could be cleaned for "the next guy."

Eric barely acknowledged Alice and me as he guided us into the break room. I couldn't determine if that was due to the strain caused on his neck to look down on us or because he was simply indifferent toward us. The break room, which doubled as a locker room, was surprisingly cleaner than I imagined. It even had a decent-sized television, on which a soccer match was playing when we entered. With little to no effort, Eric snapped the lock in two with the bolt cutters. He then jammed what was left of the broken lock into his coverall pocket. Finally, he gave a small gesture with his right arm, as if to say, "All yours," and left us to examine Javy's locker while he took a seat to watch the action on the screen.

The locker, which appeared as if it hadn't been updated since the seventies or eighties, had spots of sticker gunk and tape residue lining the inside of the door. The effect created an unintentional collage from fifty years of mechanics. Inside the locker, we quickly sifted through Javy's discarded wardrobe, everything from dirty undershirts to worn socks and a pair of Vans. Other items of insignificance included body spray and a few mainstay colored ballpoint pens. Right when I was ready to give up, Alice suggested we look closer, just in case. I did my best to avoid any direct smells coming from Javy's dirty clothes as I knelt on the floor to turn his pockets inside out and examined the inside of his shoes using one of the recovered pens.

"What are y'all looking for anyway?"

Eric, finally making eye contact with us, turned halfway around in his chair with his left arm slumped over the back. The soccer announcers, speaking in Spanish, filled the quietness in the room as we pondered a response.

"We're not really sure."

"Did you know him well?" Alice interjected.

"He was a smart kid. Had a bright future ahead of him."

"How do you mean?"

"He was a friggin' magician with computers. He worked more on the computer than in here in the trenches the past few months."

"You mean the shop's computer work?"

"No, I mean the whole friggin' place. After they had to let the IT guy go, he was the de facto replacement."

The play-by-play commentator's inflection went higher as the roar from the crowd grew louder. A player in a red jersey argued with the referee as the latter held up a yellow card. Eric straightened up in his seat to give his full attention to the replay as the striker prepared for his penalty kick. Meanwhile, I neatly stacked Javy's belongings on the floor beside me. Once I was satisfied with their appearance for his parents or girlfriend, perhaps, I pushed off my bent knee to stand, nearly hitting my head on the top shelf in the process. *What was that?* Now standing upright, I tried to make sense of a glimmer of white against a sea of rusted blue. I ducked my head under the top shelf to find a thick piece of white paper wedged into a right angle. With some applied pressure and a quick jerk, I was able to dislodge it from the locker's grip.

"Alice."

I handed her the business card of none other than our missing person, Chad Baker. She flipped the card over to reveal what appeared to be his work login and password. I confirmed Alice's disbelief with a silent, controlled nod. Before I could let out a smile, Eric bellowed his frustration when the penalty kick sailed wide right of the goal.

Larry Bridges

By the time I had arrived at the dealership, at least five patrol units and a forensic team were waiting for me. Detectives Copeland and Garcia sipped on iced coffees in front of the main doors, visibly annoyed that I was a few minutes late. The morning heat was so brutal that Detective Copeland shed her mainstay blazer, wearing only a plain white button-down, sleeves rolled up. When I had spoken with her last night, breaking the news of what Alice and Em had found, the detective emphasized her eagerness to begin the search as soon as possible. The pressure must have been mounting, because she agreed to a limited search of Chad's office and computer rather than waiting a day or two for the possibility of a more expansive search warrant. The detectives' willingness to put aside our differences, coupled with their punctuality that morning, abetted my desperation theory.

Despite my tardiness, it seemed that the detectives – for the very first time – were treating me as an ally instead of an adversary. I strategically gave them, and the forensic team, a guided tour of the showroom and prominent Big Al memorabilia, careful to keep them on a direct path to Chad's office. Once inside, I noted the location of his computer and handed them the business card, carefully sealed in a Ziploc sandwich bag for effect, that Em and Alice found in Javy's locker.

"Now, I told my partner what you told me, but he just can't wrap his head around it. You mind telling it once more?"

Detective Garcia, wearing his typical Hawaiian shirt, happily played dumb as he shrugged his broad shoulders.

"Anything to help, detectives. See, my daughter Emily and Big Al's eldest daughter Alice have been helping me as consultants on – let's call it an internal investigation. During said investigation, Emily and Alice discovered a previously unknown connection between the recently deceased Javier Perez and our missing finance officer, Chad Baker. That connection, along with Chad's login information, led to the discovery of hundreds of thousands of dollars in theft over Chad's tenure with Washington Ford. So, with that concrete evidence, I made a courtesy call to Detective Copeland."

"So generous of you, Larry."

Refusing to give Detective Garcia's sarcasm any merit, I offered him a blank face with a side of contempt. Sensing the rising tension, Detective Copeland attempted to diffuse the situation, thanking me for my time and assuring me that they would work as quickly as possible and not get in the way of dealership operations.

"Good. Then you can move the patrol cars to the back and have them turn their lights off, yes?"

"Of course," Detective Copeland agreed.

I shook Detective Copeland's hand and advised her to contact my executive assistant Brenda if she needed to reach me. As I turned to leave, I cleared my throat to prevent myself from grinning. *Everything is going according to plan.*

~

"Well if it isn't the puppeteer." The voice was strangely familiar.

"How'd you get in here?"

Sitting at my desk with her left leg crossed over her right was Big Al's second wife, Kelly Washington. Between her tailored suit and what appeared to be a fairly recent facelift, I concluded that she was somehow surviving on her divorce settlement.

"I took the liberty of letting myself in, seeing as you were a little tied up."

"Kelly, what are you doing here?"

"I didn't get a chance to speak with you at the service, so I thought I'd drop in for old times' sake."

"I'm afraid now is not a good time."

"No? Okay, you're right, maybe I'll just stop by and have a little chat with those detectives on my way out."

Kelly, overplaying her meager hand, rose from my desk and slowly marched past me toward the door. She yanked at the handle, scoffing at my inaction. I allowed the door to open by about a foot before halting it with my own.

"What do you want?"

"My fair share."

My memory of Kelly was at odds with what stood in front of me. *Has it been that long?* While my office lighting wasn't doing her any favors, I never remembered seeing grey overwhelm that once striking blonde hair. And the plastic surgery – sure, wrinkles aren't kind to anyone, but at least they help maintain a human-like appearance as people age. With her oddly inflated lips and permanent smile, I struggled to determine her true level of resentment. *After I thought about it, I realized that I hadn't seen her since the divorce proceedings.*

"You got your fair share a decade ago."

"Don't give me that bullshit."

Kelly, shaking with anger, stuck her pointer finger in my face as if she had rehearsed this confrontation beforehand in her bathroom mirror. It seemed, however, that Kelly had underestimated the depth of her emotions, as a destructive mixture of hatred, sadness, and self-doubt jumbled her speech into an incoherent mess.

"You don't know how he treated me. He was an evil, manipulative person. I still haven't recovered from what he did to me."

"Uh-huh."

"You're just as bad as he was, you know that? And you're still stuck cleaning up his shit, even after his body turned stiff."

"Look, Kelly, I feel for you after all that happened, but you signed off on the deal. Just because you already blew the money doesn't mean you get more."

"You and I both know that Al hid millions from my lawyers."

"Even if I wanted to help you, the money is tied up until the murder investigation is complete, and who knows how long that will take? I'm sorry, but there's nothing I can do."

"Oh please. Everyone knows that Bjork slut did it."

"Hey. Yes, Eva is an Icelander and a singer, but I don't think it's fair to call her a slut."

"Is a talentless hack better? And let's be clear, she's held more dicks than notes in her life."

"Oh, come on. That's uncalled for, Kelly."

Apparently determined to escalate the verbal sparring match until she got what she wanted, Kelly blathered on about how abusive Big Al had been toward her. *In with the good...*

"You have no idea how he treated me, Larry. He was a monster. Larry, what are you doing?"

...Out with the bad. After a satisfying exhale, I opened my eyes to find Kelly staring right back at me, confounded. *Al, I loved you, man, but everyone in your life is fucking insane.*

"You do breathing exercises now? You're turning soft, Larry the Lion."

"Just old."

"Al always had a way of taking the best years of someone's life."

"Al and I were good. His family, however...y'all are all kinds of crazy."

Suddenly, Kelly's eyes fell. Even her posture changed, as her tough-as-nails attitude subsided. Our sparring session had abruptly come to an end.

"Let me ask you a serious question, Larry. How can you continue to defend that womanizer even after he's dead?"

Struggling to get through a deep breath without breaking down, Kelly lifted her swollen eyes to meet mine.

"Look, I can give you some money for old times' sake, but don't think for a minute you can go to the cops or the press. Whether you like it or not, you signed that NDA. And if you breach that NDA, you're on the hook for the entire divorce settlement. What was it, five million?"

"What do I care? How are you going to take money from a woman who doesn't have any?"

I reached for my wallet, a leather fold that had faded and cracked along the spine years ago. Flipping through the bills, I quickly took inventory: One hundred, two hundred, three hundred, four hundred, five hundred. *I'll do Kelly a favor and give her four hundred. On second thought, three should be plenty.* With two hundred dollars firmly in my grasp, I went ahead and bit the bullet.

"What's the number?"

"Same as before. Five million."

"You want five million dollars?"

"My fair share."

After a deep sigh, I stuffed the two hundreds back into my wallet, then advised her not to do anything rash, and that I would be in contact over the next few days. Seemingly pleased with her opening bid and my reaction, Kelly agreed to be patient but warned me not to go dark, or she would have, in her words, "no choice but to tell the world about Big Al."

The moment the door closed behind her, I rushed to my desk – or at least, I walked as fast as a sixty-six-year-old man could without hurting himself. *Five million dollars?! That woman is out of her damn mind.* I entered the password to unlock my computer, then sat down in my chair and attempted to catch my breath. After the security camera app eventually loaded, I scrolled through the footage from the last few minutes. The detectives started by taking a blacklight to the office. Once that inspection proved not to be fruitful, the forensic team powdered down the keyboard, mouse pad, and door handle for fingerprints. The investigators then snapped a dozen or so photos and gathered the samples. Judging by their body language, they didn't seem too thrilled by the results. Next, under the watchful eyes of Detectives Copeland and Garcia, the forensic team bagged Chad's computer, the machine that had netted proof of years of embezzling. Finally, they took inventory of the contents of Chad's desk: a calculator, a sheet of stamps, and stacks of nondescript papers. Apparently satisfied, the law enforcement team packed their kits without any vial of poison to be found.

Out with the bad, in with the good; out with that fucking moron Mark. I picked up the phone at my desk, and poorly attempted another breathing exercise as the dial tone pierced my concentration.

"Hi, this is Mark."

"They didn't find it."

"What do you mean they didn't find it?"

"The poison wasn't in Chad's desk, you imbecile."

"Where could it be then?"

VII

AS I LAY LIVING

Luke Washington

As I slipped in and out of consciousness, as hard as I tried, I was unable to revisit my dream. Maybe 'dream' wasn't the right word; it was more like an alternate reality. I wore a black suit, red tie, and an American flag pin on my left lapel. There were adoring crowds and debates I had obviously won in front of TV cameras. Why couldn't I go back? Seemingly, every detail I was able to recall pulled me further from the alternate reality, not closer to it. For once in my life, I wasn't a complete fuck-up or the laughing-stock of the world. Instead of a car salesman following in my grandfather's footsteps, I was a beloved politician, one of the rare few with a strong moral compass, a leader who stood up for the voiceless and powerless. When the spotlight turned on me, I was the best version of myself. I had a purpose. Then I woke up.

On the rare moments that I did find myself awake, my thoughts were jumbled and my memory was fleeting. Yet with each awakening, I found myself more aware of my surroundings than the last. I couldn't be sure, but every time I came to, I thought I saw Lauren, and my mother sitting by my side.

Bouquets of fresh flowers and 'Get Well Soon' balloons surrounded my bed. While I had always enjoyed the smell of flowers, the mixture of twenty different types caused my eyes to water. When I attempted to express this to my mom, however, nothing came out. I couldn't form a sound, let alone a word or sentence. The moment that I became fully aware of my ineptitude, the machines hooked up to my body started to make angry noises, which caused enough concern that my mom ran out of the room to presumably look for a nurse. One eventually rushed in, with my mom a few steps behind, frantically crying out for me to "stay strong."

⌒

There was thirst, and then there was waking up after a three-day, medically induced coma thirst. My throat had that scratchy feeling, like having to swallow with a sore throat, but much more intense. The worst part was that the nurses wouldn't even let me drink a proper glass of water. Instead, they gave my mom a small synthetic sponge to dip slightly into a cup of water to wet the inside of my mouth. They even stopped me from sucking on the damn thing.

"Rest assured," the nurse said, "in a week, you'll be able to suck on ice cubes through a washcloth."

No one told me exactly how I ended up in a hospital bed with limited mobility and the inability to speak – or maybe they had, and I just couldn't remember. Racking my brain for possibilities, nothing plausible came to mind; I was far too young for a heart attack, and I didn't seem to have any scars or bruises that would suggest some sort of accident. The good news, aside from the fact that I was no longer using a feeding tube, was that my lapse of memory appeared to be short-term. While I couldn't remember how I ended up here, I recalled the faces and names of the people who visited me. Those who did walked on eggshells, careful not to discuss what happened. They would talk about recovery or about themselves, anything to avoid the topics of what happened or how I ended up in a hospital bed. After the first batch of visitors, even though I couldn't talk, I thought it was odd that they didn't ask me any questions. After the second batch, I gathered that someone probably had told them not to.

On the second day of my relative recovery, I turned a corner. My memory of the accident still failed me, but for the first time since it happened, I was able to retain new information. And more importantly, I no longer drifted in and out of consciousness. The team of revolving doctors and nurses switched their concentration from keeping me alive to planning my rehabilitation. Their focus began on my speech and motor functions, both of which were an immense struggle. With daily speech and physical therapy, the doctors believed I could be back to my usual self within a couple of months.

Now that I was conscious for most of the day, I was at least able to watch TV when I wasn't doing therapy. It was just unfortunate that my family was fodder for the local news stations' content. Day and night, the news anchors led their broadcasts with the latest update on Grandpa's murder before kicking their coverage to a field reporter on-site at the dealership, the hospital where I was staying – or the latest, Chad Baker's house. On the bright side, the news coverage provided some answers to the gaps in my memories. The latest information I learned was that Chad had stolen hundreds of thousands of dollars from Washington Ford over nine years.

"And now we go to Michelle Park, live on-site at Washington Ford."

A young, well-dressed Korean American woman stood in front of a row of cars with the Washington Ford sign towering above her in the background.

"Thank you, Erica. Chad Baker, the longtime finance officer at Washington Ford, has been indicted on embezzlement and wire fraud charges. In an exclusive interview with Larry Bridges, senior counselor for Washington Ford, I asked if there was any possible connection between Mr. Baker and the murder of owner Big Al Washington."

The reporter stared blankly at the camera, waiting for the tape to be played.

"That's a great question. Knowing what we know now, Mr. Baker certainly had the motive. And not to mention an innocent man doesn't typically go on the run."

"When did you discover something criminal was afoot?"

"Mr. Baker did not report to work the day after Big Al's murder. The next day he was officially declared missing. Shortly thereafter, we conducted an internal audit; that's when we discovered a major discrepancy in the books. We promptly handed over the evidence to Detectives Copeland and Garcia of the Charlotte-Mecklenburg Police Department. And their investigation has led to an indictment of Mr. Baker on embezzlement and wire fraud charges."

"Did you have any idea of Mr. Baker's alleged criminal activity?"

"None whatsoever. You think you know someone well enough to put your trust in them, and then this happens. It's a real shame that one bad apple could have nearly destroyed a Charlotte institution. But, I'm confident we'll get through this."

The broadcast cut back to the reporter at Washington Ford, battling her makeup from sweating off in the afternoon heat.

"As the manhunt continues without any prominent leads, Charlotte-Mecklenburg Police, with a donation from Washington Ford, are offering a $50,000 reward for any information leading to the capture and arrest of Chad Baker. Back to you, Erica."

"Thank you, Michelle. And here is a recent picture of Chad Baker and a number for the tipline. Police are urging those with any information to call this number."

A photo of Chad dressed in a blue pinstripe suit with a contrasting white collar appeared with the number for the tip line below it. I switched channels to another local news station, where a reporter stood outside of Javy Perez's parents' house.

There was a knock at the door. My mom, eager for any visitor or update from a doctor, jumped up to see who was there. Seemingly unfamiliar with the face, she kept the door cracked, perhaps wary that it was someone from the media.

"It's Mark, Mark Crawford."

"Oh, hi! So nice of you to stop by, Mark. Sorry, I didn't recognize you. Come on in."

Before Lauren and my mom had a chance to tell Mark about my condition, he rushed to my side with a big dumb smile on his face.

"Shit, I thought you were going to die on me there, bud. One second we're drinking at the bar, and the next you're on the floor unconscious. Anyway, how are you feelin,' you SOB?"

I turned my eyes away in shame, as my mom had to explain to Mark that I was unable to speak. With my head turned to the window, I imagined a combination of confusion and discomfort on Mark's face. After an awkward silence, Lauren jumped in to say that I was showing improvement, but it was going to be a long road to recovery. Finally, I turned my eyes back to the room, waiting for the conversation to continue. Mark apologized to Lauren and my mom for not knowing about my condition, but I noticed he did not address me directly.

"Say, you both look like you could use a break. Why don't you ladies get some lunch or coffee, and I'll keep Luke good company."

"Oh, I don't know."

"Nonsense, I'll watch some baseball with him, and you can take your mind off, uh, things, for a bit."

"I could use some food in me, I guess," Lauren insisted.

My mom reluctantly agreed, but only after demanding that Mark take down her number just in case anything came up. Mark proceeded to type it into his phone as Lauren kissed me on the forehead. After saving the number, Mark made a big show about looking for a baseball game on the TV while Lauren and my mom gathered their purses and exited the room.

Then the door closed. Mark continued to flip through the channels for a few seconds while keeping a keen eye on the door. After a seemingly successful charade, Mark slowly crept toward the door to listen for any sign of movement.

"What the fuck do you think you're doing, Luke, huh?"

Mark's tone and demeanor instantly shifted once he was sure that we were alone. His footsteps grew louder and more pointed as he approached the side of my bed.

"I know you can hear me, Luke."

Why is he so upset? The look of bewilderment on my face apparently didn't satisfy Mark's demand for an answer.

"The detectives didn't find the poison in Chad's desk, Luke. And then you, the person who planted it there, ends up poisoned? It just didn't add up. So I thought about it – and I remembered that I saw you near my desk that night. And what do you know, guess what I found in my drawer?"

As Mark was mean-mugging me, he lifted up his pant leg, reached into his sock and pulled out a clear plastic bag. Making sure I got a good look at the contents, he shoved it into my face. A vial.

I tried to tell Mark I didn't know what he was talking about, but nothing came out. I placed my hands over my throat to remind Mark that I was incapable of speaking. Unmoved by my frustration, Mark put his own hand over his throat, then made gurgling noises to mock me. In turn, I removed my hand from my throat, confused more than ever about what was happening.

"Listen closely, because here's what's going to happen. Fortunately for you, Larry and I have pinned this whole thing on Chad. Once he's convicted of embezzlement, Big Al's murder, and – if we're lucky – your attempted murder, Big Al's estate will be divided up among the beneficiaries. You will now be giving me half of your inheritance, pal – and then we'll go our separate ways and live happily ever after. That's the only way I see this working. And that's a pretty fucking generous offer – considering, well, you know, you trying to frame me and all."

Unable to react verbally to his demands, Mark's patience grew thin as he paced around the perimeter of my bed, too angry to articulate his thoughts. With only wisps of memory returning, I couldn't figure out if Mark's story held water. But I wasn't in a position to negotiate. *Yet, there may be one way out of this predicament.* Using my left hand, I searched through my blanket for the nurse call button, praying Mark didn't notice. *Shit. Maybe it's on my right side?* I gently patted down anything within reach. *Nothing.*

"Looking for this?"

Mark lifted his right hand, which firmly was grasping the nurse call button.

"You slimy little prick. I've only ever tried to help you, and what have you done? Stabbed me in the back, twice now."

Red-faced and teeth clenched, Mark took a deep breath. By the time he started up again, the blood vessels bulged on his forehead.

"My percentage just went up. Because of your actions and yours alone, I'm getting 75 percent now, understand? And if you don't agree, I'm not only bringing you down, I'm taking down your whole family."

Mark stepped toward my bed, leaned toward my ear, and spoke in a controlled, soft voice.

"Take the deal. Think of your wife. Or better yet, that mom of yours. I bet that's the last person that crosses your mind every night before you go to bed – isn't it, mama's boy?"

If what Mark says is true, it wasn't my most brilliant plan, but at least I now know why I did it. In my most desperate attempt yet to speak, I slowly sat up and tried to spit out a single word: "Okay." My severely chapped lips made it difficult to open my mouth, but eventually, I managed. What came out next was less of a word and more like what I imagine babies sound like before they're able to speak. To add to my embarrassment, what little saliva I had spewed out onto my chin and hospital gown. The image of my incapacity proved to be so hilarious to Mark that he practically doubled over with laughter. Then, it seemed a moment of pity came over him, but it was short-lived.

"You might not be able to talk, but you better nod your fucking head, understood?"

I nodded as much as my malfunctioning body allowed me to, satisfying Mark's demand. I could see he was already thinking of how he was going to spend my money. With a smile big enough to show his coffee-stained teeth, Mark called me a "smart man."

I slumped back into my previous prone position, which wasn't as relaxing now that the pillow was all out of place. Fighting for a semblance of comfort, I glanced at Mark, only to find him messing with something on the side of my bed with a devious glint in his eye.

"While I appreciate you accepting the offer, I wouldn't exactly call us square. I'm afraid I'm going to have to cause you a little pain and suffering."

Mark lifted my catheter bag off the side of the bed, filled with roughly three-quarters of my yellowish-brown piss.

"I've got to tell you, Luke, when I found that poison planted in my desk drawer, I felt a pain like I've never felt before. Your betrayal stung me to the core. Now, it's my turn to do that for you."

With his right hand holding my catheter bag, Mark pulled down my blanket to my ankles with his free hand. I pleaded with him to stop, but only gurgles and loud moans came out. His left hand, firmly grasping the catheter tube, slowly inched closer to my body.

"You want to know the difference between you and me, Luke? I look someone in the eyes when I fuck them over."

Shifting my eyes from Mark's left hand to his face, I found his eyes, black as night, looking directly into mine. And then he did it. With a quick tug of the tube, Mark yanked the catheter out of me. A sharp pain immediately followed. A pain so excruciatingly concentrated that if given a choice, death would have been preferable. As the burning grew, so did my howl, which was abruptly interrupted by Mark's hand over my mouth to quiet me. I couldn't be bothered to look at Mark as I rolled from one side to another, but his laughter told me he was thoroughly enjoying the moment.

In the middle of my agonizing pain, I felt a rush of lukewarm water splashing onto my gown and bare legs. I opened my eyes to discover the source: Mark emptied the entirety of my catheter bag onto my gown. Mark then threw the blue hospital blanket back over me, even mockingly tucked me in with it. Feeling utterly helpless, my eyes swelled up, and tears fell down my face. Meanwhile, Mark, thoroughly pleased with himself, began flipping channels on the television.

"Well, shall we watch that ballgame now? Your family probably won't be back for a few hours."

As yet another laugh came out of that arrogant face, I decided in that exact moment that not only would Mark never see a cent of my inheritance, but I was going to kill him.

Eva Washington

The room was too cold. *I'll never understand Americans' love affair with air conditioning.* There was no sight of Larry or any of the immediate family yet. A handful of people I didn't recognize helped themselves to a coffee and snacks near the window overlooking the city. Once Margret saw an opening, she immediately darted off to see what was being offered before I got the chance to tell her not to. *Well, I might as well get a cup of tea now.*

As I waited for my tea to steep, I thought it might be a good idea to count the number of chairs. There were four rows of chairs with an aisle in between, maybe thirty-two seats total in the medium-sized conference room. *Will there be that many beneficiaries? That seems way too many.* I figured Margret and I better sit in the first row, since we would be among the biggest beneficiaries. In all honesty, I would rather have hidden in the back, but for appearance's sake, I decided against it. *Worst case, even if I, the hated trophy wife of the family, got left out of the will, Margret should be set for life. And she'll be kind to her mother. We could get as far away as possible from this godforsaken family and enjoy a quiet life in Iceland.*

Now seated in the first row, next to the aisle, I figured I should double-check my makeup while I had a minute. Before I got a proper chance to see how I looked using my phone's camera, I saw the door opening behind me. I clicked my phone off and threw it back in my purse when I saw Courtney walk through the door. Once Margret quickly became aware that her half-sister was in the room, there was no stopping her. Against my objection to slow down, Margret ran full-speed at Courtney with open arms, practically tripping over her untied shoelaces the entire way. Courtney, putting on a show for the attendees, embraced Margret with a big hug and then picked her up.

Courtney, now carrying Margret on her hip, spotted me in the front row and approached. Their matching golden blonde hair and age difference would lead a reasonable person to believe they were mother and daughter, not sisters. But alas, here we were in the world built by the late, great Al Washington.

Courtney carefully placed Margret in the chair directly to my left while exchanging an insincere greeting with me. Despite her undying love for Margret, Courtney left an empty chair between them when she took her seat.

Next into the room was Luke's wife, Lauren. She was with a man I didn't recognize, mid to late twenties. Dressed in a suit two sizes too small to show off his unexceptional muscles, he had dark, slicked-back hair. He escorted Lauren to the row directly behind me. If Margret didn't turn around to say hello first, I know for a fact that Lauren wouldn't have acknowledged me. She introduced me to the man with her, but I tended to immediately forget someone's name the first time I met them – maybe Matt or Mike?

After a little small talk with Lauren, I stopped looking back as people arrived. Based on the footsteps and chatter, I'd estimated another dozen or so more people filed into the room as we approached the scheduled time of the reading. And then, all of a sudden, the room fell silent. Without having to look, I knew Larry had entered the room. *A lion commands attention.* As he walked down the middle of the aisle, I heard a combination of footsteps and chairs being adjusted as people found a place to sit.

Now in my sightline, Larry marched right for the table at the front of the room. To my surprise, there was a grey-haired woman with him, wearing pantyhose and a pair of geriatric-looking shoes. Both Larry and the mystery woman, carrying briefcases, found their chairs on the other side of the table, facing the crowd.

Larry sat entirely still, eyes scanning the crowd. The woman pulled a binder from her briefcase, put her glasses on, and then flipped through it until she found the desired page.

"Good afternoon, ladies and gentlemen. Thank you for coming here for the reading of Allen James Washington's last will and testament," Larry announced.

All right, Al, I gave up my better and the best years of my life for your cheating ass, you better not screw me now. If that son of a bitch leaves his daughter and me with anything less than fifty million, I swear to God...

"While a reading of a person's will is unusual for most people—"

All of a sudden, Larry turned pale. He cleared his throat as he rubbed the right temple on his forehead.

"Excuse me."

There was a prolonged lull, during which everyone looked around the room at each other, perplexed. No one appeared to have an answer. Eventually, Larry composed himself with a sip of water.

"Excuse me. I thought it was appropriate to get Big Al's close friends and family in the same room together so there won't be any misunderstandings on the dispersion of the estate."

Misunderstandings? Larry took a moment to drink more water. I took it as an opportunity to finally look behind me to get an approximate count of the attendees. Maybe twenty people? I caught a quick glimpse of Al's black sheep, Alice and her unremarkable hair, across the aisle on the right side of the room. *What is she doing here?*

"In addition, since I am one of the beneficiaries, I have decided to forgo my position as the executor of the estate so there won't be any accusations of conflicts of interest. I'm handing over my duties to Charlotte's most respected estate lawyer, Dorothy Belk. Mrs. Belk will now read Al's Last Will and Testament. Mrs. Belk."

Respected for what, living past ninety? The woman is a fossil; her pencil skirt and pantyhose reek of someone who hasn't bothered to buy a new outfit in over twenty years.

"Thank you, Mr. Bridges. As most of you are aware, in the event Mr. Washington's murder, Mr. Washington demanded his estate be frozen until the guilty party was convicted. Seeing as the suspect is still at-large, it may take months or even years until these assets can be distributed."

I've waited a decade, what's another few months? Larry, poker-faced, sat back in his chair, arms crossed. *He must be getting a nice chunk. He did work for Al for a long time, but I'd argue that his salary would be enough compensation.*

"With that said, here is Allen James Washington's Last Will and Testament:

"I, Allen James Washington, being of competent and sound mind, do hereby declare this to be my Last Will and Testament and do hereby revoke any and all wills and codicils heretofore made jointly or severally by me. I further declare that this Last Will and Testament reflects my personal wishes without any undue influence whatsoever.

"At the time of this Last Will and Testament, I am married to Eva Washington, and I have two children who are listed as follows:

Alice Washington, born 1982

Courtney Washington, born 1984

"I hereby nominate and appoint Lawrence Bridges as executor of this Last Will and Testament..."

"Wait, where is Margret?" I cried out.

"Please hold all questions or comments to the end, ma'am.

Without emotion, Dorothy Belk returned her attention to the document in her hands.

"Should the aforementioned individual be unavailable, unable or unwilling to serve as executor when needed, then I nominate and appoint Dorothy Belk as the alternate executor of this Last Will and Testament. In the event of my murder, my estate shall be frozen until the guilty party has been convicted.

"After payment of any personal debts, expenses, and liabilities, I request and direct that my property be bequeathed as follows:

Courtney Washington shall receive the W. Ranch and 50 percent of my estate.

Luke Washington shall receive 40 percent of my estate, which will be placed into a trust fund until Luke turns twenty-one years of age.

Lawrence Bridges shall receive 100 percent ownership and control of Washington Ford.

In the event of my murder, any person that provides information that leads to the arrest and conviction of the guilty party shall receive the final 10 percent of the estate. If I am not murdered, the 10 percent shall be split evenly between my living brothers and sisters.

Wait, what? Murmurs filled the room.

"I have intentionally omitted my daughter Alice Washington from this, my Last Will and Testament, as I do not agree with her lifestyle. Additionally, I have omitted my third and current wife, Eva Washington, as I believe her to be a gold-digger, and I provided her with enough gold when I was alive."

"What is this bullshit, Larry?" I screamed.

"Ma'am, please hold all questions or comments to the end," Dorothy groaned.

"In witness whereof, I, Allen James Washington, have hereunto signed this Will freely and voluntarily on the 11th day of December 2020, in Charlotte, North Carolina."

The elderly woman took a sip of water as Larry leaned forward to write something on her legal pad.

"2020? Is this a joke, Larry?" I asked.

"Please hold all comments – oh, this is the end of the document. Does anyone have any questions or comments?" The woman sneered.

I stood from my chair, took a step toward the table, and got right in Larry's face as my body violently shook with rage.

"This will is a sham, Larry."

"Sadly, it is not, Mrs. Washington," Dorothy interjected.

"Bullshit."

"Please sit down, Mrs. Washington. Does anyone else have any questions or concerns?"

"I want to hear it from him."

Just as the old fart opened her mouth to scold me, Larry stopped her with a slight wave of his hand, sat up a little straighter, and looked directly into my eyes.

"Enough, Eva. What's done is done. My advice to you is to dig elsewhere for gold while you're still... somewhat young."

"Fuck you, Larry. You'll pay for this."

I didn't give him the chance to get the last word in. I scooped Margret into my right arm, purse in left, and stomped down the aisle toward the exit. Margret, scared and confused, began to cry right before we reached the door. With my mind full of anger, I was unable to take note whether the room was in uproar. When the door closed behind me, the hallway, remarkably quiet besides Margret's crying, felt empty. After a handful of deep breaths, I whispered in Margret's ear that everything would be okay, one way or another.

VIII

THINGS COME
TOGETHER

Detective Copeland

My whole life, I dreamt about being rich. Rich enough that student and credit card debt wasn't something I worried about every day. Rich enough that I was the boss, not someone who knows less than me but was in charge because he's a white male. Rich enough that I could eat out whenever I wanted and order anything on the menu, instead of splitting a dinner or being forced to only eat only half of the plate to make an extra meal out of it. Rich enough where I didn't have to live paycheck to paycheck, praying my pension or social security would still be available to me by the time my broken-down body forced me to retire. Rich enough to buy happiness. I genuinely thought it was that simple until Big Al Washington dropped dead. Now, I want nothing to do with money. All that money does is breed problems: one daughter, an addict; another, a lazy piece of shit wasting away; a trophy wife, gave up her passion for marrying a guy twice her age; and a grandson, a complete fuck-up. Not to mention, everyone in the family hates each other. What kind of way to live is that? If I had to choose between my life or being a Washington, I'd take mine any day of the week and twice on Sunday.

"Any sign of him? Over."

"Negative. Over."

After putting away the police radio mic, Garcia carefully slurped from his coffee tumbler and leaned back in the seat. There hadn't been one peep on Chad Baker's whereabouts for almost a week. That was until we got a tip this morning that he might be mulling around in Boone, a college town nestled in the Appalachian Mountains. Typically, Boone bustled with students, but the town proved to be pretty sleepy this time of year due to summer break. With the assistance of Boone PD, we established a five-mile perimeter from where Mr. Baker was last reported, which happened to be at a Cookout, a burger joint on the main drag of town. We probably went up and down that road damn near fifteen times and saw nobody resembling Mr. Baker. At least, the chilly mountain air meant we weren't sweating our asses off in the squad car. I even rolled down the windows for a few minutes before Garcia complained.

"You ever hear the one about a crawfish whistling on a mountain?"

"No," I replied.

"Well, we have a better chance of finding a crawfish whistling on this mountain than catching this guy up here."

"Mr. Optimism."

"An ex-girlfriend calling in the tip just seems unlikely to me. Who willingly seeks out an ex-girlfriend?"

"You never tried to reach out to the one that got away, Garcia?"

"See, that's different – we're talking soulmates vs. ex-girlfriends here."

"Nothing like a little reward money to come between soulmates."

Garcia and I devised a new plan: painstakingly check each and every one of the parking lots on the main drag. Going east, we surveyed the parking lots of Bojangles, Dunkin', Hardee's, a laundromat, a couple of churches, the post office, and finally a tattoo parlor. After forty-five minutes, and no sign of Mr. Baker, I turned the car around to check out the parking lots on the other side of the street: Mellow Mushroom, a few cafes, a sushi spot, and another church. There was no sign of anyone resembling Mr. Baker anywhere. Even though most of the college students were gone for the summer, the majority of people we saw were still college-aged or parents touring the campus with their kids. *Baker would stick out like a sore thumb in this town.*

"There's no way Baker would be on a street like this with college kids and their parents. That's it. We're wasting our time," I relayed to Garcia.

"Where do you propose we look then, boss?"

"Where would you go if you were Baker?"

"Well, I can't use a credit card, so hotels are out. Maybe some motels still accept cash, but that seems unlikely to me."

"So where?"

"Plenty of campgrounds around here."

"Now that's a great theory, Garcia. And to think, everyone calls you a brainless meathead."

"Who calls me that?"

"Oh, no one really – just Markinson, Bacon, Walker, Peralta, Williams, and sometimes Taylor."

"Fuck off."

"Yeah, and a few others. But not me. I set them straight...well, I never have, but now I will, after this genius theory of yours."

Garcia, in his typical humorless way, displayed not the slightest hint of a smile. He honestly might confront them all one-by-one, the next time he sees them.

With some quick Googling, Garcia found two campsites just southwest of our position: Flintlock and Honey Bear Campground. First up, Flintlock Campground – which, we would come to find out, featured more tiny house cabins than campsites. First, we stopped at the office to find a "camp ranger," a college kid who was likely mailing it in for the summer. We kindly asked him if we could see the log of people staying in the campground, figuring he wouldn't be paid well enough to care or put up a legal fight. Sure enough, the college kid gladly turned over the log. The kid even expressed an interest in our presence, offering to help in any way possible. With no sign of Chad Baker or any solo travellers in the logbook, we returned it to him and asked for a map of the campgrounds. Garcia and I knocked on roughly fifteen doors, with about a third answering. We showed a recent photo of Mr. Baker, studying their behavior as they looked at it. Without any luck, we drove to the campsites, where we discovered only a handful of tents.

"Excuse us, ma'am? Have you seen this man?"

Another six or so people camping in tents or mulling around common areas didn't recognize Mr. Baker. Realizing our time was limited, we called in reinforcements. The Boone chief of police informed us that there were six campgrounds within fifteen minutes or so of downtown and another ten within thirty minutes, and those were only the sanctioned ones. Hell, Eric Rudolph, the bomber at the 1996 Summer Olympics, spent five years in these mountains undetected. We informed the Boone PD that our manhunt came up empty at Flintlock, and we planned on searching Honey Bear Campground next. Meanwhile, the chief said he would send his guys to the other four campsites in closest proximity to downtown Boone.

"Here we go. Honey Bear Campground has 3.6 stars on Google

reviews. Listen to this, Shane Cleary gives it three stars, 'Pros: Friendly staff, strong coffee, duck pond. Cons: Outside firewood not permitted, filthy bathrooms, no ducks.'"

A single road led to Honey Bear Campground, just a few minutes' drive from Flintlock. Similar to our last stop, the welcome center stood adjacent to the main entrance. Armed with a few photos of Mr. Baker, we tried our luck to see if anyone had a line on our suspect.

"Good afternoon, and welcome to the Honey Bear Campground."

Garcia flashed his badge to a baby-faced campground attendant with bloodshot eyes, presumably named JB from the nametag on his ratty polo with its Honey Bear logo. Rather than follow me to the counter, Garcia took a lap around the lobby, undoubtedly in search of that strong coffee. I can't say I blamed him; we had a long night ahead of us driving back to Charlotte.

"Hi there, JB, my name is Detective Copeland, and the one helping himself to your fine coffee is Detective Garcia. We're looking for a man, traveling by himself, in his late thirties. Have you seen anyone matching that description?"

"Whoa, I don't think so. Is he, like, wanted or something?"

"Take a look at his photo, would you?"

I pulled up the photo of Mr. Baker on my phone; a headshot we'd found on the Washington Ford website, dressed in a suit and tie, looking off into the distance, smiling but not showing any teeth. JB scrutinized the photo with high intensity; if there was any previous doubt he was stoned, that had now been removed.

"I don't know – he looks familiar, but then again, doesn't everyone kinda look familiar?"

"Do you keep a logbook of your guests?"

Garcia finally joined me at the counter, coffee cup in hand. The young attendant greeted him instead of retrieving the logbook. Only when I reminded him to kindly retrieve the logbook did he open a nearby drawer to pull out a spiral notebook with a sticker of the camp's logo on the cover. Opening it on the counter in front of him, JB flipped the pages back and forth at an excruciatingly slow pace, licking his index finger before every page turn.

"How's the coffee, Garcia?"

"As advertised. Going to have to check out that duck pond next."

At the mention of the duck pond, JB abruptly stopped page-turning, looking a little crestfallen. *Must be a sore subject around here.* Garcia, annoyed with JB's leisurely pace, opted to wander through the kitschy welcome center, sipping his coffee. On what must have been the fiftieth page turn, I turned the logbook 180 degrees to face me, where I located the current date in fewer than two seconds. JB appeared to be genuinely impressed with how quickly I found it. The logbook had about fifty entries from the past few days. Each entry listed the primary guest, the number of people in the party, and the license plate of their vehicle if they had one.

"Do the guests supply this information, or do you verify?"

"We only verify the license plates; otherwise, they'll get towed."

Examining the logbook, I failed to find an entry for Chad Baker – not that he'd use his real name. There were four entries for a single guest and about a dozen entries for exactly two guests. At that point, it was more likely than not Chad was alone, especially if the supposed reunion with the ex-girlfriend went sour. I figured if we checked out those four camp-sites, we would've done our due diligence, with time to hit up one more campsite before trekking back home for the night. A knock at a window on the opposite side of the room suddenly diverted my attention. Garcia opened said window and called out to someone, presumably an employee within earshot. After some indistinct chatter, Garcia turned to me.

"Hey, Copeland, you got that photo?"

Without asking JB's permission, I brought the logbook with me, using my index finger as a bookmark. A young female employee, equally as chipper but a hell of a lot less stoned, wearing the same polo as JB – name tag 'Nicole' – greeted me on the other side of the window. Just as I did for JB, I pulled up the photo of Baker on my phone.

"Huh. I think I saw a guy who looked something like that near the bathhouse, yesterday or the day before. The guy didn't have a beard, though."

Garcia and I exchanged glances, and a beam of hope crossed his face. He blurted out that he would locate a map, while I flipped the logbook back open to the bookmarked page.

"Nicole, do you remember his name?"

"No, I didn't check him in. I'm sorry."

"That's all right. Was he traveling with anyone, or by himself?"

"I didn't see him with anyone."

Nicole's dark hair started to blow across her face as she patiently waited on the outdoor side of the open window. Garcia, now next to me, quickly unfolded the brochure-like map across the windowsill between Nicole and the two of us. The illustration, crudely drawn with some rudimentary program – some ancient version of Microsoft Paint? – featured the campground layout, with a legend of outlandish icons in the lower right-hand corner.

"So, just the one road in and out, right?"

"That's right."

"What's the plan, Copeland?"

Nicole, the natural choice to help us block the road, backed the campground's Gator utility vehicle next to our cruiser, mostly obstructing both lanes. Meanwhile, Garcia, referencing the license plates in the logbook, cross-checked the guests traveling by themselves with our system.

"Any hits?" I asked.

"Nothing for Chad Baker or the ex-girlfriend."

"How many of them have autonomous cars?"

"Two out of four. I immobilized them."

"All right. Backup is ten minutes out."

"Fuck backup, he's our man."

I sternly reminded Garcia that this wasn't our jurisdiction, and it wasn't his call. Meanwhile, a few guests wandering the campground had begun to take notice of our impromptu operation. Garcia, gun unholstered, started pacing back and forth between the Gator and our car. Before I sent Nicole out of harm's way, I asked her to circle, with a red pen, the two campsites on the map where the two individuals traveling alone and without autonomous cars were staying. Just as Garcia readied himself to inspect the two campsites, a car filled with a young family pulled up to our makeshift roadblock, looking to enter the campground. Overhearing their exchange, Garcia informed the driver that the road was temporarily closed and to return later that evening. The driver pleaded with Garcia that his family had a reservation. Just then, an older Ford pickup truck pulled in behind the irritated family. Unable to get a good look at the second driver, I moved in closer, spotting a male, who appeared to have no other passengers with him. *Could it be?* Before I could get closer, the driver threw the truck into reverse, forcing us to duck for cover to avoid the gravel he kicked up. Once the dust cleared, I sprinted to the cruiser, where Garcia had already climbed into the passenger seat. The engine roared as I pressed the push start on the car and spun it around as fast as I could. In my rearview, I saw Nicole assisting the poor guy whose car was pelted with gravel, and JB standing dumbfounded nearby.

"Dispatch, we're in pursuit of a black Ford Ranger, license plate VRK-7302, that's Victor Romeo Kilo-7302, heading north on Honey Bear Campground Road, soon to be, uh – "

Garcia clicked the pad on the laptop to try to figure out where the hell we were going.

"Poplar Grove Road South. Heading east. Over."

"Copy. Self-driving? Over?"

"Negative. Looks like we're doing it the old-fashioned way. Over."

"Copy. Attention all units, be on the lookout for a black Ford Ranger, License plate Victor Romeo Kilo-7302 heading east on Poplar Grove Road South toward Highway 105."

The radio clicked off, leaving nothing but the sweet sound of pursuit – an engine in high gear and sirens blaring. Garcia, holding onto the grab handle above his head, looked like he might throw up from the winding roads. I didn't feel great about doing 80 mph in low visibility on unfamiliar mountain roads, but there was zero chance that I was about to lose our guy.

Finding ourselves on a rare straightaway, the suspect wove precariously in and out of both lanes, passing a handful of cars over the double yellow.

"You read the plates out, I'll do the rest."

"Echo Tango Oscar-4478."

Garcia, using the hunt-and-peck method, struck the license plate number into the keyboard of the computer in front of him. After a slight delay, the car in front of us drifted off to the shoulder. I had to admit, even though it had become a normal part of police work, controlling someone else's car still seemed like an infringement on a person's rights. At the same time, it was an extraordinary feeling to control traffic, almost God-like. There was a rumor that the TCU, or Taking Control Unit, would soon be proximity-based, meaning any self-driving car within one hundred yards would automatically be veered off to the shoulder when the squad-car lights started flashing. But until then, at least Garcia had something to do.

"Mike Alpha Hotel-0727."

Another one bites the dust. Now there was just one more car between Chad Baker's Ford Ranger and us. As the pursuit persisted, news flashed over the scanner that Boone PD was setting up a remote-controlled spike strip at the fork ahead. Garcia updated dispatch on our position. They estimated we were roughly two miles away from the obstruction. The car wedged between ours and Baker's resigned from the race on the next straightaway, a human-driven car with what seemed like a glacially slow reaction to our blaring sirens. Now it was just the Ford Ranger and us. We kept a healthy distance so as not to scare our suspect into taking an unwanted turn. However, even that tactic proved difficult with his reckless speeding.

"You should be coming up on the fork in thirty seconds," dispatch buzzed. "There's a sharp left turn and then a tenth of a mile downhill 'til the fork. Over."

"Thirty seconds? He's doing damn near eighty. Get those officers out of there! Over."

As Garcia yelled into the mic, the sharp curve came into sight. Baker hadn't slowed down one bit.

"He is going to kill someone!"

Radio silence lingered for what felt like forever but was probably only a few seconds after Garcia let go of the mic button.

"Attention Units 151 and 173, be advised, suspect in the Ford Ranger is doing 80 mph toward the roadblock. Abort the spike strip. Over."

Flying through the curve, the pickup began to swerve erratically, its left-side tires catching air for a brief moment. Somehow, the driver miraculously regained control as he approached the fork, darting past the two police cruisers, one on each side of the street, to the right of the fork. As I followed, Garcia yelled out to me that the road led directly to campus. Meanwhile, in the rearview, the officers who'd pretty much gotten caught standing with their dicks in their hands frantically rushed to join the chase.

"What the fuck is going on? My men were in position. We could've had him," the radio squawked.

"Chief, he was doing eighty, it was too dangerous," Garcia replied.

"Too dangerous?! He's headed directly for campus!"

"But sir, we need him alive."

"This has gone far enough. I'm not going to let you endanger the lives on our campus. Stand down detectives, do you hear me?"

Maintaining our distance behind the truck, Garcia and I quickly debated what to do. Garcia argued that this was our man, and we were the ones who found him – worse case, we'll get a slap on the wrist.

"Do you copy, detectives?"

"We copy," I radioed, grabbing the mic.

Against Garcia's objections, I fell back, letting the patrol cars take the lead. As much as I wanted to be the one to catch Baker, the chief had a point; it was now a matter of public safety – not to mention, our knowledge of these roads paled in comparison to local PD.

Now entering Appalachian State University property, our suspect pushed on in his attempt to evade authorities. The radio buzzed on again, this time from an officer who asked for permission to engage. A dispatcher quickly granted the request. Then, in the blink of an eye, an empty black self-driving luxury Uber seemingly appeared out of thin air to join the pursuit.

"What in God's name do they think they're doing? He's going way too fast for this shit."

There was nothing more Garcia and I could do but sit back and watch our operation go up in flames. The suspect had slowed to a modest 60 mph in a 35 mph zone as he navigated through campus, which meant the Uber was driving at least seventy to catch him. Now just a few car lengths behind Baker, the Uber moved into position for the pit maneuver.

"Ah shit, he's turning!" Garcia yelled.

The suspect made a hard right turn, truck tires screeching in the process, in a desperate attempt to ditch the Uber. Unfortunately for Baker, the pit maneuver was already underway. The Uber slammed into the body of the vehicle instead of the rear bumper for which it was aiming. The move launched the Ford Ranger into the air, and caused it to roll across the immaculate lawn crested with the Appalachian State Mountaineer logo. After three or four rolls, the beat-to-shit Ford Ranger came to an abrupt stop when it slammed into a fully grown pine tree.

Seeing no reason to try preserving the damaged lawn, I drove straight to the wreckage. Before I could even put it into park, Garcia, gun drawn, jumped out of the car to inspect the accident. By the reaction on his face, I knew immediately that Chad Baker, our only suspect, was dead.

Larry Bridges

For the last ten years, I knew I could run Washington Ford better than Al, and now I had the chance to prove it. While Al's marketing prowess was unmatched, he had zero sense of innovation. Everyone and their uncle could see the world transitioning to autonomous cars. Everyone except Al. He insisted on calling it a fad that would pass, as if it was something as insignificant as wood paneling on a station wagon. Hell, the 2010s were some of the best years in Washington Ford history. "Why fix it if it ain't broken?" Al loved to recite, anytime I broached the subject. As a result of this stubbornness, Washington Ford had gone from being one of the largest car dealerships in the country, operating in thirty-seven states, to a low-level regional player in a matter of five short years. Now, Washington Ford operated in just two states: North Carolina and Alaska. Never once did Al take responsibility for its decline; instead, he chalked up his failures to market cycles. Yet through all the downsizing, Al's personal wealth never took a hit. That was because Al immediately sent me out to shut down a dealership if it didn't turn a profit for two consecutive months. He did make one exception – his flagship dealership in Charlotte. Even Al didn't have the gall to close his baby. But today began a new chapter, and as the new owner and general manager of Washington Ford, I would usher in a new era, one in which we embraced self-driving cars.

I had it all planned out – well, the sales pitch anyway. *Why rely on Uber and Lyft when you can just own an autonomous car outright? Instead of paying exorbitant prices to live near a city, you can sleep on your way to work in the morning with your own self-driving vehicle.* We would finesse the message, but with a big marketing spend, Washington Ford could be on a path to profitability again. I planned to honor Al's legacy, of course, but it was time to either adapt or die. Hell, if I did nothing and let Washington Ford go under, what kind of legacy would Al have left? *This way, he'll be remembered forever.*

I told Em to meet me at the dealership at 2 p.m. I called in a food truck that made customizable cookie ice cream sandwiches. I figured I could treat the employees and properly thank Em for a job well done. *Two birds, one stone.* Preferring the air conditioning over the blistering sun, I stood just inside the main entrance waiting for her. I rechecked my watch. Butterflies tingled inside my stomach – it almost felt like one of those "bring your daughter to work days" when she was little, but this time I would be the boss, not an employee. Right as I reached for my phone to see if Em was running behind, an Uber pulled into the dealership. I even bore the summer heat to receive her embrace.

The few employees who waited in line for the ice cream truck quickly moved aside when Em and I approached.

"Order whatever you'd like, dear. My treat."

The ice cream started dripping between the freshly baked cookies before we even got a chance to bite into them. We walked our tasty treats to a shady spot under an awning attached to the service building.

"I just want to say I'm really proud of you, Em."

"C'mon Dad, you're not going to get all sappy on me, are you?"

"Can't a dad be proud of his little girl?"

A hint of a smile emerged. Long gone were the days that I was Em's one and only hero, but at least she still laughed at my terrible dad jokes once in a while. I wondered if she would want to take over once I turned old. I wouldn't make the same mistakes Al did with his kids, that much remained certain. Which was precisely why it was time for me to give up on Em being a lawyer and support her in whatever she desired to do with her life.

"Say Em, I know about the bar exam."

Her shoulders tensed, and the playfulness faded.

"What do you mean?"

"If you really didn't want to be a lawyer, you could've just said something instead of bombing the test on purpose."

"But Dad, I did tell you."

"Suppose I just didn't want to listen. But that's over now. Let me assure you, I love you and will support you in anything you choose to do with your life."

"Thanks, Dad. It's just not for me."

Em finished the final bite of her ice cream sandwich, being extra careful to avoid any drips on her clothing, before leaning over to give me an unexpected hug. *I love this girl.*

"Say, I want to give you a gift for helping me out by finding Al's killer."

"You don't have to do that, Dad."

"True, but I want to do for you what Al did for me. When I was your age, Al gave me a car, and now I want to give you one."

"Ah, thanks, Dad, but –"

"Don't worry, it's a self-driving car. That way, I don't have to see you taking Ubers everywhere. Don't you know they're putting us out of business?"

Em and I shared a laugh, a tender moment to file away in my memory, just in case she ever found out the ugly truth about me one day. I forced myself to continue smiling, even as that thought made my heart sink and my stomach churn.

Alice Washington

When I first hatched my plan, I tried to convince Emily to come along, but she thought it was a waste of time, since the case was closed. I pressed further, but she gave an excuse that she had already made plans and then asked if a bar was the best place for "someone like me" to go.

Without any windows or proper ventilation, the smell of piss and cheap beer wafted throughout the basement. The temptation for a drink persisted nonetheless. I had only been to Jeff's Bucket Shop once before, but that was a lifetime ago. It was one of those places you only went to when one of your friends was way too into karaoke, and the rest of the group couldn't think of anywhere else to go – that, or an alcoholic looking for cheap drinks. The place was much livelier on that night, many years ago, than it was when I met Eva.

When I arrived, I found Eva sitting by herself at the bar with an empty shot glass and a nearly empty mixed drink on the counter in front of her. To get her attention, I tapped her on the shoulder, but it was only after a second tap – a much more forceful one – did Eva acknowledge me. To my surprise, her face lit up with delight, and she quickly offered the open stool next to her. As I settled in, she called out to the preoccupied bartender for her next drink, a vodka cranberry. It took several requests to annoy him sufficiently that he finally refilled her empty glass.

Okay, Alice, remember – you're here to get answers from Eva, not to drink. You have to ask her if Big Al ever talked about Chad. Why did he want to kill Big Al? Why did she think the will was bullshit? Why did she try to buy a gun after Big Al died? And why was she going to leave for Iceland after the memorial service, but ultimately didn't?

Just looking at Eva's freshly made vodka cranberry gave me bad ideas. Fighting the temptation, it took me a moment too long to decline the bartender's offer to take my drink order. Meanwhile, Eva downed her drink and then slammed the glass onto the countertop, much harder than she intended. Her exuberance quickly transitioned into irritation. She ran her hand through her hair; what I recalled as perfectly coiffed and dyed was now greasy and showing its roots.

Cue the next karaoke participant. A man drunkenly yelled the lyrics of *We Didn't Start the Fire* into the microphone at the far side of the bar. With her liquid depressant settling in, it was Eva who broke the ice first.

"So, why'd you really come here tonight? Call me a bitch to my face? Or a gold-digger who deserved what she got?"

"No, not at all. As someone else who never got a fair shake in this family, I wanted to hear your side."

Before I got the chance to ask about Big Al's relationship with Chad, Eva frantically explained that Larry had blindsided her at the reading of the will. When I requested that she elaborate, she explained that she knew for a fact Big Al had updated his will just last year. Eva spewed a sad handful of half-baked theories as to why the will was illegitimate, each one more incoherent than the last.

"Up next, we have Eva!" The DJ's voice boomed into the microphone.

"Oh, that's me!"

Suddenly, Eva leapt out of the barstool to take her place on the stage. Only when she grabbed the mic from the DJ did she realize she'd forgotten her drink, so she quickly doubled back to the bar just as the music began. The song started with a quick tempo; it sounded old but familiar – I couldn't quite place it. When she reached the bar, Eva didn't bother to take the drink with her; instead, she slammed the rest of it before wandering back to the stage.

"And oh, my dreams
It's never quite as it seems
Never quite as it seems."

The Bjork wannabe could shockingly hold a tune, even if some of the lyrics were unintelligible. She exuded confidence on the stage, a makeshift platform with blue Christmas lights stapled against the wall and a peculiar 'CHEERS' sign in block lettering. The few patrons in the crowd even stopped their conversations to appreciate Eva's singing. It was one of those rare performances that teetered between greatness and a train-wreck at any given moment.

"I want more
Impossible to ignore
Impossible to ignore."

As the song continued, though, Eva became less and less intelligible. Eventually, it got to the point where the only lyrics she was able to articulate were the lines of the chorus, albeit slightly ill-timed. The DJ eventually shut her down for, during a musical interlude, swinging the microphone cord in a circle as if she was Mick Jagger.

"This is what happens when you don't listen. How many times have I warned you? Huh?"

The abrupt ending confused both Eva and the audience to the point where people didn't know whether to clap or not. After the DJ's lecture, she stumbled back to the bar, flirting with a male patron along the way.

Sadly, it was only when Eva returned to her stool and ordered another drink that I realized I had made a mistake by meeting her at a bar. I figured my best hope at not getting blackout drunk was to cling to a false obligation that I needed to get her home safely.

"I never heard you sing before. Didn't you have a hit record or something?"

"I had a song in Iceland's Top 40 for a couple of weeks."

"So, what happened?"

"Same thing that happened to the best years of my life, I gave it up for Al."

As she downed another vodka cranberry, I saw my best chance to get her out of there. It took some persistence, but I convinced Eva into leaving with me for another drink at a different bar. Once in her car, Eva's energy crashed, and she dozed in and out of consciousness for the first few miles. It was only when we left the city that she realized I was driving her home instead of to the bar that I'd promised, causing another sudden mood shift.

"The bait and switch, eh? All you car salesmen are the same. You'll say anything to get what you want."

"Good thing I'm a car saleswoman then."

I cracked the front windows to catch some of the night breeze in hopes that it might prevent her from yacking on the elegant interior leather.

By the time we got to the famous W. Ranch gate, Eva had reclined her seat and was subdued in a full-on drunken stupor. After a few vigorous shakes, Eva showed signs of life and slurred the gate code to me. Just the sight of the plated iron gate brought back a flood of unwanted memories. I punched the passcode "0724#" into the keypad, turned out it was the same code from when I was a kid. I wondered what Eva thought every time she had to enter that code, knowing it was the wedding anniversary date of Big Al and my mom. *Maybe she didn't even know.* The keypad accepted the brazen sequence, and the gate slowly parted in the middle of the crested 'W.'

Facing vast darkness, I switched to the high beams and wandered farther into the place I once called home. The first stop on memory lane came as we passed the guest house. From what I heard, Courtney now lived there. It looked nothing like I remembered – *when did Courtney add a pool and horse stables*? Deep down, I genuinely hoped for some sort of reconciliation between Courtney and me, but didn't hold much optimism that it would ever happen. After all, any grown woman who still referred to her father as "Daddy" could prove difficult to reason with.

The next stop on the tour was what I had been avoiding since I came back: my childhood home, the place we were once a happy family, now burnt beyond recognition. It was as if the forgotten foundation and ashes that remained were a symbol of my life within the family. I turned the car off to soak in all the memories – both good and bad, a reminiscing of sorts. Eva, now totally passed out, didn't seem to mind or notice the delay. The sound of crickets chirping triggered some nostalgia. *Where did it go wrong?* The answer was obvious, but we were a happy family once. Why couldn't we stand united after she died? In hindsight, I think we all underestimated my mother's power as the linchpin. Big Al didn't know how to handle a rebellious teen and a confused pre-teen. I couldn't blame Courtney for sticking beside him as she grasped for any semblance of normalcy. Of course, she was going to take his side – she was young and had been entirely dependent on him. *Stop dwelling, it's only going to cause more heartache.* I turned the car back on, rolled up the windows, and gently pressed on the gas pedal.

Finally, I caught sight of the pine trees lining each side of the drive-way to the lake house. The same trees I recall being freshly planted many years ago had now blossomed into an impressive height. The house certainly was big, a product of modern aesthetics without any character or history to it. At first glance, it appeared to have more windows than bricks. Eva didn't respond to any of my gentler tactics to wake her. It was only when I dragged her out of the car and accidentally dropped her on the cement driveway did she awaken, with a chihuahua-like yelp that broke the harmonizing of the chirping crickets. I quickly pulled her up to her wobbly feet, holding her as best I could as we stumbled to the front door.

Inside the dimly lit house, I placed Eva at one of the seats around the kitchen table. Using a cloth napkin, I applied pressure to her wounded chin. But when the fabric quickly changed in color from white to dark red, I figured I'd better look for something more practical.

"Just maintain the pressure. I'll go look for some bandages."

Eva couldn't provide much direction in helping me find a first aid kit, but considering her state, I shouldn't have expected much. The pantry proved fruitless, so I moved on to the nearest bathroom. As I pillaged through her cabinets, I remembered that I still needed to ask Eva why she bought the tickets to leave the country, and then days later attempted to buy a gun. In any event, the fall should have sobered her up enough to get her talking.

Opening and closing an additional dozen drawers, I finally found the elusive alcohol wipes and bandages. I scooped up whatever I could carry, holding the assorted boxes against my chest.

"Hold tight, Eva. I found them!" I yelled from down the hall.

Running through the house, my steps were swift but also cautious enough to ensure I wouldn't need any of the contents in my arms for myself. *Did she hear me? It could just be the house is too damn big.* I hollered again to reassure her that I was on my way. Still nothing. It had only been a couple of minutes – *what'd she do, pass out?* Finally, back to the living area, I looked up to find two people sitting at the kitchen table. The unexpected sight of another person startled me so much, I accidentally launched half of my first-aid cargo into the air.

"Sorry Alice. I didn't mean to scare you."

Sitting at the table, applying pressure to Eva's wound, was none other than Larry. Transferring his gaze from mine to Eva's chin, Larry pulled out the chair next to him, motioning for me to sit. As I retrieved up the bandages and alcohol wipes from the floor, I glanced toward Eva, sitting stiff as a board, her hands shaking beneath the table.

"Come sit, Alice. Help me get Eva fixed up so we can discuss some business."

With that, I realized as if gut-punched that I had discovered the answers as to why Eva tried to leave the country – and when that failed, to buy a gun: Larry.

Courtney Washington

There was so much damn noise. Maybe I should have gone to the Ritz for a few days until all the construction was over. *No wait, you can't do that, you have the horses getting dropped off any day now.* Outside on my patio, I couldn't even enjoy my morning coffee, for the deafening sounds of the jackhammer and trucks beeping. I felt my phone buzzing in my back pocket – someone was at the gate. *Oh great, maybe the horses are finally here. I can hang out at the new stables with them instead of dealing with the construction workers today.* When I finally opened the app to buzz the driver through the gate, I saw it was just another Amazon delivery truck.

My phone vibrated again. I looked down to see a text from an unknown number. Swiping it open, I came to find a note from my former stepmom:

"Hi, Court. It's Kelly. I know it's been a while, but I was wondering if you're free for lunch today. There are some things I'd like to discuss with you. Also, I'd love to catch up and hear what you've been up to after all these years. Let me know. Sending my love, Kelly."

Kelly?! God, how long has it been? Interesting timing on her part to reach out after all these years, just after Daddy's death. You'd think if she wanted to "catch up," she would've sent more than an impassioned greeting. I stepped inside to refill my coffee, mulling over a response – or whether to even bother. Inside, the drills and the shop vacs overwhelmed my train of thought. *Don't let your anxiety talk you out of it, Courtney. A lunch with Kelly can't be any more unbearable than this place right now.*

Kelly, sporting oversized designer sunglasses, a sun hat, and a floral printed dress, drank most of her mimosa before I arrived. The rooftop restaurant featured plenty of shade and mist fans for the plethora of bankers on their lunch breaks. When I finally reached Kelly's table in the corner overlooking uptown, she let out a yelp loud enough to annoy every suit within earshot. After a big hug that lasted a few seconds too long, I happily found my chair on the opposite side of the table.

"So Court, how have you been? Tell me everything."

"Honestly, it's been a tough stretch, you know, just with everything going on – "

"Of course, your dad, and now Luke. I'm so, so sorry. I can't imagine what you're going through."

"Yeah, it's been, uh, it's been really tough – "

"Excuse me, waiter?" Kelly interrupted.

I turned my head to see our clean-cut waiter approaching. Before he'd even had a moment to ask if he could get us anything, Kelly managed to order another mimosa for herself and insisted I get one as well. I relented to her persistence – it was clear she hadn't been listening to me from the start – *why waste my energy?*

As our lunch date wore on, the "conversation" became even more one-sided. I might as well have been a bobblehead sitting across from Kelly, forced to nod in agreement to her pointless ramblings. In the moments that I could concentrate long enough to listen, I learned that Kelly had been devoting her time and energy to any and every nonprofit organization imaginable. But reading between the lines, it was also apparent that she enjoyed bumping elbows with big shots at the galas and fundraisers more than taking up a noble cause. As I found myself less and less engaged, my thoughts drifted to memories of my childhood while I nibbled on the eggs benedict in front of me.

Kelly hadn't been the worst stepmom. Putting myself in her shoes, I wouldn't have known how to parent two girls who'd just lost their mother, either. To her credit, or perhaps detriment, she never tried to take my mom's place as she mostly stayed out of our way. But a girl like me needed boundaries at that formidable age. *Maybe I could've been somebody. Instead, you got yourself knocked up in high school. That was it. Game over.*

"Court? You there?"

"Hmm?"

I snapped to. The waiter stood above me with a concerned look. Kelly, quick to recognize that I had been zoning out for the last few minutes, shot me a look of disgust before requesting the bill. The waiter scurried away.

"What was I thinking?" Kelly muttered under her breath.

"Excuse me?"

"You were never one to listen, Courtney. Just like everyone else in your fucking family."

"Seriously?"

The sudden tension hung over the table as Kelly downed the last drops of her mimosa.

"Look, I hate to do this to you since I'm a believer that no daughter should pay for her father's sins, but it's his money you've got now."

Kelly's grip on her empty glass tightened to the point where I noticed the veins bulging on her ghostly, old-lady hand.

"Ah, we've finally gotten to the real reason you wanted to see me, huh?"

"You have no idea what your father did to me."

"Actually, I do. Daddy gave you wealth, and the only thing you ever did for our family was to burn our house down – and every memory of my mother down with it."

Kelly sat back in her chair, speechless for the first time since our luncheon began. As she pouted, the waiter dropped off the bill, placing it directly in the center of the table. Neither of us budged.

"You still think I burned that house down?"

I lifted my eyes up from the bill to study Kelly's face. I struggled to decipher whether she was bluffing or not, with those ridiculous sunglasses blocking her tell. But if I had to bet, I'd say she was about to spew some more bullshit.

"But you did burn it down. Sauteing mushrooms. It was all over the news. You were the joke of the city, don't you remember? Or has your memory become as bad as your cooking?"

Kelly scoffed at my outburst, finally removing her sunglasses to look me directly in the eye.

"You naïve little girl. Let me ask you something: when you were growing up, how many times did I do the cooking?"

While maintaining my poker face, I quickly tried to think back to that time in my life without giving her the satisfaction that I was doing so. A slight smile returned to Kelly's face. *In my defense, I've never actually played poker.*

"That's right. I never cooked – hell, I still don't. So that begs the question – "

Kelly paused, held her palm out toward me, presumably to ask what really happened, but I refused to play along. Frustrated, she pulled her hand back and rolled her eyes. While her cooking or lack thereof didn't jog any memories, that eye roll certainly did.

"Your father wasn't exactly like his character on TV – but you already knew that, right? Sure, he was charming when he wanted to be, but for the most part, he was a real son of a bitch with a bad temper. And anyone caught in the vortex of that temper would be in some serious danger, you know? Like, let's say, an older boy who knocked up his daughter and then left her in the dust. Let me ask you a question, did you ever hear from Jake after he left you?"

"Enough. You're out of line."

"You should know the truth, Courtney. You're old enough now; you can handle it. See, your dad beat that boy so badly his face swelled up to the point where he couldn't breathe. He died right there, in the basement of that house. Problem was, his mother reported him missing, so they traced his phone to your house. Larry couldn't exactly sweep the DNA under the rug, so they burned it down. And blamed it on me, with that cheap excuse."

"You're lying."

"Nope. Al even got the insurance money from it."

That's it. I'd had enough. I rose to leave only to be swiftly forced back into my chair when Kelly latched onto my arm for dear life.

"Get your hands...off...me." I gasped at Kelly.

"I'm afraid we're not done here. Like I was saying, I don't think any daughter should have to pay for her father's sins, but since you got his money, it's now your debt to pay."

"What debt?"

"The debt to me for keeping my mouth shut – five million dollars."

"Excuse me?"

"Tell you what; I'll give you and Larry until Washington Ford's 'Giant Anniversary Sale' that I keep seeing ads for to pay me before I go to the media, the police, your son – anyone who might want to know the truth about Big Al Washington."

And with that, Kelly slid the bill from the center of the table toward me and put on her sunglasses to leave, all in one vindictive motion.

Luke Washington

O n Tuesday, the hospital served chicken noodle soup for lunch. Nevermind, I guess, that we were in one of the hottest summers in recorded history. In fact, four out of the seven days of that week, they served soup for lunch. Monday was split pea; Tuesday was chicken noodle; Wednesday was tomato bisque; Thursday was minestrone. When I was bored, which was nearly every minute of my stay, I tried to imagine the reasons why a hospital would insist on torturing its patients, and I believed I had come up with a sound theory.

First and foremost, the hospital wanted to save money. At some point, The cheap bastards realized there was nothing more economically efficient than making an oil drum worth of soup for hundreds of people. By strategically serving soup during lunch Monday through Thursday, the days and times with the least amount of visitors, the hospital conveniently avoided potential complaints from overly concerned family members. My second-best theory was that the hospital hadn't noticed or cared enough to reset its robot chef since winter. But until I got confirmation that the hospital had a robot chef, I was sticking with my first theory, that they were just cheap asses.

My other hobby to pass the time between my daily physical therapy and Netflix binge-watching was plotting against Mark. After Mark's visit, I needed to regain the upper hand. The fact that Mark, one of my best friends, was now extorting me for family money that was rightfully mine only proved that I had underestimated him when I initially set him up for Grandpa's murder. But not anymore. I just had to figure out how I was going to get out of his greedy grasp for good. A knock at the door distracted my train of thought.

Lauren opened the door, dinner in hand. Her visits had become less frequent. During my brief coma, she was allegedly here nearly every hour of every day. When I woke up, she would visit every day for hours, but no longer slept by my side. Now that I was a couple of weeks into my stay and alert, she brought me dinner – always takeout, I noticed, nothing ever homemade. Then she would stay maybe an hour or two, but that was it. I sensed that spending time with me felt like more of an obligation than something she wanted to do. And lately, when Lauren did visit me, she seemed more interested in my inheritance than my well-being.

"I still can't believe Eva. I mean, she completely lost her shit at the reading of the, uh, will."

"You don't say?"

"Yeah, I mean, she let Larry have it. Ripped him a new one. But, that gold-digger got what was comin'. Say, has Larry said anything to you, timeline-wise?"

"No."

"Well, maybe you should ask him. I mean eighty million ain't nothing to sneeze at. Can you talk to Larry about it the next time you see him?"

"Sure."

"Good. I mean, we can do a lot with eighty million, babe. A lot of good, too. Maybe we could start a charity or something in a few years once we get settled into our new lifestyle."

"Uh-huh."

I should have never let Lauren go to that reading of Grandpa's will. *How am I going to tell her that Mark blackmailed me for sixty of that eighty million?*

"What's wrong?"

"Nothing's wrong."

"Luke, don't you lie to me. What's going on?"

I turned the TV on in an attempt to get her off my back. My plan appeared to work, as Lauren scoffed at my emotional ineptitude when her frustration overtook her curiosity. It was only when the commercials began that my plan blew up in my face.

"Hey, Charlotte! Big Al Washington's longtime friend and business partner Larry Bridges here. As you probably know, Big Al has tragically passed away, but we're going to honor his memory by pressing on – just as he'd want us to – with Washington Ford's 47th Anniversary Blowout Sale.

This Saturday, every car and truck is 47 percent off! Yes, you heard that right, 47 percent off! And for the first time in Washington Ford history, we'll be selling fully autonomous cars. So come on down to Washington Ford this Saturday. Saturday! Saturday! Saturday!"

After the ominous, obnoxious voice echoed the word 'Saturday,' an unfamiliar jingle played as Larry stood near a row of self-driving vehicles, pointing enthusiastically at an oversized '47 Percent Off' sticker on each windshield.

"Unbelievable."

"What?" Lauren exasperated.

"Larry! That's what! That should be me in that commercial, not Larry. This is a family business, and Larry ain't family. People act like I was the one who died. I've been passed over and forgotten. First, Mark walked all over me to the tune of sixty million fucking dollars, and now Larry's taking away my birthright. Fuck that! It's time Luke Washington took back what's his."

"What do you mean, Mark took you for sixty million?"

"Huh?"

I averted my attention from the wall-mounted TV to find Lauren's very angry, very confused face staring back at me.

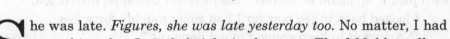

She was late. *Figures, she was late yesterday too.* No matter, I had everything that I needed right in the room. The foldable walker, the one with the tennis balls on the legs, so it didn't scratch up the floor, rested just a few feet away from the bed. *Take it slow, Luke. Easy does it.* Despite my caution, the first step nearly did me in, but by grabbing onto my bed, I was able to catch myself from falling at the last second. The next step proved to be just as tricky when something prohibited me from moving any farther. The culprit, as it turned out, happened to be my hospital gown. With the tails caught in the bed rails, the fabric pulled tightly against my bare skin, constricting any further movement. After a few unsuccessful yanks of the gown, I considered reversing course back to the bed. But I reminded myself that Washington Ford's 47th anniversary was just two days away – the day when I planned to put the wheels in motion to take it all back. *But before I can do that, first things first. Get to your walker, you pathetic fat man.* With all my might, I yanked on the tails of the flimsy gown. I broke free from the bed, but the force caused me to lose my balance and tumble to the ground. Now on the cold laminate flooring, I sucked air through my nostrils in an attempt to subdue the pain.

"That's it. One step at a time. You're doing great."

I forced a polite smile as I grimaced through the pain. As it turned out, small talk didn't come naturally after a person finds you lying on the floor, bare ass exposed, unable to move. To the physical therapist's credit, she didn't bring up the incident once on our walk. I hoped that the silence would allow time for me to plot against Mark; instead, I couldn't help but replay my last conversation with Lauren. Specifically, her last words to me after I told her about being blackmailed.

"I refuse to associate with losers, and I certainly don't marry them. So you need to figure this shit out, or I will divorce you and truly take every penny to your name."

I had never seen that side of Lauren before. Admittedly, if her goal was to motivate me, then it worked. *That's all it was, a motivation tactic, right? People who are in love like us don't get divorced over something like this.*

"Okay, that's enough for the day. Let's get you back to the room, and we'll pick it up again tomorrow," the physical therapist instructed.

I looked back to see how far I had gone: roughly forty feet.

"No, I want to keep going. I'm not done yet."

CRIME AND VINDICATION

IX

CRIME AND
VINDICATION

Emily Bridges

It didn't have to be perfect, but it had to be me. The problem was, every office I visited or viewed on Redfin was either in need of a severe makeover or out of my price range. Well, out of my price range until I received the payout from my work on Big Al's case, but who knew how long that might take?

Arriving at the available office, I studied its exterior features: plenty of parking, a modern looking building, and easy access to the highway. *So far, so good.* I punched the access code from Redfin into the keypad, which granted me entry. The inside proved to be even more impressive. New wood floors – and not that cheap vinyl stuff – a granite reception desk; and a freshly remodeled bathroom. I double-checked the price on my phone again. *What? That can't be right. How is this place so cheap?* It was so reasonable that I scrolled frantically through the listing for the number to call. As the phone rang, I visualized how I was going to transform the office space. After workshopping a dozen or so names, "Bridges Investigations" was the one I settled on as the winner. For the logo, I figured it was best to keep it simple – a black and white illustration of a bridge under a magnifying glass.

"Hello, my name is Emily Bridges. I'm inquiring about the office space on Independence Blvd. near I-485. Is it still available?"

"Yes, ma'am."

"Great. How soon would I be able to move in?"

"Oh, wow! You're ready, huh? Terrific. You can move in today, if you want. You'll just need to sign the lease first, of course. It's such an enchanting space – recently remodeled, too."

As the leasing agent rambled on about the logistics, I took another look around my future headquarters. The lighting didn't do it justice, so I opened the blinds to discover precisely why the space was so cheap. Blinking back at me was an oversized neon sign that flashed the word 'TOPLESS' in pink, cursive lettering. My view from Bridges Investigations headquarters would be... a strip club.

"Can I get your email, so can I send over the documents?"

Wait, I know that sign. It's the same one across the street from Alice's hotel. Speaking of Alice, I haven't heard from her in awhile. I think I remember her texting me a few days ago.

"Sorry, something came up. I'll call you back."

"Oh, okay. Can I give you my direct – "

I hung up and searched for my last text message from Alice.

"Hey Emily, things aren't adding up. I want to talk to Eva. Are you free tonight?"

I hadn't responded.

"Eva said she'd meet me tonight. She suggested Jeff's Bucket Shop, that weird karaoke bar. I guess she wants to sing? Can you make it?"

After no response for fifteen entire minutes, she texted me again: "???"

Finally, I had texted Alice back to explain my reasoning. The case was solved, after all – everyone knew Chad did it.

"It doesn't feel right to me. Chad was a thief, but he didn't have a violent past. And what about the break-in at the ranch? Why would Chad do that?"

"Look, just because we can't rationalize the truth doesn't make it any less true," I texted back.

Thinking back to that exchange, I recalled feeling that I might have been too harsh, but Alice needed to hear it if she ever wanted to move on with her life. I also remembered seeing text bubbles appear and then disappear a couple of times after I sent it. Finally, after what felt like a minute of her debating exactly what to say next, she'd made a final appeal:

"Would you be able to come anyway? I could really use your support."

"I already have plans. I'm sorry." I replied.

Scrolling through the conversation again, I knew I'd been unnecessarily cold. Alice had a lot on her plate. *You need to go see her, Emily. She's just down the road.*

T he hotel, relatively quiet for check-in hour, like all modern hotels, lacked any humans on the reception staff, which made it incredibly easy to gain access to just about any spot on the property. I passed one couple checking in, excited to eat their complimentary cookies that the computer just spat out, and sauntered toward the elevators. Remembering that Alice was staying in Room 212, I got off at the second floor, and followed the signs. When I reached the door, I forcefully pounded with the butt of my fist. After a minute of futile attempts, I sighed, knowing I was going to have to employ the same technique to gain access that I did the last time I paid her a visit.

See, in all of these modern hotels, the lack of staff created an interesting predicament: what happened when you locked yourself out of your room? The hotel industry's brain trust decided to have guests provide their fingerprint when they checked in so they could confirm their identity when a key was lost. Privacy aside, there was one major practical problem with the policy. Because the guest was required to give only one set of fingerprints, a person claiming to be a spouse or child could call the hotel's automated call center, answer a few security questions, and voilà, you now had a key to someone's hotel room. For someone like Alice, whose information was easily accessible in an online search, it was alarmingly easy to gain access to her room.

"To provide you with another key, please answer these three security questions: Number one: what is your mother's maiden name?"

With the phone in my hand, I quickly typed in "Elizabeth Washington obituary" and clicked on the first link, which brought me to the *Charlotte Observer's* archived obituary section. In the first sentence, I located her maiden name.

"Murphy."

"Thank you. Number two..."

The next thing I knew, the kiosk spat out the keycard to Alice's room, along with a fresh-out-of-the-oven cookie. Of course, that was almost two weeks ago, but I'd saved that key for some reason – maybe too lazy to have thrown it out? Or perhaps I knew I might need it again.

I scavenged my purse for the keycard and held it up to the door. Access denied. I double-checked the room number and tried again. Access denied. *Shit. Alice didn't check out, did she?*

I banged on the door again, twice as loud as before.

"Alice! Open up."

Still nothing. *I suppose I can just call her. C'mon, pick up.* Straight to voicemail. Either Alice had turned her phone off, or it was dead.

"Hey, sorry I couldn't make it the other night. I'm at the hotel. Want to grab a coffee?"

Right after I sent the text, the door opened as wide as the latch allowed. Through the narrow gap, I saw an unfamiliar woman, clearly irritated at my harrasment.

"Can I help you?" The well-dressed business type asked.

"I'm so sorry. I think I have the wrong room."

I returned to the elevator, checking my phone for a reply at least twice along the way. *She's okay, right?* I still hadn't received a response by the time I pressed the elevator's down button. The cold steel doors finally opened. *Where are you, Alice?*

⁓

I only had one mantra in my life, a slogan that my dad got more annoyed with every time I said it: "If you put things off, they tend to work themselves out, one way or the other." I was happy to say that once again, my inactivity had paid off, since I'd never taken those car trackers off of my initial prime suspects in Big Al's death: Eva, Courtney, and Luke. Alice's last known whereabouts were two nights ago at a bar with Eva, so it was a no-brainer to start with her. On the night in question, Eva had parked her car outside of Jeff's Bucket Shop for a few hours, and then it went back to the W. Ranch, with no stops in between. Rather than going straight to the ranch, I figured it would be smarter to bump into Eva in the wild, catch her off-guard. According to the GPS log for Eva's Ford Edge, she frequented Amélie's, a French bakery and café, in the late mornings. By the time I arrived, Eva had already been there for ten minutes. Not wanting to miss my window of opportunity, I had my car drop me at the front door, leaving it to park itself.

Once inside, I scanned the bustling room for any sign of Eva. *Where is she?* I was about to give up when I found her sitting in a nook by the door that I'd just walked through. On her plate, nothing but crumbs; her latté was almost empty. *Shit. You need to act now before she's gone.* In a move to avoid suspicion about the circumstances of this coincidence, I quickly improvised, discreetly removing a coffee cup from the compost bin.

"Eva? Is that you?"

Eva, wearing a yellow pullover and matching yoga pants, lifted her eyes from her phone but hesitated to look directly at me or offer a response. *Better use her full name.*

"Eva Washington! It's Emily Bridges, Larry's daughter."

Now confident that I'd called out for her specifically, Eva offered a polite wave, but couldn't entirely hide her confusion. I hoped to elicit a telling reaction from her, but got only her look of bewilderment as I maneuvered my way to her table.

"Mind if I join you?"

I didn't wait for her to respond as I claimed the chair that blocked her most accessible exit. Judging by the yoga outfit but lack of sweat, I couldn't tell if she actually planned to attend a class or if she just preferred the comfort of athleisure.

"I'm not sure if we've ever officially met, but I wanted to introduce myself. I'm Emily Bridges."

Before I offered my hand, I gently placed my secondhand coffee cup on the table, careful enough to hide the name written on it. Eva, visibly nervous, eventually extended her hand to meet mine. She had one of those dead fish handshakes, and it didn't appear that she had any interest in chatting. *Better make this quick, but don't forget the flattery.*

"That's a great outfit. Mind if I ask where you got it?"

"Lululemon."

I waited a moment for her to expand on her answer or return a compliment, but it never happened. *Let's try one more time.*

"Well, it's 'gorge,' and it really brings out the, uh, brightness of your soul."

Too much? I can practically smell the bullshit.

"That's nice of you to say. Did Larry send you?"

A half-question. I'll take what I can get.

"No, of course not. You know, it's funny running into you here because Alice – you know, Alice Washington – tried to get me to go out to karaoke the other night and mentioned you would be there. I was so bummed I couldn't go because I have always wanted to meet you."

"Hmm. What a – what's the word I'm looking for?"

"Coincidence?"

"Yes, that's the one."

Squirming in her chair, Eva took the last sip of her latté, an uncomfortably long gulp that took her several seconds to get down her throat. *She's trying to get out of here as fast as she can. Just go ahead and ask before she leaves.*

"So…are you going to tell me what happened that night?"

"What do you mean?" Eva muttered, collecting her sunglasses and purse.

"Where's Alice? I haven't heard a peep out of her since that night."

"What is this, huh? We both know she went back to Alaska, all right?"

Eva, sunglasses and phone in one hand and keys in the other, got up abruptly to make her exit. Luckily, I foresaw her circumvention – and I, too, stood up, completely blocking her escape route.

"Excuse me, I need to go now."

"What do you mean, 'We both know?'"

Eva dropped her eyes and lowered her voice to a whisper.

"Look, I'm not going to say a word, okay? Can you please tell your dad that he doesn't have to check up on me?"

And with that, Eva, trembling with fear, brushed past me to leave.

Afterward, I sat in my car, replaying the interaction again in my head. *What did Eva mean – 'Tell your dad he doesn't have to check up on me?' And why the overt sarcasm when she talked about Alice going back to Alaska?* With a quick Google search, I found the number for Washington Ford in Anchorage, but I hesitated to call. After a deep breath, I finally tapped the screen and brought the phone to my ear.

"Washington Ford – Anchorage. This is Kimberly. How may I direct your call?"

"Hi. I'm looking for Alice Washington."

"May I ask who's calling?"

"Yes, this is her sister. Courtney, Courtney Washington."

"Oh, you don't know?"

"Know what?"

"Alice resigned a couple of days ago."

"Resigned?"

"Yeah, she didn't provide notice or anything. We just got an email from our new owner telling us that she quit and to have HR hire a replacement."

"The new owner being Larry Bridges?"

"Yes, Mr. Bridges. He didn't tell you?"

Larry Bridges

Why couldn't she let it go? After everything I did for Alice, she just couldn't let it go. Disowned by her father for an archaic reason, I helped her when no one else would – by giving her a generous inheritance, enough for a new start. But that wasn't good enough for Alice. No, she just had to keep prodding for answers to unanswerable questions.

Alice finally joined Eva and me at the kitchen table after my invitation turned into an obligation.

"Sit, sit."

I slowly peeled the cloth napkin – the second I had gone through – off Eva's face to inspect the wound. The bloody mess varied in severity, resembling a city's grid plan with certain streets larger than its offshoots. Alice, startled by my presence, tossed me a hodgepodge of first aid items. Before I sorted through them, I flipped over the second napkin to the side that hadn't been soaked with Eva's blood. Then, I laid out the most useful items in front of Eva on the table so I could, as quickly as possible, treat and dress the wound.

"Oh, Alice. You just had to go poking around where you didn't belong."

"You hired me, remember?"

Using one of the few remaining dry spots on the cloth, I wiped away the blood before cleaning the cut with the alcohol wipe and applying the oversized band-aid. The sting of the alcohol wipe must have jolted Eva awake because she finally sat up on her own, though not enough to join the discussion.

"I gave you a chance to retain a portion of your inheritance. And for that gratitude, what have you done, huh?"

I finally looked to Alice and sighed. Her hands were crossed, resting on the table's surface. The polish on her fingernails was badly chipped.

"I just want to know what happened."

"So do I, Alice, but you know what? The truth doesn't change a thing. We both know that you'll still be an addict, whether or not you figure out who killed your father."

"So it wasn't Chad then, was it?"

"Do you know how much your father despised you? He truly didn't want to leave you a cent, but I always had a soft spot for you – against my better judgment. So I thought, stupidly, I'd do right by you, even if Al never did while he was alive. And this is what I get in return."

"If it wasn't Chad, who killed him?"

The booming sound of a hand hitting the table caused the room to fall silent. I looked down to see my right palm flat against the wood table. As my fingers began to throb, I slid my hand toward my lap to conceal any sign of pain.

"What are you guys doing here? Let's do shots!" Eva slurred.

Ignoring Eva, in hopes that she would fall back into her drunken stupor, I returned my attention to Alice, who appeared to grow ever more stubborn by the minute .

"It doesn't matter who killed him. Don't you get that?"

"Doesn't matter?"

"He's dead, okay? 200 million dollars would have sat in a bank collecting dust if I didn't do something about it."

"So, why did you set up Chad, then?"

"He's a thief. He could have fought the murder charges if he wanted to, but he chose to run. I didn't make him do that."

"Isn't that convenient?"

Alice slumped into her chair, as if defeated. Meanwhile, Eva, eyes glossed over, furrowed her brow in confusion as to why we were talking more than drinking.

"Speaking of choices, it's time for you to choose, Alice."

"Choose between what? Death and getting a murder charge pinned on me?"

"No, no, nothing like that. Remember that 10 percent of Al's will that I generously offered you? That's gone. Emily and Eva will be splitting that now. You get nothing."

"That doesn't sound like a choice to me."

Just then, an idea came to my mind. I chuckled at the thought of it. It was a hell of an idea, if I said so myself. But first, I needed the proper components to execute it properly. Excusing myself from the table, I made my way to the kitchen to locate what I needed.

"You're right, Alice. Let me fix that for you."

I found what I was looking for in a cupboard above the refrigerator, concealing it behind my back until I rejoined the women. Once I sat down, I gently placed a bottle of Gran Patron Silver Tequila on the table along with three shot glasses.

"Shots! Shots! Shots!" Eva screamed out.

I uncorked the expensive bottle of tequila, lined up the glasses in front of me and started pouring.

"Here's your choice, Alice: whether or not you want to be sober when you show up to rehab tomorrow."

"Excuse me?"

With each glass filled to the top, I placed one in front of each of us. Eva, bandage hanging off her chin, threw hers back without so much as a "cheers." Alice, meanwhile, was much more hesitant, studying what appeared to be the amount of tequila in the shot glass as she twirled her dark hair.

"See, tomorrow morning, I'm sending you away to rehab for ninety days. You will never speak to anyone in this family – ever again. Once you're clean, I'll find you housing and a job in a state where no one knows you, so you can start your new, sober life."

"Some choice."

Alice's thorough inspection of the tequila continued as she lifted the glass into the air.

"I didn't poison it if that's what you're thinking."

"You first, then."

Does this bitch seriously think I poisoned Al? The man who was like a father to me. With a straight face and a scowl, I threw back the shot. As I swallowed, I felt a drop of tequila sliding down my lip toward my chin, I wiped it away with the back of my hand. Seemingly satisfied, Alice shrugged her shoulders, smiled, and took her turn. She slammed the shot glass onto the table and then leaned forward to grab the bottle for another.

*T*ime to lead, Larry. Go in there and inspire them. This is no longer the stagnant, old-school business. With your leadership, Washington Ford will not only rise from the ashes, but will become the dominant player in the autonomous vehicle market.

The conference room was packed to its gills. Between managers, veteran salespeople and the new hires, there wasn't an empty seat to be found around the conference table. When I officially took over, one of my first actions had been to get rid of the suit-and-tie mandate and hire a younger, savvier sales team. The fact was, despite my love of formal wear, the workplace had been trending casual for years. Dressed up like bankers, the salespeople had been uncomfortable, and the customers were intimidated. As far as going younger, it not only fostered more competition between the salespeople, but allowed for more autonomous, forward thinkers at Washington Ford.

The room fell silent when I opened the glass door. Without a word, I positioned myself at the front of the room. Every face looked to me for guidance. Soaking it in for a moment, I couldn't help but grin.

"It's a new day at Washington Ford, and I'm so excited that each and every one of you will be a part of it. Washington Ford got caught in the business cycle: we peaked, and then we refused to innovate with the times. Because of that, our business plummeted – and to be frank, we're hanging on for dear life. But, by switching our focus from traditional, antiquated cars to autonomous ones, we are on the precipice of another boom. That's where you all come in. We need you to convince the everyday working man and woman that they absolutely need an autonomous car. Is it actually cheaper to take Uber and Lyft everywhere – or does a monthly car payment make more fiscal sense? And if Uber and Lyft are in fact cheaper, which I doubt, then make it about class. The American Dream has never been about opportunity. It's about showing off to your neighbor; saying, 'I'm more successful than you.' Now, get out there and sell some damn cars!"

The room erupted with applause; some might have called it a standing ovation. I couldn't remember the last time I'd seen that room so alive. As the employees slowly poured out, I thought about all those laborious meetings that had gone on under Al. By the time they were over, everyone had either forgotten or lost interest in actionable items. Now that I was in charge, I pledged to be concise, especially with time and productivity at stake. I stuck around by the exit to note which people showed exuberance on the way out. I suspected the ones that looked away or at the ground wouldn't last very long under my new regime, so I made a mental note of their names or faces. Just as the last few waited their turn to leave, an anomaly caught my eye. It appeared that Em had sat in on our meeting.

"What are you doing here?"

"I thought it was 'bring your daughter to work day,'" Em quipped, flashing that infectious smile of hers.

Wearing jeans and a muted blouse, she came around the table on the opposite side of the stragglers making their exit. I gave her a hug when she finally reached me, but the question still remained in my head as our embrace came to a close.

"Really, what are you doing here?"

"There's just something that's bothering me."

"Okay, well, sit down. I'll get the door."

The last person in the room not named Bridges had left by the time I reached the glass door. As I closed it, I wondered what could be bothering her – another career change or a boy, perhaps? Instead of joining her at the table, I began collecting the coffee mugs and discarded paper the team had left behind.

"So, what's bothering you, dear?"

"Alice."

Just hearing her name made my shoulders tense. Unsure of what to say, the best I mustered was repeating it, but in question form. I purposefully concealed my face, turning my focus to putting the chairs back in their correct spots around the table.

"I can't get hold of her. Have you seen her?"

I instinctively cleared my throat, a tick my father had that always annoyed me. Just like his tell, mine came out whenever I wanted to carefully formulate an answer or just to buy time to think about how to change the subject. Most people would never catch it, but Em knew me inside and out.

"Not recently. Why?"

Technically the truth. Em studied my face as I finished up tidying the room. She wasn't convinced, but I wasn't about to lay my cards down first. To quote the best sales movie of all-time, *Glengarry Glen Ross,* "You never open your mouth till you know what the shot is."

"She's gone, checked out of the hotel. She won't respond to my texts. I'm worried, Dad."

"I'm sure she's fine. But, I'm happy to look into it, if you want me to."

"Maybe I'm being paranoid, and she went back to her life in Alaska. But, if you wouldn't mind, I'd really appreciate it."

"Sure thing, Em."

"Thanks, Dad."

Em rose from her chair, kindly put it back in place, and asked me to keep her posted. I told her I loved her as she left, but instead of returning the phrase, she just offered me a faint smile.

Alice Washington

When it's your third stint in rehab, it's no longer a feeling: you are *a failure. You are a forever fuck-up that's been crossed off by all your friends and family.* At least on the third time, I no longer had any illusions that my future would magically get better when I got out. Best case scenario, I would get a new life like Larry promised. I only hoped it would be somewhere warmer than Alaska but colder than North Carolina. How many states did that leave – like, seven? Maybe Larry would be gracious enough to send me to Hawaii. I had never been, but those dumb Internet surveys always rated it the happiest state, and I had grown accustomed to living outside the lower forty-eight. *But who am I kidding? He's probably going to send me to fucking Utah, where alcohol is sacrilege.*

Even after what he did, I couldn't muster up too much anger toward Larry. I mean, he tried to give me some money when my father didn't want me to leave me a dime. Then I started asking too many questions, questions that didn't bring us any closer to the truth of who might have killed my father. Even now, when Larry could've cast me away for good, he'd footed the bill for rehab and promised me a new start. Were his tactics a bit unorthodox or even extreme? Sure, but it was hard to argue his heart wasn't in the right place.

I couldn't help but think that Larry chose my new inpatient facility for me at least partly for its name: Legacy Freedom Treatment Center. Now that Big Al was dead, his legacy became a matter of the utmost importance, to keep the dealership in good standing with the city. *And a daughter who is an addict ain't good for business.*

At my first rehab stint, the twelve-step program was all the rage. Nowadays, facilities like the Legacy Freedom Treatment Center loved to claim they weren't your "typical twelve-step program." The mission behind the treatment center, as I had quickly learned, was to help addicts find a passion in life. Every session, whether brief or lengthy, began with a "passion update," in which you shared whatever progress you had made in finding your true calling. To help facilitate the process, the counselors would take the "passionless" – people like me, who apparently had yet to find meaning in their life – on field trips to discover what might make us whole. Most of these outings involved going to museums or adult education centers. On one particular occasion, we visited the U.S. National Whitewater Center, to participate in an array of activities: ropes courses, ziplining, whitewater rafting. I highly doubted the counselors expected one of us to discover our passion strapped to a wire as we flew through the air, but instead hoped we might learn something about ourselves. At least the outing provided an excuse to get outside after being cooped up for the past few days.

After signing a waiver and sitting through a fifteen-minute safety class, our team of twelve split into two different rafts. Even wading in the water to get to our raft felt heavenly in the ninety-degree morning heat. Our instructor Maya, jarringly lean and tan, introduced herself to us as she recapped the paramount rules from the safety training class. To be honest, I paid very little attention to her instructions, since her light-up-a-room smile distracted me. *If I was that tan, would my teeth be that white?* Looking down at my pale arms, I quickly realized my question was moot.

"Now, who's ready to have some fun?"

"Hold on one minute, Maya. I'd like to say a few words."

Oh no. Maybe I was too distracted by the oh-so-refreshing water or Maya's aura, but I failed to notice that Instructor Tom had made his way into the same raft as me. I had only known Instructor Tom for less than seventy-two hours, and could already tell we were not going to get along. There were Type A people; then there was Instructor Tom. Immediately upon meeting him, he insisted upon a "debrief," sitting way too close to me and refusing to break eye contact. At one point, when I stared at the floor for too long, the man literally got out of his chair and put his face on the rug in his office to make eye contact with me.

"Okay, y'all, this is going to be an exciting day. As addicts, we often forget we're capable of having fun adventures sober. Today, I want you to focus on the importance of teamwork, okay? See, if we don't work as a cohesive unit, we could lose someone or even flip the raft."

"Thank you for that – what was your name again?" Our guide indignantly asked.

"Instructor Tom!"

"Why, thank you, Instructor Tom. Could you do me a favor and move to the front of the raft? Just to even out our weight distribution."

Knowing precisely what Maya was up to, I happily volunteered to switch seats with Instructor Tom, who had no clue that he was about to take a swim. Meanwhile, I took the position directly in front of Maya, who sat on the very back of our boat. I then anchored my right foot under the tube for some semblance of support. As we approached the first rapids, Maya stressed the importance of listening to her commands and to always hold onto the T-grip of our paddle, since getting hit in the face by one was the most common cause of injury when rafting.

"Right side – two strokes forward; left side – one stroke back. All together now – two strokes forward."

Maya's last command sent us directly into a Class Two rapid, where we plunged a few feet down before slamming the front of our raft into a boulder. The swift collision shot Instructor Tom overboard and into the water. Before she reached out a paddle to help Tom back into the boat, I swore that I caught the quickest of glimpses of Maya chuckling to herself. Eventually, Tom found his way back into the raft, albeit soaking wet, his shorts riding high enough to expose an unimpressive bulge. Tom, embarrassed from his mishap, didn't say much after that. Even his paddle strokes seemed less enthusiastic. Once we got to the bottom of the run, there was a bit of a lull as we waited in line for the 200-foot conveyor belt to take us back to the upper pool and make another whitewater run, so I decided to open my mouth.

"So, Maya, how long have you been a guide?"

"A few years. I'm a teacher, so it gives me something to do in the summer. Plus, teaching doesn't exactly make you rich."

"That's awesome...not the low pay part, but that you are a teacher and do this in the summer."

"Yeah, I like it."

God, I sound like a bumbling fool. "That's awesome?" Just shut up.

"Okay, everyone, keep your paddles inside the raft as we go on the conveyor belt," Maya announced.

In unison, everyone pulled their paddles into the raft as Maya guided us gently onto the belt. The giant structure collected the raft, and with a quick jerk, we began our ascent.

"And what do you do – Alice, right?"

"I sell cars," I shouted over the loud, whirring sound of the motorized pulleys.

"People still buy cars?"

"Not really."

"Hmm...car saleswoman, huh? Can you believe that someone murdered Big Al Washington? Do you remember those commercials? *If you want a car or truck, go see Al. If you want to save a buck, go see Al. Go see Al, go see Al, go see Al.* I used to love those growing up."

"Actually, he was my father."

"Oh, I'm so sorry."

"Don't be. He was a piece of shit."

Maya didn't respond; instead, she studied my face to see if I was serious or not. I couldn't see her eyes with the mirrored lenses on her sunglasses, but her friendly facial expression changed. As our brief conversation came to an unceremonious end, the raft dropped off the conveyor belt, and back into the water.

"All together now – four strokes forward."

Following the motion of the woman's strokes ahead of me, I timed my paddle as best I could with hers. By the fourth stroke, I must have temporarily lost interest, because her paddle knocked into mine on the backstroke. I apologized under my breath, in hopes that Maya didn't notice my mistake. While we approached the second run – the one Maya described as "advanced" with dangerous Class Three and Four rapids – I debated whether my new crush had been completely turned off now. *Why didn't you just say you were in finance like everyone else in this city? On the positive side, you did a great job coming across as a girl with daddy issues.* Before I got a chance to hit the restart button on flirting, our raft entered the advanced run.

"Right side – one stroke forward. Left side – two strokes forward."

The first rapid sent a jolt through the raft, followed by a massive wave over the left side. Even though the incoming wave failed to reach my side of the raft, a few droplets of the frigid water temporarily refreshed my sun-baked skin. Without much time to recover, we immediately bounced into the next set of rapids. Maya screamed out instructions over the sound of the rushing water. Her commands eluded me, however – because, in the next moment, I flew out of the raft. Even though I wore a helmet and life vest, the safety devices felt more like weights dragging me down than a lifeline. Just when I thought I could safely take a gasp for air, I encountered another rapid that prevented me from getting a clean breath. Starting to worry, I did my best to locate the raft, but all I got was a blinding sting of chlorine when I opened my eyes underwater. The real panic set in when I felt the water entering my lungs. Despite what appeared to be my imminent death, I was too embarrassed to call out for help.

My obituary – if anyone bothers to write one – will read, Alice Washington, died unexpectedly on a whitewater rafting trip with her adventurous rehab group after she refused to ask for help. Well, if nothing else, it would be an appropriate ending for a pathetic life.

As my arms grew tired and the rapids more intense, I accepted my fate; an addict without a home or family, it wasn't like I had much to live for anyway. But before my lungs completely filled, I felt a single, swift tug on the straps of my life vest. Struggling to breathe, I found myself halfway onto the rafting tube. With another yank, Maya pulled my dead weight into the middle of the raft, where I violently coughed up the water invading my lungs.

"You all right there, Alice?"

Doubled over on my hands and knees, I sensed the raft slowing down as the rapids ceased. For the first time since going overboard, I opened my eyes for more than a few seconds. Finding my bearings, I saw a few inches of water lining the floor of the raft, and calm waters surrounding it.

"You all right there, Alice?" The manly voice repeated.

After another productive heaving fit, I turned myself over and sat up on the floor of the raft. I lifted my eyes to find Instructor Tom staring back at me with the most concerned expression.

"I'll live."

"You scared us for a minute there," said the familiar voice from the back of the raft.

Still catching my breath, I decided not to acknowledge Maya. *If she has complete control of this raft and intimate knowledge with the run, then she must have thrown me overboard on purpose. Was that her way of flirting? Fuck. If that's the case, she's even more hopeless than me. No, the only logical reason is that I make her sick, just like every other person who knows me.* As we approached the conveyor belt to return to the top, I stumbled my way back to my position in the raft. Usually, I would never pick a wedgie or readjust my bra in public so nonchalantly, but after a near-death experience, one tends to stop giving a fuck.

"Are you sure you're okay?" Maya whispered so that only I could hear her.

"I'm fine."

"You want to keep going? We can drop you off when we get to the top."

"No, I'm fine. I can go again."

"Fantastic. That's the spirit."

What I didn't tell Maya was that the only reason that I wasn't getting off was because I planned on killing myself on the next run. The way I saw it, I wouldn't get another opportunity in the next three months to do it, so I wasn't about to waste it. Once I accepted my imminent death, I could honestly say that I felt happier than I had been in a long, long time.

As the conveyor belt threw us back into the upper pool, I discreetly unzipped my life vest, since it had been the primary factor keeping me alive when I went for a swim just minutes ago. Following Maya's instructions, we paddled back to the advanced run. With my clothes dripping wet and head spinning, I forgot to paddle. Luckily, Maya didn't give me any flak, apparently opting to ignore me than scold me at that point. As we quickly approached the churning waters of the advanced run, I envisioned my end: After the first major rapid, I would slip out of my life vest and jump as far as I could from the raft. It would have to be instantaneous, leaving no one the chance to pull me back into the raft. I figured intentionally swallowing water or bashing my head against the rock should speed the process up – which reminded me, I would need to ditch my helmet, too, after I jumped in.

"All together now – three strokes forward."

With my left hand on the T-grip of my paddle, I used my right hand to unbuckle my helmet strap and unclip my life vest. *This is it. I can't say it was a great life, but better to end it now before it gets any worse.* As the first rapid quickly approached, I detached my right foot from under the inner tube. And then, for some reason – *one that I still can't fully explain* – seconds before I prepared to jump, I looked up and who did I see? None other than Emily Bridges. Coincidentally, she stood on her namesake: a bridge that spanned across the width of the channel. After I spotted her, Emily raised her right hand toward me. While she seemed relieved to see me, her face carried a grave weight. Turning my attention back to the rapids, I dug my foot back into the tube and bore down.

Courtney Washington

*F*ive million dollars?! Kelly is out of her damn mind if she thinks she is going to get that much money. Trying to blackmail my family and me like that – who does she think she is? If she thinks I'm going to take this lying down, she's got another thing coming. C'mon Larry – pick up, pick up...

"Hello, this is Larry Bridges, owner and general manager of Washington Ford. I'm sorry to have missed your call. Please leave your name, and number after the tone and I'll get back to you as soon as possible."

"Hey, Larry. It's Courtney, again. Call me back. It's urgent."

Fuck. C'mon Larry. I tried his office line next.

"Washington Ford. This is Brenda."

"Hi, Brenda. It's Courtney. Is Larry there?"

"Hi, darlin', Umm, let me see – no, I'm sorry, Courtney. He's unavailable at the moment. May I take a message?"

"Was that him in the background?"

"No, he's out for a, uh, doctor's appointment."

"Brenda, c'mon – I wouldn't ask if it wasn't an emergency."

"Okay, hold on." Brenda sighed.

Listening carefully, I became convinced that I heard Larry's muffled voice in the background.

"Hi, Courtney? Are you there?" Brenda asked.

"I'm here."

"Great. Well, I just double-checked, and Larry is, in fact, at the doctor's office. I'm so sorry. May I take a message?"

"Sure, but first, could you do me a favor and put me on speaker?"

"Why would I put you on speaker? It's only me here."

"I'm asking you to do me a favor here, Brenda."

"Okay, I got you on speaker now – even though it's just me here. What's your message for Mr. Bridges?"

"Tell Larry that it's still my family's name on that dealership, and if he doesn't call me back after his phony-ass doctor's appointment, he'll have *five million reasons* to see a real doctor after I get done with him!"

"Okay, darlin'. Is that all?"

"That's all, Larry! Now call me back!"

I hung up before Brenda got a chance to play dumb again. *What the hell is Larry's problem? I know he's busy with the anniversary sale tomorrow and all, but I'm a Washington, not some nobody that he can brush aside.*

After an hour of not hearing from Larry, I gave him the benefit of the doubt. After two hours, I grew impatient. After three hours, I was dressed and out the door. Using the address from Detective Copeland's business card, I headed uptown to make sure someone would stop Kelly, because Larry apparently had no interest. I would be lying if I didn't say a range of thoughts crossed my mind on the trip over to see the detectives – the most alarming of which I couldn't quite shake. *What if Kelly is telling the truth about Luke's biological father? Now that I think about it, a fire of that magnitude caused by someone sauteing mushrooms does seem a bit far fetched. But, if it's true, that would mean that my father is a cold-blooded murderer and a bald-faced liar.*

Soon, I was at the Charlotte-Mecklenburg Police Department headquarters, located near the Charlotte Hornets arena. Parking around the venue was always a cinch due to the Hornets' irrelevancy, which rang especially true now, in the middle of the off season. On my way into the building, I passed a few cops visibly overheated in their black uniforms, coming and going. It wasn't long after I checked in with the receptionist and found a seat in the lobby that Detective Copeland strolled out of the elevator wearing a blazer and jeans, to offer a chilly, impersonal greeting. Already looking impatient, she took a seat on the flimsy plastic chair next to mine.

"Well, Ms. Washington, I have to tell you, my partner thought it was a waste of time to come down here to meet with you. But there's just something about this case and your family that doesn't sit right with me."

"It's not a waste of time, I promise."

"Mmm."

I couldn't blame her for hating us. Larry had stonewalled her at every turn, but all in all, it had mostly worked out for the detective. She got her man, after all.

"It's about Al's ex-wife."

"Not here. Follow me."

The detective led me past the security checkpoint and into an elevator, rebuffing my small talk about the month-long heatwave with a dismissive head shake. We eventually entered an interview room, which unabashedly resembled every cop procedural on TV: a table, two uncomfortable chairs, and a one-way mirror.

"Coffee? Soda? Water?"

"Okay, I'll take a coffee with two creams if you have it?"

"This is a police station — of course, we have it."

Detective Copeland tapped her knuckles against the one-way mirror and repeated my order. Refreshingly, it appeared as though the detectives took the threat as seriously as I did. While I waited, I wondered how many people were on the other side of the glass? *Detective Garcia for sure, then the chief of police, and the DA, maybe?* Detective Copeland assured me that my coffee would be arriving shortly and in the meantime, invited me to sit down at the bare table.

"So, what brings you down to the station today, Miss Washington?"

"As I was starting to say in the lobby, my father's ex-wife, Kelly Washington, is extorting me to the tune of five million dollars."

"And why would she do that?"

Just then, the slightly ajar metal door to the room fully opened as Detective Garcia, wearing a colorful short-sleeve button-down, carried two coffees into the room. Garcia apologized for interrupting and found a spot against the empty wall to lean upon after setting the coffee cups on the table.

"Why would Kelly blackmail you?" Detective Copeland rephrased.

"Who the hell knows? She claims to have dirt on my father or something."

"What dirt?"

"Nice try."

"What does Larry think of all this?" Garcia chimed in.

"Larry? How should I know? He's too busy with the huge Washington Ford anniversary sale tomorrow. Forty-seven years strong."

"Forty-seven years? I understand having a big sale for a 50th anniversary, but 47th? Seems trivial." Detective Copeland questioned.

"You see it all the time. Any car dealership, furniture store, or lemonade stand will use any holiday as an excuse to get people in the door. Hell, just a couple weeks ago, it was National Ugliest Dog Day, so some store was giving away a brand new seventy-inch TV to the owner of the ugliest dog. Can you believe that?" Garcia interjected.

"You're missing the point. I'm being blackmailed. Isn't that a crime?"

"Sure. If you have evidence. A taped conversation or a text would suffice," Detective Copeland informed me.

"No, I don't have that. Kelly just told me to my face that, 'If you don't give me five million dollars, I'm going to tell everyone the truth about Big Al Washington,'" I pleaded.

"Hearsay, I'm afraid. Your word against hers."

Detective Copeland leaned back in her chair, disappointed. Detective Garcia, unimpressed with the reality of blackmail, straight up left the room. *Are they for real? Don't they know how much influence the Washington name carries in this city? Instead of giving Kelly five million, maybe I'll threaten to donate one million to the mayor's opponent if these two bozos aren't fired.*

"Say, have you heard from your sister Alice lately?"

"No. We don't really talk. Why?"

Detective Copeland pierced her lips together and blew cold air into her compostable coffee cup. She proceeded to sip the coffee before letting out an audible "Aaah."

"Well, she's missing."

"Didn't she go back to Alaska?"

"Nope. Apparently, Alice checked herself into rehab earlier this week, and then yesterday, she disappeared during a field trip."

"A field trip?"

"Some fancy rehab BS. Anyway, we have reason to believe she may be planning something."

"Like what? Getting drunk in a dive bar?"

"Larry has reason to believe that Alice will retaliate against him and/or Washington Ford for being omitted from the will."

"Sounds like – what did you call it? Oh yeah, hearsay." I taunted.

Detective Copeland leaned forward, close enough that I could smell the coffee on her breath.

"You ever heard the phrase quid pro quo?" she Copeland asked.

While the term sounded vaguely familiar, I couldn't define it – but I sure as hell wasn't going to let Detective Copeland know that. She already acted like she was better than me.

"Yeah, why?"

"Tell you what, we'll have a unit watch Kelly over the next forty-eight hours – if she does in fact blackmail you, we'll get it on tape. And in return, you will call me about any news on your sister, deal?"

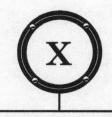

A STREETCAR NAMED AUTONOMOUS

Larry Bridges

God, I loved Saturdays. That feeling of waking up early, knowing the day will push your mind and body to its limits, was unparalleled. The easiest way to find out if a new salesperson would sink or swim was to throw them on an all-day Saturday shift. If he showed up on Monday morning without bitching or moaning – well, then, I knew he was born to sell.

Feeling generous, I stopped by Krispy Kreme on the way to the dealership to pick up a few dozen hot-out-of-the-oven glazed donuts for the sales team and any customers who visited that morning. However, even I couldn't resist the powerful temptation on the way out of the drive-thru line. Within seconds, I'd scarfed down two of the mouth-watering donuts as the car made its way to Washington Ford. They were so soft that I didn't even have to chew them.

Being the first to arrive, I exited the car and unlocked the dealership gate. The gate and metal posts on the perimeter of the property were eyesores, but deemed necessary about a decade ago by the insurance company. Once I unlocked the gate, I returned to my car, where I couldn't help but play Sam Cooke's "A Change is Gonna Come." As Sam belted out the first verse through those impeccable speakers, I programmed the car to park in my newly minted spot labeled, "Larry Bridges, Owner." *It has been a long time coming, Sam.*

Juggling the box of warm Krispy Kreme donuts in one hand and the keys in the other, I entered the security code at the door, then hurried through the decorated showroom and into the kitchen. There I carefully stacked the boxes of donuts on the communal table. *Now, where are the plates and napkins?* Digging through the disorganized cupboards, I found an assortment of other items. *Why in God's name is there an oversized industrial fire extinguisher in here?* Bewildered by its existence, let alone what appeared to be a signature scrawled on it, I pulled it out of the cupboard and placed it on the counter to remind myself to inquire about it later. But first, plates and napkins.

Inspecting the lot before the day officially started was, in my opinion, the most important task of selling cars. Whether we wanted to believe it or not, the customer could see everything. When someone looking to buy a car came onto our lot, a discarded soda can or dirty windshield could ultimately make or break the sale. It might not be a conscious decision, but those little things added up. The other important detail I checked on that morning before we got swamped was the placement of the cars. I instructed my team to park all the autonomous cars front and center, and hide the old-fashioned models in the back parking lot. Whether it was a news crew or potential buyer driving by, a discernible shift would be visible at Washington Ford.

As I finished up with my spot check, Brenda, clipboard in hand, scurried out to check in with me. The time on my phone read 7:47 a.m. and sweat beads had already formed on her temple by the time she reached me. *Shit. Why are the tents not set up? The customers are going to roast on this pavement.*

"Good morning, sir. And happy 47th anniversary!" Brenda said with a welcoming smile.

"It's already too fucking hot. Why aren't the tents set up yet?"

"The team is looking for the instructions now."

"They're fucking tents. Just set them up."

"Yes, sir."

"And where is the water for the guests?"

"Chad always ordered those, sir. No one knows how to contact the vendor."

"Are you serious? How hard is it to go to a fucking grocery store? Do I have to do everything myself?"

"No, sir. I'll send Mark."

"All right, then. Run down the schedule for me, would you?"

"Yes, sir:

10:30 a.m. - The warm-up band goes on stage.

11 a.m. - Press conference: You'll say a few words, and we'll show a

video on the autonomous future for Washington Ford.

11:30 a.m. - Immediately following the press conference, the Washington family will join you onstage for a photo op.

12 p.m. - Lunch. We'll grill hotdogs and burgers. Traditional and plant-based.

1 p.m. - Cake and a 'Big Al Washington and his dog Teddy' petting zoo tribute."

"Thank you, Brenda. It's going to be a hell of a day."

*S*alespeople these days, I swear to God, think the customer will just *fall into their laps. With more tools at their disposal than any other generation before them, they fail to generate leads and are socially inept when it comes to the ducks on the pond. On the bright side, the ad buy seems to be working. The lot hasn't seen this much foot traffic in ten years.*

I checked the time on my phone. It was almost 10:30 a.m., and Mark still was nowhere to be seen with the cases of water. *How fucking hard is it to go to the grocery store and pick up some water?* With the sun and temperatures on the rise, the lack of shade and a hydration station loomed large. To take my mind off our poor execution, I grabbed one of the last remaining donuts from the box as I sent a Slack to Mark about his ETA. The donut tasted dry, and the glaze turned thick.

"Five minutes," Mark messaged me back.

"Hey you, come here."

A young, new salesman – whose name I hadn't cared to learn – avoided eye contact with me.

"Yes, you. Come over here."

Reluctantly the kid, wearing a golf polo with our logo, moseyed over to where I stood.

"How we looking? Any sales yet?"

"Not yet, sir."

"Why not?"

"Sticker shock, sir."

"That's what financing is for, all right?"

"But, sir – "

"The prices aren't too high, dammit. Did you explain to them how much they'll save a month on ride services, or being able to live in the suburbs with a cheaper mortgage?"

"Yes, but – "

"No one comes to a car dealership for the free donuts. They are here for a reason. It's your job to find out why and to exploit it. Understood?"

"Yes, sir."

"Good. Now go help set up those tents and then sell some damn cars."

As I watched the salesman run for cover, I caught a glimpse of a news van turning into the lot. *Shit. The press is already here, and the heat is only getting worse. That water better get here soon.*

"Mr. Bridges?"

The voice startled me. When I turned around, I found Detective Copeland and her partner Detective Garcia staring back at me. Garcia's ugly Hawaiian shirt-of-the-day distracted me long enough to forget to offer a proper greeting.

"Mr. Bridges, I thought we should talk in person," Detective Copeland began.

"Yes, thanks for coming down on our big day, detectives."

"All this for the number forty-seven, huh?" Detective Garcia sneered.

"Yes, well, they say time is unforgiving. You never know if you'll see the next zero."

I held up a donut for effect before offering the box to the detectives. To my surprise, neither seemed the slightest bit interested. *Even cops are eating healthier these days.*

"I'm afraid we haven't found Alice," Detective Copeland declared.

"Why not?"

"We're not your fucking lackeys, that's why," Detective Garcia chirped.

"Excuse my partner. What he meant to say is that, after a thorough search, we have been unable to locate Alice, and we don't have the resources to continue looking for her."

"So, that's it?"

"Well, she voluntarily checked herself into rehab, so it's my understanding she can leave at any point. Even if it was an untraditional exit."

"Uh-huh. I see."

"It was voluntary, right?" Detective Garcia questioned.

These fucking detectives. Talk about short-term memories. Didn't I just hand-deliver a murderer to them? It looks like I'll be making another call to their supervisor later to discuss this harassment.

"Thanks for coming down, detectives."

"One more thing, Mr. Bridges. Are you aware that Courtney Washington has claimed that her ex-stepmother Kelly Washington is extorting her?"

Courtney actually went to the police?! It never ends with this fucking family.

Courtney Washington

I thought about cleaning out the Porsche, but who was I trying to impress – Eva? It wasn't like she had Daddy's ear anymore. Hell, she technically didn't have a house anymore, but Larry asked me if I would let her stay in the lake house rent-free for a year to get her life in order, as a sort of peace offering. *What's another year?* In a way, if she weren't a gold-digger, I would feel kind of sorry for her. I mean she spent – what, ten years with Daddy? And it wasn't his glory years either; it was the 'take him to the doctor every other week' type years. Then there was poor Margret, my half-sister, who I didn't have much of a connection with because Eva never let me see her. That and well, she was only five years old.

Regardless, I wasn't entirely sure why Larry wanted me to take Eva to the anniversary party at the dealership, but I figured it would finally give me a chance to have a face-to-face with him about Kelly. Hell, he couldn't even be bothered to call me for the favor; Brenda, his executive assistant, had to do it. Assuredly, Larry wouldn't be able to ignore me in person. Between Kelly's extortion and allegations about Big Al murdering Jake, we had an awful lot to discuss.

When I reached the lake house, I laid on the horn a couple of times instead of texting her. When she finally came out – with Margret, throwing a tantrum, trailing behind her – Eva didn't seem too pleased.

"Hi Eva," I yelled through the open passenger window.

"C'mon Margret. We can't be late for the family event," Eva said sarcastically.

Eva opened the rear passenger door, which brought the sound of Margret's tantrum into full volume. That's when I turned my head to note confusion on Eva's face.

"Where's the booster seat?"

Ah, shit. I knew I forgot something. Brenda even paid extra for one-day shipping, but it just seemed like so much work, I must have subconsciously put it off.

"I'm sorry. I guess it slipped my mind. We can go back to my place to install it, or maybe we can take your car instead?"

"No, Larry took away my loaner from the lot. New policy, he said."

"Shit. I'm sorry. We're short on time. Maybe I'll just call a Lyft with a car seat?"

While we waited for the Lyft, Eva suggested we go inside to escape the heat. Upon entry, I couldn't believe the stark contrast from the last time I visited: the place was immaculate. I wondered if she planned on staying longer than the year we all agreed on with Larry. *I hope not, because if she thinks she's staying longer than that, she is sorely mistaken. I won't have my kindness confused for weakness.* Unsure of how to kill the time, we all gravitated to the dining room table. I could tell something was weighing on Eva when she skipped the small talk.

"It's just been a tough couple of weeks, and without Al here, it feels like everyone is against me."

Seeing Eva in full view for the first time that morning, I couldn't help but stare at her chin, where a thick layer of caked makeup was covering something. Despite my curiosity, I figured it was best to avoid the topic.

"It's been tough for everyone in the family."

"I truly did love him, you know."

"Eva, no offense, but I'd respect you a whole lot more if you just said you married him for his money. He was – what, seventy-five when you met him?"

"What's wrong with falling in love for money? It was still love. Who cares about the how or why when both people are happy?" Eva asked heatedly.

The sharp rise in her tone sent Margret into another tailspin. As Eva tried to calm her down, I reminded myself why I had generally stayed away from the lake house for so many years despite its close proximity.

"While we're speaking our minds, tell me, why does everyone in this family hate me?"

Where the hell is this Lyft?

"And why do you all ignore Margret? She's blood, yet you all treat her as if she is a foreigner like me," Eva continued.

I covertly checked my phone under the table to see the ETA. *Five minutes, still? C'mon. Hurry up, for the love of God.*

"Are you looking at your phone? Are you fucking kidding me?"

"No, it's just, um, I'm just checking status on our Lyft. That's all."

"See, this is what I'm saying. I'm trying to talk to you – for what reason, I don't fucking know – but I'm trying. And in return, I get laughed at or just straight up ignored."

This is going to be an excruciatingly long ride.

"Hello? Are you listening to me? Un-fucking-believable. I just want Margret to be included in this family. Hell, I want to be included."

Now both Eva and Margret were crying. To Eva's credit, I was inclined to believe the tears were real. I wasn't quite there with Margret, though.

"Hey, don't cry now," I said.

"Look, I'm really sorry that Daddy screwed you over. I'm not saying you deserved the entire family fortune or anything, but to leave you and Margret with nothing, I mean…that's bullshit."

Eva pulled a tissue from her purse and quickly unfolded it to wipe away her tears. After swallowing the lump in her throat, Eva turned deadly serious.

"There's something else…"

"What's that?"

"I think Larry killed him."

Emily Bridges

I had only owned it for a few days, but I started to believe my new autonomous car wasn't worth it. *I mean, don't get me wrong; it's a beautiful vehicle and all, but it's becoming more of a hassle than anything else.* Between the insurance (why you needed insurance for a car incapable of causing accidents was beyond me) and parking tickets, I had already spent more on it than I would have in an entire month for Lyft rides.

I ended up parking my car around back by the dumpsters to keep it out of view from the main drag. I knew I had to hide Alice somewhere that no one would look for her, and luckily, I had stumbled into a perfect situation. Did I feel great about signing a year lease on an office space with a blinking 'TOPLESS' sign as its backdrop? No, but it served an immediate purpose. To her credit, Alice understood the need for me to stay with her. We made the most of it, though. The experience almost reminded me of a sleepover as a kid; we had junk food, sleeping bags, and stayed up all night talking. I had heard stories of Alice growing up since our families overlapped, but they were biased. Listening to Alice's side of things for the first time opened my eyes to how awful Al had treated her, especially after her mom died. When it was my turn to open up, I pretty much had a full-on breakdown about my dad. It could have been easy for Alice to air all of her justified grievances against my dad; instead, she simply listened, because she knew that was exactly what I needed. Over the years, I had heard rumors about my dad but never took them too seriously, because I knew him. At least, I thought I did. He was a devoted husband and father who coached my soccer games and drove me to and from school every day. Perhaps I was naïve to think my dad was perfect, but after learning about some of the allegations against him the past week, I worried that he could genuinely be a monster. Theft, fraud, and murder? All seemed at least in the realm of possibility.

After airing out our daddy issues, we circled back to the black cloud that had presided over Washington Ford for the past few weeks.

"Could Chad have really orchestrated this entire thing?" I asked.

"I don't see it. But, for the sake of argument, let's say Chad was stealing money from the dealership for the past decade. Why does he kill Big Al?"

"Self-preservation, maybe."

"Then why go on the run immediately after Big Al dies? It's not like he's a suspect at that point."

"Hmm. That's interesting. So, you're saying it's either one or the other?"

"Exactly. Unless Chad was completely incompetent, either he would have killed Al to avoid being caught, or gone on the run to evade capture. Not both."

"And then there's Javy. What was the link between the two?"

That was the question that kept me up long past the moment Alice fell asleep. I thought it was plausible that Chad was the main culprit, but no matter which way I looked at it, Javy didn't fit into the equation. *How did a lowly mechanic end up involved in this thing?*

Using Javy's obituary, I quickly found Javy's parents' names, and with that information at my disposal, it didn't take long to find their home address. According to Waze, they only lived about twelve minutes away. Now, we just had to get them to talk.

The next morning, on the way to Javy's parents' house, we stopped at a convenience store to get some basic toiletries and coffees. In what you could call an oversight or sheer ignorance, we quickly discovered the problem with hiding out at an empty office was the lack of basic necessities. Sure, you could buy a toothbrush and deodorant – as a temporary patchwork, but realistically, how long could Alice and I stay there without a proper place to shower and sleep? Neither of us broached that topic; however, because then we would've had to acknowledge the sheer dysfunction of Alice's current situation. Her life was in shambles, and the pieces could never fit back together.

Back in my car, I entered the location of Javy's parents' house into the navigation. Alice didn't look so hot as she sipped her morning coffee. Figuring she was exhibiting the symptoms of withdrawal, I didn't bother asking how she was feeling. Only when we passed a sleek, fifty-foot billboard, featuring my dad lounging in the backseat of an autonomous car for Washington Ford's 47th anniversary sale, did she perk up.

"So, what's the plan?" Alice asked.

"Selective truth."

"Selective truth?"

"Yeah, we tell Javy's parents that we are working on behalf of Washington Ford to see if anything can be done to, uh, help ease the pain for the family."

"Ease the pain?"

"Perhaps the dealership provides a life insurance payout to employees' families? I don't know."

"So, lie then?"

"No, no. That's such a harsh word. Like I said, selective truth."

"Uh-huh. Whatever. You do the talking, but I swear to God, I'm not buying another useless fire extinguisher this time."

My car stopped on a cul-de-sac of a suburban neighborhood lined with cookie-cutter, two-story houses built in the nineties or early aughts. I cross-checked the address on my phone with the house numbers. Like all the others in the neighborhood, the Perez home had a mixture of brick and vinyl siding. It stood out for only one reason – the yard was unkempt, as the weeds were winning the invasion against the bermudagrass.

Immediately after I rang the doorbell, both Alice and I instinctively took a few steps back to appear less threatening. And then we waited...and waited. I checked the time on the phone: 9 a.m. *I suppose it is a tad early, but it's a Saturday morning – someone should be home.* Alice wanted to leave, but my stubbornness got the best of me. And after the third attempt, the front door finally opened.

"May I help you?" An exhausted-looking man in his robe asked.

"Hi, Mr. Perez? My name is Emily Bridges, and this is Alice Washington, we're from – "

"Washington, as in Washington Ford?"

"That's right," I replied.

The man's annoyance quickly transitioned into relief. He profusely apologized for his scruffy appearance and insisted we come inside. Before I walked through the door, I looked back at Alice and gave her a wink – a gesture that wasn't well received.

Upon entering, a repugnant smell abruptly stung my nostrils. I couldn't place it until I saw a black cat roaming around the untidy living room, and realized what I smelled was a neglected litter box. From that point on, it was a struggle attempting to breathe through my mouth. Mr. Perez eventually welcomed us to sit on the couch, where he first had to brush away the crumbs. The offered coffee tasted a day old that someone reheated minutes before we arrived. *Dare I ask for cream and sugar? God knows the cream would be cottage cheese, if he even has any. Better not.*

"So, you're a Washington, huh? How are you related to Big Al?" Mr. Perez asked Alice.

"He was my father."

"Hmm. You taking over the family business then?"

"No, that would be her father."

Mr. Perez, confused, initially thought Alice was joking, but I assured him that she was not. Selfishly, it felt good to hear that Mr. Perez wasn't even familiar with my dad, making a connection between Javy and him less likely.

"Since neither one of us knew Javy personally, would you mind telling us about him?" I asked.

"Javy was a good kid. He got into some trouble in high school, but had really straightened out the past few years. He was even planning on going to community college this fall."

"What about his life at Washington Ford?"

"What do you mean?"

"Did he hang out with anyone from work?"

"Not that I know of, I think most of his co-workers were older than him."

"Did you ever hear Javy mention the name Chad Baker to you before the police named him as the primary suspect?"

"Never."

Alice, relatively quiet since the initial introductions, gave me a look that said we should leave the poor man alone as she pretended to sip from her coffee cup. I noted her objection but pressed on anyway.

"Moving on to the night of the incident, it's my understanding that was your boat that was involved, yes?"

"Yes."

"Did the police return it yet?"

Shortly after that question, Mr. Perez led us through the house toward the back door. Both Alice and I jumped at the chance to breathe fresh air again. The backyard resembled that of a hoarder – playsets, multiple grills, car parts, and the fifteen-foot boat. As I gravitated toward the boat, I almost ran over a young boy, maybe four or five years old, sitting on the burnt grass below me, playing a game on his iPad. He stopped to see who almost ran over him before getting off the ground to hide behind his dad's legs.

"There she is. The police were kind enough not to take responsibility for all of the scratches," Mr. Perez said, pointing at the boat.

Upon closer inspection, it seemed the scratches on the hull were more likely due to its age rather than police malfeasance, but I wasn't about to voice my opinion aloud. Meanwhile, the young boy had taken an interest in Alice, who followed a few yards behind me.

"Where did the police say they found it?" I asked Mr. Perez.

"Some old boat ramp off the beaten path. No cameras around, apparently."

I continued my assessment of the boat, circling the perimeter, hoping for a clue to pop out at me. Just before I finished my inspection, my shirt got caught in the propeller of the motor. *Could this be something?*

"Any fingerprints?"

"Nope. Police said the guy flipped it over into the water to destroy any evidence; killed my motor in the process. Again, the police said that is my problem, not theirs. Can you believe that?"

A dead end. I thought for sure that Javy was the key to figuring this thing out. After letting out an audible sigh, I checked on Alice. It appeared that the young boy was now trying to get her attention, but Alice wanted nothing to do with him. Regardless, the boy followed her with every step she took away from him. I wondered why he'd become so persistent, and I drifted closer to them as Alice continued to rebuff her new shadow.

"The boat – " The boy's muffled voice trailed off.

"That's the boat – " He repeated.

Alice, no longer annoyed, knelt next to the boy as he showed his iPad to her. Now within full earshot, I finally understood what he was saying, as Alice's jaw dropped. She stared at the iPad and then at me, completely dumbfounded.

"That's the boat in the pictures."

Luke Washington

Everywhere I looked, I couldn't help but see them. Larry had the ad agency place the anniversary sale ads across every digital billboard, social media and streaming platform you could imagine.

"Larry Bridges here. C'mon down to Washington Ford's 47th Anniversary Blowout Sale this Saturday. Saturday! Saturday! Saturday! And for the first time in our illustrious history, we will be selling fully autonomous vehicles. Look how comfy this backseat is – you can fall asleep in Charlotte and wake up in New York or D.C. without the hassle of traveling on an airplane or taking an Uber."

The video, which began with gleaming rows of autonomous cars in the Washington Ford parking lot, cut to Larry, outstretched in the backseat with a nightshirt and pillow, pretending to sleep as the car drove through the night. After Larry woke up against an obvious green screen of the D.C. cityscape, the video inexplicably transitioned back to Washington Ford. And it got even cheesier. The children's song – "London Bridge Is Falling Down" – played as Larry leaped from one hood to the next, tossing the price stickers to the ground and replacing them with cheaper ones. Only Larry had unimaginatively altered the lyrics to, "Autonomous prices are falling down, falling down, falling down. My fair prices!"

I saw the entire campaign boasting about Washington Ford's transition to selling autonomous vehicles as a personal insult to Grandpa and our customers. I firmly believed that people still wanted traditional cars, not some computer-driven bullshit. *Grandpa must be rolling over in his grave right now.* The fact that Larry had promoted himself to the role of company spokesman made it even more egregious.

The good news was that his farce wouldn't last for long. I had finally put together a plan that would help me take it all back – and in my humble opinion, it was rather genius. In essence, the idea was to kill Mark in a car crash so I could keep the full share of my inheritance. I would then use the proceeds to buy Larry out and force his retirement, so the dealership would once again be under family control.

The details of the plan were a little hairier, but with all the time I had in the hospital, I finally worked those out, too. For every waking hour since Mark's unwelcome visit, I had tunnel-like focus. Over the past week, I'd busted my ass to get the doctors to discharge me from that god-forsaken place. The physical therapist, no thanks to her, said I was her 'most successful patient' in terms of expected recovery time. I still couldn't pee straight, but my doctor was optimistic that I would eventually be able to go standing up.

I was released the morning before the anniversary sale. Without a word to Lauren about my discharge, I took a bus – something I hadn't done since middle school – to my bank, so I could access my rainy day fund from my safety deposit box and then, caught another bus to a nearby used car dealership. With a sufficient disguise (a Carolina Panthers hat and sunglasses) and a wad of untraceable cash, I purchased the biggest car on the lot: a 2023 Ford Expedition. Well, the second largest, after a 2024 Chevy Suburban – unflinching loyalty to Ford was in my blood. Initially, I was wary that the dealership wouldn't accept my all-cash offer without proper identification, but a desperate business knows how to bend the rules.

Waking up the next morning in a cash-only motel, I had to figure out exactly where Mark would be and when. With the help of Slack, our internal messaging software that the dealership neglected to boot me from yet, it was all too easy. I learned that Larry tasked Mark with picking up some cases of water for the customers. According to the app, Mark left the dealership at 10:15 a.m., but only after arguing for an hour that the job was beneath him. I sat near the dealership in my newly acquired car, waiting for my window of opportunity, knowing that otherwise, I would have had to hang around until Mark went home for the night.

By 10:25 a.m., I positioned my car in the empty parking lot of an abandoned gas station, about a mile between Washington Ford and the grocery store where Mark ran his errand. I figured it was the perfect site, with a side road quiet enough that I could easily escape unnoticed after my Ford Expedition plowed through Mark's Mustang. Whether it was nerves or the feeling of driving an unfamiliar car, I couldn't stop squirming in my seat. *What's with everyone's obsession with leather seats? I mean, anyone who has worn shorts in a North Carolina summer has lost at least one layer of skin to a leather cushion. And why is my seat so close to the steering wheel?* Eventually, I found the button on the bottom of my seat and adjusted it to a more acceptable position. With the skin under my knees stuck to the leather, I refreshed Slack once again – probably the twentieth time since I'd parked – in hopes that Mark would soon message everyone his ETA.. Even if he didn't, his flamboyant "Need for Green" Mustang wouldn't be difficult to spot as it hurtled down the street toward me. And once I spotted it, I would calmly pull out with my five-star-safety-rated behemoth, accelerate and take aim. I figured if my vehicle swiped his at that speed, the force would be enough for the Expedition to obliterate the Mustang without compromising my car's ability to continue driving. Even if mine unexpectedly crapped out, it was in no way tied to my name, so I could quickly ditch it and escape through the woods to reassess an exit strategy.

And then on the twenty-first refresh, at 10:33 a.m., Mark messaged that he "got the water" and was "coming back to WF now." When I saw his name next to the Slack message, for some reason, I thought back to all the words that we exchanged throughout our friendship. Between the texts and work DM's, I must have seen his name pop up on my phone more than ten-thousand times. *You can't get nostalgic, Luke. This guy is the only thing standing in the way of your dream of running Washington Ford. And if you're being honest, he deserves it – he's a dirtbag who has been masquerading as your friend. The bottom line is that when times got tough, he blackmailed you. Fuck him.* With my right foot on the brake, I put the car into drive and waited for any sign of that obnoxious green Mustang.

My eyes glued to the road, I saw a silver car in the distance, let out a deep breath and temporarily took my hands off the wheel to crack my knuckles. I casually glanced at the silver car as it drove past me – a brand new, autonomous Ford Destiny. In the backseat, I caught sight of two hollow eyes staring back at me as the car continued down the road toward Washington Ford. *Fuck me; he's not driving his Mustang.* I took my foot off the brake and stomped on the gas, spinning my tires in the process. *Shit, shit, shit, shit. Okay, you have a mile until you get to Washington Ford. Think, Luke. Time to improvise. Okay, okay. Here's the play: Just ram the shit out of him from behind. That little car won't be able to take a beating from my Expedition.* As I accelerated, I glanced at the speedometer to see I was already doing fifty-five and closing in on Mark's car. With the speed limit at 45 mph and Mark's car's restrictions to follow the speed limit, I gained on him quickly. In the back window, I saw Mark gesturing frantically, panicked. I couldn't make out exactly what he yelled, but I knew it was obscene and directed at me. By about the half-mile mark, I had caught up to him. My engine roared as I went in for the final push. *Eighty million dollars. You can do it.* Just as my front bumper prepared to make contact, Mark's Ford Destiny pulled ahead to avoid the collision. *What the fuck?* Frustrated, I went for the car again. The speedometer read 75 mph as I made my second attempt to take my life back – and once again, Mark's car jolted ahead right as I readied to make contact. *Shit. Shit. Shit. It must have an emergency override or something to avoid accidents.* With the Washington Ford billboard now fully visible atop the pine trees, I figured we were about a quarter-mile from the dealership. *No. No. No. Time is running out. Should you abort?* I let off the gas. *Mark's going to get away with it again. Unbelievable.* All of a sudden, an idea sprung to mind. There was a stoplight ahead. If the light was red, there would be no way the autonomous car would dart into a busy intersection to avoid a rear-end collision. If the light was green, I figured I would abort my plan. *Okay. It's a solid plan. You should create some distance between the two of you to maximize impact.* I let off the gas. Mark, arrogant as ever, started laughing as the gap between us widened. It was only when I returned the smile that his disappeared. To my benefit, the light showed red. Mark's car slowed to a complete stop as cars passed the intersection perpendicular to his. *Goodbye, Mark.* I barreled toward his car, topping out at 70 mph. I would have given anything to see the look of terror on Mark's face again when impact appeared imminent. But a second before impact, Mark's car darted into the shoulder to avoid the collision. Meantime, as I shot past the red light into the middle of the active intersection, all I could think about was what people would say when they heard Luke Washington died in a car accident. *Will I be mourned? Will I be remembered? Will anyone care at all?*

Alice Washington

A bright young woman, life turned upside down, sat next to me in the backseat – and instead of trying to console her, all I could do was think about how I most related to the person who destroyed her. It's not a lie that destroys families, it's the truth. For Emily, the fact that her dad was a sociopathic murderer would no doubt destroy their relationship. Similarly, the relationship with my father concluded when I told him my own truth, that I am gay. Waiting for Emily to figure out where we were going next, I posited a world in which those truths never came to light. Ignorance is supposedly bliss, after all. Would Emily and I be living normal lives if we were unaware of our fathers' wickedness? Perhaps every Sunday after a family dinner, Big Al would treat me to frozen yogurt while we reminisced about the good times. Would we be happy? I simmered on that question for a moment.

Snapping back to reality, I checked in with Emily. She put on a brave face, but I knew a million thoughts were racing through her mind, none of them positive.

"Hey, nothing I can say will make it better. I just want you to know that I'm here for you if you want to talk."

"Thanks."

"Do you want to go home?"

"No. I need to look my dad in the eyes. I need to see if he'll tell me the truth or not."

There it was again – that pesky notion of truth. I revisited the imagery of eating frozen yogurt with Big Al. Like today, it was a hot summer day. My father and I sat across from each other at a picnic table, shaded by a nearby oak tree. He couldn't ask me any questions because he didn't want to hear my answers. I refused to talk to him because I was too upset. All

I wanted was to be happy – in a normal, loving family. But he obstructed my goal; no one else. It was then that I realized I needed to stop making excuses for two abhorrent men. The truth didn't crack the foundation of our relationships; no, it was our fathers' reprehensible actions. *Frozen yogurt is overrated anyway.*

With our destination set for Washington Ford, Emily's car pulled out of the Perez's driveway. According to the touchscreen in the front seat, we would be arriving at the dealership in eight minutes. Before we confronted Larry, I wanted to take a second look at those photos to ensure my eyes weren't deceiving me. They might have been dark and blurry enough that Larry would claim it was not him in the boat with Javy.

"Mind if I look at those photos again?"

Emily sighed, eyes downcast.

"Go for it."

She unzipped her purse, pulled the iPad from it, and then handed it to me. The iPad, unlocked, opened right to the photos. Suddenly, the car dropped the music volume on the sound system, and the route on the touchscreen display buffered.

"Accident ahead. Rerouting. Updated ETA: eleven minutes," the navigation system stated.

Indeed, the photo was dark around the edges with a vignette effect from the flash, but the center was fully illuminated. No matter how hard I attempted to scrutinize its quality, the picture unmistakably showed Larry sitting in the Perez's boat, with a gun pointed at the camera. Even the expression on his face conveyed guilt. I figured I would let Emily take the lead questioning Larry, since it was her dad. But because of their relationship, I figured she would likely freeze the moment she saw him. If that were the case, then I would be the one tasked with questioning him. *How can I get him to confess? Maybe I should pretend that I'm going to him for help, so he can relax. Then, when the moment is right, I'll turn the tables on him.*

As I contemplated my strategy, my thumb inadvertently double-tapped the iPad and brought up a photo strip at the bottom of the screen. Upon closer inspection, it appeared there were more photos on the device. We were so absorbed by the sight of Larry's guilt that we hadn't even bothered to look for additional evidence. I swiped right to discover a series of photos, of what appeared to be pieces of paper. After a few more swipes, I came across the document: "The Last Will and Testament of Allen James Washington." The declaration was dated May 26, 2028 – just a few months ago. *Holy shit. There is another will. Eva was telling the truth.*

"Emily, You need to see this."

I held the iPad out to Emily, who appeared to have zero interest in revisiting the contents of that device. At least it provided a likely answer as to why her dad did what he did, although I wasn't sure knowing Larry's motive would help heal Emily's fresh wound. After a moment of hesitation, she reluctantly took the iPad from me. I carefully monitored her body language as she read through Big Al's legitimate will. At one point, her face froze, mouth agape, almost as if her level of shock had reached full capacity for the day. When she presumably finished reading, Emily calmly turned off the iPad and placed it back into her purse. I waited for her to speak first.

"I just can't believe it. In some ways, I'm envious."

"Envious?"

"Yeah, I wished I loved anything as much as my dad loves that car dealership. I mean, the lengths he went to, and number of lives ruined – or ended – all to own and operate that stupid dealership, makes me jealous that someone has that kind of passion. If only he had that kind of passion for his family, huh?"

"I'm so sorry, Emily."

"You know, it's too bad your dad didn't actually leave the dealership to my dad. It would've been a fitting succession from one self-centered asshole to another."

Relieved to see her at least attempt to make light of the situation, I laughed, harder and louder than my typical laugh. I couldn't help but think of one particular sentence in Big Al's will: "I have intentionally omitted my daughter, Alice Washington, from this, my Last Will and Testament, as I do not agree with her lifestyle." Almost everything else had changed from the previous will, but that one sentenced remained. *Thanks for leaving that one in there, Dad.*

"You have arrived at your destination," the navigation uttered out of the blue.

The knot in my stomach tightened as soon as I looked up to see the all-too-familiar massive Washington Ford billboard. My anxiety did every-thing in its power to make me run from our half-assed confrontational plan. *Never underestimate Larry. Hell, maybe he's in the process of framing you for everything you're accusing him of having done, and you're walking right into his trap.*

As I took in the crowd of people on the lot, I heard a strange noise and turned toward Emily, the apparent source of that noise. She was having a breakdown – the kind where you try your hardest to keep your composure, but your emotions come pouring out anyway. Tears streamed down her face, as she covered her nose and mouth to muffle her sobs. The way I saw it, there was now way she was getting out of the car.

"Hey, don't worry. I got you."

I carefully plucked the iPad from Emily's purse and opened the car door, with every intention of taking down Larry Bridges for good.

THE LION IN SUMMER

XI

THE LION IN SUMMER

Larry Bridges

At some point on the morning of Washington Ford's 47th anniversary, I decided that nothing would ruin my moment in the sun. I hadn't patiently waited on the sidelines for decades and declined dozens of lucrative job offers just to be railroaded when I was finally handed the keys. *Alice is missing after escaping rehab. So what? Big Al's ex-wife is attempting to blackmail us. So what? The cops are poking around because Courtney went behind my back. So what? Errand boy Mark can't even procure a few cases of bottled water on a hundred-degree day. So what? Get over it. I'm on top now, and none of that peripheral bullshit matters.*

The turnout wasn't as big as I had hoped, but as long as the television crews captured enough content for their news segments or social media bullshit, I wasn't going to sweat the size of the crowd. Standing on the side of the stage – admittedly, a splurge for the momentous event – I told Brenda to go ahead and give the band the signal to wrap up. The group, consisting of middle-aged men with hair too long for their own good, had milked their moment for the cameras. For a minute there, the only thing that I 'stopped believin'' in was that the song was going to end. When the set finally finished, the band took a bow to a temperate reception, and exited the stage.

Then, my time had officially come; time for me to introduce myself to Charlotte as the next leader of Washington Ford. The beloved staple of the city would rejuvenate its relationship with its residents, supplying them with their own, state-of-the-art automotive tools to thrive in our new world. Just as I was going over the talking points of my speech one last time, a piercing noise interrupted my train of thought. After a moment of trying to place the sound permeating the parking lot, I figured it out – dozens of sirens in unison, responding to a call – police cars, ambulances, and a fire engine. On the bright side, their destination wasn't Washington Ford, but within close enough proximity to interfere with my press conference. It was enough of a commotion that Detective Garcia rushed over to his car and appeared to radio their dispatch, most likely to see if he and his partner were needed. But our show would go on. Brenda stepped to the mic.

"Please welcome Washington Ford's new owner and general manager, Larry Bridges!"

I took to the stage to tepid applause – due, I'm certain, to the pandemonium down the street. As I passed Brenda on the platform, she mouthed, "I'm sorry," and darted past me before I got a chance to scold her for introducing me to a distracted crowd. When I reached the podium, I surveyed the attendees in hopes of killing time for the sirens to die down. Also, it gave me a chance to note the people in attendance – or more importantly, those who hadn't shown up to support me. This turned out to be a challenge, when all but three people had the backs of their heads facing me, craning instead to learn more about the emergency. And who were the only three people not watching the events unfolding down the street? Why that would be Eva Washington, Courtney Washington, and her sister, Alice. They stood side by side, arms folded across their chests, staring daggers at me. *Oh, God. What is it now? And what the hell does Alice think she is doing here? Where are those useless detectives?* As I rescanned the preoccupied crowd to alert the detectives, the house music dropped out, and the microphone produced horrific feedback. I pulled it away from the podium, but the damage had been done. *I'm surrounded by incompetence.* Even the maddening sound of the feedback didn't bring the crowd's attention back to the stage. Moreover, the majority of the people began to drift toward the sirens, like mindless insects to a bug zapper. *Stupid rubberneckers.* Even the TV crews packed up their gear to cover the mysterious incident.

"Excuse me, everyone? Hi, due to unforeseen circumstances, the press conference will be postponed by a half-hour. Let's reconvene then, so I can tell you all about the next exciting chapter of Washington Ford."

I placed the mic back on the podium and walked as casually off stage as someone in my circumstances could. Taking one last look into the crowd with as big a fake smile as I could muster, I once again saw the Washington women, whose eyes followed me across the stage as they simultaneously began walking in my direction.

"Brenda! Find the detectives, would you?" I shouted over the sirens. "And make sure those TV cameras stick around, understood?"

Brenda nodded and, to my dismay, disappeared once again before I got a chance to lecture her about the importance of being flexible when it comes to unexpected events during live stage productions.

"And find out where the hell Mark is with that water, please!" I shouted across the stage.

As I descended the stage stairs, my mind was spinning. *How can we salvage this disaster? Let's offer our tow truck for free to the scene, so they can clear it as quickly as possible.* Just as I retrieved my phone from my suit jacket to call the service department, I looked up to see three familiar faces blocking my path at the bottom of the stairs.

"Larry, we need to talk," Courtney insisted as her sister Alice stood next to her. Eva, now holding her daughter Margret, wasn't too far behind them.

"The photo-op has been pushed back. Just stand by, okay?" I blurted out.

The sisters stood their ground as I politely attempted to push past them. *They can't be serious right now.*

"Please excuse me, ladies."

"Maybe you didn't hear her, Larry. We need to talk to you," Alice added.

"You really want to do this, Alice? Or do you not remember our deal?"

"Oh, I remember, but I'm living my truth now, no matter the cost."

"Is that right? Fine. Let's go inside and talk then. This heat is unbearable."

With my arm outstretched toward the dealership, I awaited the women's decision. Truth be told, I wasn't too worried – if they were going to turn on me, they would've already done it. After a short deliberation amongst themselves, they agreed to relocate our impromptu meeting.

The showroom was noticeably quiet compared to the unexpected bedlam outside. Not a single salesperson or support staff member could bother us. As I led Big Al's kin to a more private location, I remembered to call the service department for the tow truck, since I was so rudely interrupted the first time. While on the phone, I studied the women's body language. *What do they want to talk to me about? Courtney probably wants to tell me how Kelly's latest blackmail attempt is keeping her up at night. Eva, no doubt, is here to complain about not getting her fair share of Big Al's inheritance. And Alice – well, I have to say I'm genuinely surprised she is here.* I initially thought the conference room might be the right spot to lead them, but the glass windows didn't offer much privacy, so I guided them down the hall toward Big Al's old office. The door still had his name on it. *While I don't love the idea of taking over Big Al's office, I probably should for appearance's sake. The boss has to have the largest office in the building; I don't make the rules.* I took the keycard from my pocket and unlocked the door. Once inside, between the memorabilia lining every inch of the walls and lack of natural light, I immediately felt uneasy. *I'll need to get rid of this crap and remodel before I move in here for good.* After I closed the door behind us, the women looked anxiously at each other. Apparently, none of them wanted to air their grievances first.

"Well, spit it out, would you? I'm rather busy today."

"It's over, Larry. We know everything," Alice finally started.

"Oh yeah, what is it that you think you know?"

"We know the will is bogus," Eva asserted.

Turning my attention to Eva, I studied the scab on her chin. *Hopefully, the photographer can fix it in Photoshop.*

"What are you talking about?"

"Show him," Eva said.

"Show me what?"

"You know that poor kid you murdered on the lake? Well, he took some photos before he died. You must know the ones."

Shit. How would they know that? Alice, remaining stoic, took my silence as a cue to continue.

"We visited Javy's family, Larry. Turns out all the photos from your adventure were uploaded to the family's cloud. I have all the proof, right here."

Alice, without breaking eye contact with me, held up an iPad in her right hand. On the small screen, I could see the photo Javy took of me seconds before I knocked him overboard. It already seemed like years ago. *You fucking idiot, Larry. Why did you trust that kid? You finally made it to the top, and it's all going to implode because you got bested by a twenty-*

year-old nobody.

"Why did you do it, Larry?"

"You have the will right there, and you're asking me why I did it? Did you not read it? You all should be thanking me! Al just gave away his entire fortune to some charity with no regard for any of us."

A cry filled the room. After pausing for a moment, I found Margret to be the source. Her face revealed terror; she was petrified of me. If I was being honest with myself, she had the right instinct. I took a step back and studied the faces in the room. It wasn't just Margret; every single person in that room looked scared to death of me. Still, I couldn't help but come back to one question: Why hadn't they gone to the police yet? They had the smoking gun right there on that iPad, which meant they either wanted a bullshit cathartic moment where I confessed to ruining their lives – or they wanted to make a deal.

"So, what now, huh? Courtney, are you prepared to give away 99 percent of your inheritance to the Breast Cancer Research Foundation? Or you, Eva – are you and Margret prepared to live on, what did he leave you two, fifty-thousand dollars for the rest of your life? Well, I suppose you could always get a job. But answer this for me: how much does a has-been lounge singer make these days? And then there's you, Alice. What's going to happen to you when you relapse, if you haven't already? Who is going to help you? You're going to kill yourself with booze or drugs, and you will die alone – because no one gives a shit about you except for me."

I scanned the room for the expressions on their faces. Each and every one stared at the carpet. *A person who lives their entire life in the lap of luxury isn't about to throw that away.*

"You can call me whatever you want, but you all know that if you turn that iPad over to the cops, then you have to give up everything. No amount of donations to the Breast Cancer Research Foundation will bring your mother back, so you might as well keep it all."

Silence once again. It appeared they had changed their tune. I won them over because they knew I was right. Better yet, I won them over because I was a damn fine salesman.

"Okay, here's what's going to happen. I'm going to go back out there to finish the press conference. You three hammer out the numbers you can all agree to, and once everyone's happy, you come out with those multi-million-dollar smiles and pose for the camera with me. Understood?"

While none of the women verbally agreed to my proposal, their desperation to resolve their financial stability was overt. Feeling good about where things stood, I checked the time and headed for the exit. But right as I clutched the door handle, a voice stopped me from leaving.

"Wait, Larry?"

"Yeah."

"Tell me the truth about Jake," Courtney demanded.

"Jake, who?"

"Are you serious? My Jake! Luke's Jake! Kelly told me that Daddy killed him, and you helped cover it up by burning down our house."

"So, you're going to believe the woman blackmailing you over me, the person who has looked after you your entire life?"

"Tell me the truth, Larry."

The truth? If I tell her the truth, then the deal will be off. If I lie, then everyone wins. The truth is perilous.

"Courtney, no one killed Jake, all right? The truth is that he was a deadbeat who ran out on you and Luke."

I didn't wait for Courtney's reaction before I pulled at the door handle again. Big Al's office fell silent as I stepped out into the hallway and waited for the door to close behind me. The moment the door latch locked in with the frame, I stood frozen and replayed the conversation in my head. *Unbelievable. The deal was rock solid until Courtney opened her mouth. Jake? Really? That was twenty-five years ago. Who gives a shit? And it was Big Al that killed the guy, not me. The question now is, does the deal still stand? Would they all be willing to flush millions of dollars down the toilet just to punish me?* I put the odds at fifty-fifty, which was too high for comfort.

I reached back into the pocket of my slacks for the keycard, and replayed the conversation in my head one more time, deciding that a couple more steps were needed to hedge my bet. Knowing cell reception was sketchy in Big Al's office, I scanned my card to lock the door, and then unplugged the wireless router for the entire building. As I returned to the parking lot for the rest of the anniversary sale festivities, I felt optimistic that the Washington women would come to their senses and fall in line, but a man in my position always planned for the worst-case scenario.

Emily Bridges

After I'd already repositioned my car twice to get a better vantage point, I figured a third time would almost certainly raise a few eyebrows. On the other hand, I couldn't see a thing with the tow truck completely obstructing my view. I impatiently waited for a minute or two in hopes that it would move, but the driver remained idle. Just the thought of getting out of the car to wander the parking lot made every bone in my body stiff. *What if I see him? There's no way I wouldn't break down the second my dad says hello or even waves to me.* As I contemplated my next move, a woman I vaguely recognized strolled past my window. My eyes followed her as I tried to place exactly how I knew her. She was an older woman, maybe in her late sixties, carrying an extra-large designer handbag over her right shoulder. It was not until moments later that I figured out not only her identity, but also why someone might need an excessively large purse, in light of the object noticeably protruding through a gap in the top zipper. It was undoubtedly the nozzle of a bright red, plastic gas can, in the bag carried by Kelly Washington.

By the time I opened the car door and stuck my feet to the pavement, Kelly had vanished. I stood on tiptoe to stretch above the surrounding cars and around the tow truck, to no avail. *Why would Kelly be sneaking around the parking lot with a container of gasoline?* I needed to find it out.

Although the fire engine and most of the police had left the scene down the street, the chaos remained. I followed what I thought might have been a glimpse of an older woman with grey hair – but after a few strides in her direction, it became apparent that the inscrutable shape was Madison, Washington Ford's receptionist, a platinum blonde. Without proper guidance, I shuffled toward the twenty-foot stage as my magnet. Similarly, the crowd, sparsely scattered throughout the parking lot, began to return to the base of the elevated platform, steered by the overzealous sales staff. To my mind, the threat of a catastrophic event seemed likelier by the minute. *Where is she?*

"Em? What are you doing here?" An all-too-familiar voice.

I didn't even have to turn around to know who stood right behind me. I could feel the insincerity of my smile, but hoped he might not notice.

"Hey, Dad."

"Hey, Em, what are you doing here?"

Had Alice already confronted him? What did he know? What should I say?

"I came to see you, Dad."

"Oh yeah? Support your old man, then?"

I quickly scanned the crowd for any sight of Alice. *Did she bail? I don't think he would be this callous if Alice had shown him the evidence.*

"Never goes quite as scripted, huh?"

"What do you mean?"

My dad pointed in the direction of the police cars and ambulances that had clogged the roads surrounding the dealership. *I can't believe Alice flaked on me.*

"Say, can I get you something to eat? We're grilling out, you know."

"Oh, that's okay. I'm sure you're busy."

"Eh, the schedule is all messed up now. Come on, have lunch with your old man."

I strolled beside my dad across the parking lot toward a well-used, not-so-stainless steel grill, the knot in my stomach twisting. The thought of eating anything made me nauseous. *Just spit it out, Em. If you don't call him out now, you'll never be able to.*

"Dad?"

"Yeah, Em?"

"I know everything."

My dad stopped in his tracks, took a second to look into my eyes, and then smiled. He actually smiled. I had essentially told him that I knew he was a monster, and he just smiled at me. How could he do that? In response to my existential crisis, he basically shrugged me off.

"Who would've thought my biggest mistake was underestimating my own daughter?"

As we stood on the pavement, my hands clammed up and sweat dripped down my forehead, and it wasn't because of the heat.

"To be honest, that's my only regret," my dad continued, "and for that, I apologize. But, you have to believe me when I say, my initial intentions when I hired you to find Big Al's killer were genuine."

"So, you're telling me you didn't kill Big Al?"

"Of course not."

"And why should I believe you?"

"He was like a father to me, why would I?"

"Because then, the dealership would be solely under your control."

"The morning Big Al died, he told me that Luke was out. He finally saw what everyone else already knew: Luke would run this place into the ground. His life's work would've been destroyed within a year. The problem was that, at the time of Big Al's unexpected death, his will said otherwise."

"You know, I've been thinking a lot about that Confucious quote you told me. How did it go? Oh yeah, 'Everyone has two lives but the second doesn't begin until when you realize you only have one.' Well – "

"Em, you're young, you have your whole life ahead of you. You're not going to understand until you're older. I mean, when I die – in the not so distant future – what am I going to have to show for it?"

Wow. How thoughtful, Dad. It's not as if I'm standing right in front of you.

"No, that's not what I meant, Dad. I kept wondering, what was so wrong with his first life that he wanted to destroy it?"

For the first time since our conversation began, my dad appeared sincerely apologetic as his eyes fell to the pavement, jaw clenched. But, I refused to give his remorseful facade any merit. As I turned to walk away, I caught sight of a perplexing amount of smoke billowing from the direction of the grill. Only after a subtle shift in the wind did my view become clear: Washington Ford was on fire.

"Dad, look!" I instinctively shouted.

After a moment of confusion, he, too, discovered two very different types of smoke. In the foreground was the transparent, concentrated smoke from the grill; in the background, thicker black smoke, pouring from the building.

"Fuck me," my dad muttered under his breath.

As I dialed 9-1-1, I kept a watchful eye on his body language. While there was, without a doubt, a brief moment of unbridled anger, it seemed that he quickly accepted the situation. And then, something strange happened – he struggled to hold back a smile. As the 9-1-1 operator asked me for the cause of my emergency, two thoughts entered my brain. First, Kelly was most certainly the culprit, and I'd let her slip away. Second, why on Earth would my dad be elated about the thing that he'd literally killed for being set ablaze?

"There's a fire at the Washington Ford dealership."

"Is this about the car accident?"

"No, this is a separate incident."

"Okay. Well, it looks like our fire engines just left that area."

"You need to send them back, right now!"

"Okay, ma'am. And what is your name?"

My dad continued to stand in place with a glint in his eye, as he watched the fire that was sure to wreak havoc on his life's work. *Why isn't he doing anything?*

"Emily Bridges."

"Thank you, Emily. Do you know if there is anyone – "

I shoved the phone back into my pocket before approaching my father. By the time I reached him, there were bright orange flames visible through the glass windows of the showroom.

"Dad, why aren't you more upset?"

"You know, I used to hate the nickname that Al bestowed upon me, Larry the Lion. Do you know why?"

"Why?" I sheepishly asked.

"See, lions are social creatures. They live in groups, called a pride. If an outside lion challenges the king and wins, the usurper will then kill any existing young cubs from the deceased. Before taking over Washington Ford, that tidbit always troubled me. But now, I get it."

"Dad, please tell me you didn't – "

"Of course not. Hell, between Luke killing himself in that car accident and Kelly burning down the dealership with the Washington women inside, I didn't have to do anything."

"Wait, what?"

"You didn't hear? Luke died at the scene."

Before my dad spewed any more bullshit, I took off running for the main entrance to the showroom. I had hoped the humid, stagnant air hitting my face would wake me up from this nightmare, but no such luck. Right as I reached the door, I looked over my shoulder for any sign of a fire engine or first responder, only to realize that I was on my own.

Inside the fiery showroom, my visibility was so limited that I bumped into one of the model cars as I attempted to find my bearings. If *they are still here, they must be in the conference room or one of the offices.* I had walked every inch of the building more times than I could count, but for the life of me, I couldn't figure out which way to go. It was only when the smoke started filling my lungs that my survival instinct kicked in and I recalled a fire safety demonstration from elementary school. The advice – "crawl low to avoid inhaling smoke" – echoed in my mind. Now on all fours, inching forward on elbows and knees, I could see better. Once I made it past the showroom, my first stop was the conference room where Alice and I had spent a week investigating Big Al's murder. After I discovered the space was empty, I briefly rested in the doorway on my back, with my eyes closed. Assuming my dad was telling the truth about him not killing Big Al, I couldn't help but wonder about an alternate timeline – one in which I'd found the real murderer. Maybe if I had, my dad never would have taken his nefarious path. I could've worked longer hours. I could've interviewed more people. I could've done more surveillance. Then I opened my eyes, and clearly saw that the destruction around me had been caused – either directly or indirectly – by my father. I realized I couldn't have done anything differently. It wasn't my fault things played out this way; it was his burden, and his alone. I could already feel my joints swelling, but I pressed on, on knees and elbows. What else was I supposed to do?

Next stop: the kitchen. When I reached the doorway, I pulled myself inside using the door frame. Once again, I found an empty room – well, devoid of people, anyway. But I gasped, then laughed aloud at the sight of a familiar, bright red object sitting on the kitchen counter. I sprung to my feet and rushed over to examine the comically large fire extinguisher. *Oh shit, can't fire extinguishers go bad? How many years does that take? What year did that pawnshop clerk say this was used by that NASCAR guy? 2019 or 2020, maybe? That has to be borderline on its lifespan, no?* I pulled out the small safety pin, lifted all twenty pounds of metal into my arms, pointed the nozzle at the doorway, and squeezed the handle. As soon as I applied pressure, a white-colored chemical surged ten feet through the smoky air. *It works.* Now that I was able to navigate the hallway, I yelled Alice's name at the top of my lungs. To my dismay, I discovered every door required a keycard to unlock it. With no response and no way to open any office doors, I seriously considered heading for the exit.

"Help us. We're in here!" A faint voice cut through the hissing sound of the flames.

I aimed the extinguisher's nozzle low to the floor and swept it back and forth, coughing at chemical fumes that were almost as bad as the smoke, inching down the hallway until I identified the office door where I believed the sound originated.

"Alice! Are you in there?"

"Yes! Open the door!" A muffled voice pleaded.

I took a step back to study the door in front of me. Like the others along the corridor, Big Al's office showed a red light at the edge of the door frame, indicating it was locked.

"It needs a keycard!" I yelled through the door.

Through the door, I heard Alice repeat what I had just said verbatim to the other Washington women in the room. I scanned the hallway; my efforts to slow the flames and smoke had been moderately successful, but the fire had engulfed the walls and was quickly spreading to the ceiling. Being mindful not to squander the entire contents of the fire extinguisher, I squeezed the trigger again, aimed low at the base of the walls, and swept the nozzle back and forth to suppress the flames within five feet on either side of the door.

"Get us out of here!" A voice hollered. Maybe Courtney?

I quickly scanned the hallway again for some sort of tool that might help me open the door, but the smoke restricted my view, and I doubted that Washington Ford had an axe on hand anyway. Forced to improvise, I used the butt of the fire extinguisher to repeatedly strike the door where the lockset met the frame, but it barely flinched. *Even if the door doesn't break, maybe the handle will.* In one fell swoop, I desperately lifted the fire extinguisher above my head and brought it down on the golden handle with all my might. The metal-on-metal impact created a bright spark, and the handle snapped off at the base. *Shit!* I picked the broken handle off the carpet and tried to put it back together again.

"Help us!" Voices screamed on the other side of the door.

A dreadful coughing spell prevented any update on my part; I could feel the soot collecting in my lungs and scanned the hall to see the flames regaining their strength. *If we all die, my father will not only get away with every single one of the terrible things he has done, but he will be rewarded for it. No one will be left in his way to stop him. I can't let that happen.* I once again lifted the fire extinguisher over my head and pounded what remained of the door handle. With each strike, memories flooded my thoughts. A spectrum of images – from my dad cheering me on from the sidelines at my soccer games to vacations at the beach – flashed across my mind. With each vignette, I struck the door harder and harder until I could no longer lift my arms. As my body collapsed against the door, I thought about giving up. Time was running out. With seemingly no immediate help on the way and the fire accelerating, the Washington women behind that door were going to die a horrible death. *Hell, maybe I should die with them. Honestly, what do I have to live for? Not only will I have no family or future, but I'll forever have to live with myself for letting those women die.*

"Emily!" Alice cried out.

Something about her voice sounded different – distinctly louder than before, as if no longer muffled by the barrier between us. I looked over my right shoulder and saw a light beaming through a hole where the door handle used to be. I jumped to my feet and pressed my eye against the makeshift peephole. Huddled in Big Al's former office were the women who shared his last name: Alice, Courtney, Eva, and young Margret. With the exception of Alice, the look of sheer panic on their faces was palpable. Alice ran to the far side of the room to dig through Big Al's desk.

"Where are the firefighters?" Courtney asked.

"It's just me."

"Just you?"

I ignored Courtney for the moment to inspect the inside of the lockset, but was suddenly sidetracked when perspiration dripped past my brow and into my left eye. As I reached to wipe it away, my shirt sleeve turned out to be so drenched in sweat that the slightest contact came with an unbearable stinging to my eyes, temporarily blinding me. I desperately patted down my clothes for any material that wasn't soaked, as the pleas for help on the other side of the door grew more desperate. I brushed the back of my left hand back and forth against the carpet before dragging it across my closed eyelids. The stinging returned, but it was a duller, more constant pain. I must have blinked nearly thirty times in a few seconds, and when I finally willed my eyes to open, I saw the barrel of a gun being pointed at me through the hole in the door. I screamed at the top of my lungs and ducked for cover.

"Em, are you okay?" Alice's voice trembled.

I managed to fully open one of my eyes to discover that my mind had deceived me – what I'd seen was a black ballpoint pen, not a gun. At that moment, I knew the photo of my father on the boat, just moments before he killed that young kid, would haunt me forever.

"Help!" Eva cried out at the top of her lungs.

I snapped to attention. Seeing the flames lap at the door once again, I held down the trigger on the fire extinguisher for a few more seconds. *Forget about your dad. Focus or die.* As I fought my paralysis, Alice methodically guided the black pen inside the hole where the doorknob had been, like a surgeon with a scalpel. Through that same hole, I watched as Courtney smashed a glass trophy case with her high heel, picked up a gold plaque and used it to slash at the drywall. And then, through the chaos, I heard the breakthrough: "click." Alice had somehow cracked the locking mechanism with her pen. With visual confirmation, I stepped back a few feet from the door and rammed my shoulder into it with what energy I had left. After impact, I felt a sense of satisfaction like I had never felt before, despite the agonizing pain of crashing through a door and then falling awkwardly on the thinly padded floor. Face down on Big Al's office carpet, I lifted my head to find Alice grinning ear to ear, holding the incriminating iPad, as she stood over me. I rolled over and took her free hand to get to my feet.

"I thought you left me behind."

"Same."

"Hey y'all, can we get the fuck out of here?" Courtney interjected.

Alice, maintaining eye contact with me, chuckled as tears trickled down both of our faces. Now beaming, I turned around to grab the fire extinguisher, so could I oblige.

Even without a physical barrier blocking our exit, the expedition proved more complex than any of us envisioned. Impaired by the overwhelming amount of smoke, we had no choice but to crawl our way out blindly. I took the front of our human chain; Eva held onto my ankles, Margret took the middle, and Courtney and Alice rounded out the back. At first, I limited my use of the fire extinguisher, knowing the dire consequences if it ran out of juice. But after having to stop our convoy to cough my lungs out a couple of times, I figured it was time for a more dramatic measure or the smoke was going to kill us all.

"We're going to need to hurry this up if we want to get out of here alive," I yelled hoarsely behind me. "So, on the count of three, take as deep a breath, stand up, hold on tight to the person in front of you, and don't stop until you see daylight. One, two..."

"Wait, what about Margret?" Eva asked.

"I'll carry her," Courtney answered.

"Okay, are we good? One, two, three."

Unable to manage a deep breath, I rose to my feet anyway and squeezed the trigger on the fire extinguisher as hard as I could. Aiming the nozzle at the nearest baseboard, I planned to follow a wall for as long as I could; if it turned into a dead end, then I would move along the opposite wall. The first wall proved to be just that: a locked office door. I could sense the uneasiness of the group, but I didn't have time to worry about morale. Pressing on, I moved to the next wall, which fortuitously led to the main showroom. Even with the haze of smoke and ten-foot flames, for the first time since the rescue mission began, I had the tiniest bit of optimism that we were going to get out alive. We found ourselves at the edge of the sales bullpen. If memory served, I estimated there were about a dozen desks. Moving forward, I slammed my knee into the side of a desk and tripped over a chair at another. I felt like a pinball bouncing back and forth off the bumpers, and I rejoiced when, finally, I collided with the trunk of a brand new sedan – because I distinctly recalled that the floor models always faced the front entrance.

"Almost there!"

I lugged the fire extinguisher with my left arm, and my right hand felt its way along the autonomous car, leading our bedraggled convoy to the front of the vehicle. There appeared to be fewer flames surrounding us, but a noticeably thicker cloud of black smoke ahead made for one last, formidable obstacle. And then a troubling thought hit me: if I was wrong that the car was pointed at the front entrance, then we'd undoubtedly be disoriented as we ran out of precious time. *Trust yourself; no second-guessing now, Em.*

I took my right hand off the car's hood and into the void, one foot immediately in front of the other. Without a wall, desk, or car to guide me, each step proved to be a balancing act between caution and speed. After my tenth step, the doubt started to creep in again. It only ceased when I looked up to see the glass ceiling of the showroom atrium meet the front windows roughly ten yards ahead of me. *Holy shit. We're going to make it out of here alive.* No longer required to walk like I was performing a field sobriety test, I lunged toward the entrance, desperate for the chance to breathe fresh air again. Then it appeared. After what felt like an impossibility, the front door had finally materialized. I'd almost decided that I might have been hallucinating from the smoke inhalation, but the door indeed opened to the outside world. I held it open for the rest of the women before doubling over into another coughing fit, violent enough that my breathing constricted substantially. I dropped the heavy fire extinguisher onto the cement.

"You okay?" Alice asked.

After a desperation heave, the mucus exited my lungs in the form of what could only be described as a giant loogie. I tried once again to inhale a deep breath, but failed; it felt like I was suffocating.

"Short breaths. Nice and easy," said a voice I couldn't immediately place.

As I worked to calm myself and listen to the advice, the insatiable feeling of catching my breath was a relief. I looked up to see that it was Detective Copeland comforting me.

"Where the fuck is the fire department?" Courtney asked.

"They're on their way," Detective Copeland replied.

"What's taking them so long? We can't just let it burn to the ground!"

Courtney went to pick up the discarded fire extinguisher but struggled with its weight.

"Alice, help me!"

"No."

"What do you mean, 'no?'"

"I'm not going back in there."

"It's our legacy. I won't let it go up in flames."

"I will."

"Fine, is everyone else going to just stand there, too?"

Still doubled over, I glanced up to find Alice, Eva, Margret, and the detectives standing in a semi-circle around Courtney, who was attempting to drag the fire extinguisher back to the entrance.

"Courtney, you're going to kill yourself," Alice said.

"Luke can't preside over ashes. Washington Ford is rightfully his now."

Shit. Courtney has no idea, does she?

"Wait, Courtney!" I yelled.

"Emily, thank you. Hurry up, we're running out of time."

"Put it down. You need to go to the hospital."

"I'm fine."

"The accident down the street. It was Luke."

Courtney dropped her flimsy grip on the fire extinguisher and got in my face just as I finally stood up straight.

"Is he okay?"

"Uh –"

"Is he okay?"

Courtney, eyes soaked in desperation, shook her head in disbelief. She already knew the answer.

"Tell me he's okay."

"I'm so sorry, Courtney."

Courtney's eyelids slightly fell before she adjusted her gaze toward the scene of the accident. In the distance, you could see the Washington Ford tow truck loading up a totaled vehicle. And then, Courtney took off running. Alice instantly followed and was there to console her when she dropped to the ground in agony. *More pain, pain caused by my father. Enough is enough.*

"Hey detective, you got a minute?"

M y dad's desperate charade to play the unflappable leader continued, as I saw him directing the fire engines down the fire lane
when they finally arrived. By that time, I had shown detectives
Copeland and Garcia all the evidence they needed to see for an arrest.
When they confronted him, I couldn't stand to be anywhere near him.
Instead, I hid like a coward behind a nearby parked car and watched, eyes
glued to my father's every move as he was being cuffed.

"What do you think you're doing?"

"Mr. Bridges, you're under arrest for the murder of Javier Perez."

"You're making a big mistake."

"You have the right to remain silent."

"Don't fuckin' read me my rights! I'm a lawyer, dammit. I know my
rights. My business is on fire, and you're wasting the city's resources on
falsely arresting me?"

A crowd of onlookers began to form around the quarrel as my father's
tirade became more exasperated.

"You'll both be fired come Monday morning, you hear me?"

Detective Garcia tightened the cuffs on my dad and gently guided
him toward their squad car.

"I demand that you show me your arrest warrant. No warrant? How
about your probable cause? I'm going to sue both of you for harassment."

I couldn't take any more of the farce. After the myriad of selfish acts
that had destroyed countless lives, he had the gall to deny his involvement.

"Hey, Dad!"

The eyes of the crowd turned to me as I stepped from the shadows
into the bright, almost debilitating sunlight. Without taking my gaze off
my father, I floated straight toward him.

"It was me, Dad. I gave them everything."

A flicker of hatred flashed briefly across his face, the same look that
I recognized from the photo taken just before he killed Javy.

"Why?"

"Because you taught me what's right and wrong, remember?"

He let out a single chuckle. Without uttering another word, he turned to face the squad car, ducking as Detective Garcia placed him into the back seat.

"I'm proud of you," Alice said as she joined me to watch my dad being driven away by the detectives.

"For what, betraying my father?" I muttered, in between my sniffles.

"It takes courage to do what you did. Do you know that we seriously debated in that office to take the money or not? I don't even want to admit what side I was on before you showed up."

I turned my attention to Alice, who pointed at the dealership behind me, now completely engulfed in flames. The firefighters, set for battle, descended anyway upon the lost cause.

"Ah, you would have come out on the honorable side, eventually."

"How can you be so sure?"

"We may be our fathers' daughters, but they can't define who we are. We get to make that choice on our own."

A few surprising moments of undisturbed tranquility passed. I couldn't speak for Alice, but for me, I felt an unimaginable level of catharsis watching Washington Ford burn. I threw one arm around my friend and held her close.

"I suppose it's fitting, isn't it?" Alice finally asked.

"How so?"

"Your dad had to kill mine for all of this to unfold."

"Hmm – " I started a thought aloud, then stopped.

"What?"

"I'm not so sure my dad killed Big Al."

"What makes you say that?"

Alice pulled away from our embrace and wiped her tears to examine the sincerity of my facial expression.

"When I confronted my dad about all of his terrible deeds, he only denied one thing: killing Big Al."

Alice, confused, paused for a few seconds before asking a version of the same question that had brought us together in the first place.

"Wait – who killed Big Al, then?"

THE DEATH

Big Al Washington

It will get better. It always works out in the end. Those were the words that Big Al Washington said to his wife, Elizabeth, on the drive for what turned out to be her final treatment for breast cancer in 1997. Those same words echoed in Big Al's thoughts on what proved to be his last drive to Washington Ford. Big Al had thought about those words almost every day since Elizabeth's untimely death. Over the years, he had convinced himself that those words had become nothing more than a hollow assurance that had violated Elizabeth's trust in him.

Instead of having time to cope with the grim diagnosis and say her proper goodbyes, Elizabeth must have felt blindsided when her condition quickly took a turn for the worse, despite Big Al's insistence that everything would be fine. She wanted so much to believe him. But, within a matter of days, she had died. In her final moments of consciousness, hysteria set in, as she realized her life was ending before she had time to come to terms with it. For Elizabeth Washington, everything did not work out in the end, and Big Al lived with that burden every day after the love of his life passed away.

Years later, as fate would have it, Big Al faced his own uphill battle against cancer. First diagnosed with stage III prostate cancer four years earlier, he underwent a grueling chemotherapy regimen that predictably caused the loss of his hair and stamina. What neither Big Al nor his doctors could predict, however, was the closure of his thirty-odd dealerships across the country as consumers transitioned away from owning cars. The entire cancer treatment and recovery experience – one he initially thought might help bring him closer to his late wife – ended up being nothing more than a series of harrowing events that made him question every consequential decision, both professional and personal, of his life. And now, after years of remission, as Big Al's cancer returned, so did his existential crisis.

The doctors suggested an aggressive treatment plan, involving a combination of chemotherapy and radiation therapy to combat the disease that had metastasized to his liver and bones. Knowing the toll it took on him the first go-round, Big Al elected against the debilitating treatment, choosing instead to live his last six months to a year on his terms. The most important of those terms included lying to his family about receiving treatment. In Big Al's eyes, he figured the pity would be just as threatening to his livelihood as the cancer. With whatever precious time Big Al had left on Earth, he pledged to make Washington Ford viable once again – or die trying.

The first month after the diagnosis, Big Al felt reinvigorated. He filmed a series of new "My 'dog' Teddy" commercials, schmoozed with city council members, gave interviews to reporters, and worked longer hours than he had in years. His optimism continued into the second month, despite a lack of customers. In the past, Big Al had famously – and somewhat ruthlessly – closed any of his dealerships that couldn't turn a profit for two straight months, his flagship location had become his blindspot. Over those two months, Big Al sunk nearly ten million dollars in advertising and renovation costs into his failing business. Even advice from his attorney and closest confidant, Larry Bridges, was quickly dismissed.

After the third month of bleeding cash, Big Al's frustration manifested into increasingly irrational decisions. When a news story ran that estimated he'd sold just under a million cars in his life, Big Al lowered the prices well below cost on every vehicle at his two remaining dealerships in order to reach the one million benchmark. In the process, he also put off his mentoring duties with Luke, his publicly named successor, insisting that he would "get to it later."

At first, no one in the family dared to question Big Al's reckless actions, for fear that any slight would be seen as cause for him to write someone out of the will. Instead, Washington family members bombarded Larry with their litany of concerns that their patriarch's erratic behavior could cost them their inheritance. Larry, who always had an open-door policy with the family, readily lent an ear. In turn, Larry leveraged the opportunity to gain critical insight into each member of the family. And what an earful he got. This was how he learned, for instance, that Eva was the only one with knowledge that Big Al had recently updated his will. And with the certitude that none of the other family members would stand up for Eva, the idea to use an outdated version of the will had been planted.

⌇

By the time Big Al walked into his dealership on the morning of his death, feeling a gamut of emotions, nearly five months had passed since he had decided against treatment. Where the diagnosis had initially given him newfound purpose and energy, with each passing business failure, Big Al had become more and more somnambulant.

Meanwhile, tensions had only risen between Big Al and his inner circle in the intervening months. Larry's unrelenting plea for a transition to autonomous cars fell on deaf ears; Luke failed to grasp the fundamental duties of running a business; Eva became indignant at the lack of time Big Al spent at home; and Courtney lashed out against her father for neglecting to train Luke. Famously stubborn, Big Al begrudgingly listened to his contingent's desperate pleas, promised he would do something about all of it, but never seriously entertained the notion of taking action. After all, he hadn't sold one million cars without the ability to blatantly lie to someone's face.

Knowing full well that the window of time his doctors had given him was coming to a close, Big Al struggled to think about anything other than his impending death. While the lazy sales staff and the improper commercial setup irked him, the real source of his anger that morning stemmed from his fear of death. Even after eighty-five years of life and two cancer diagnoses, Big Al had never had come to terms with his ultimate fate. Whenever the thought popped into his head, he'd sought any and every distraction. There was also the vivid memory of panic on his late wife's face in her waning moments, a scene had occasionally permeated Big Al's dreams over his illustrious life. But lately, the nightmare had become a regular occurrence – and, with no control over his subconscious, Big Al desperately clung to any sense of power he had left. The incessant micromanaging and lashing out at Washington Ford staff became emblematic of that desperation.The television crew there to shoot the new commercials that day saw it firsthand.

"Get...out...of...my...showroom. Now!"

"Sir, Mr. Washington told us to set up inside and..."

"Don't you know who I am?"

"Yes, but Mr. Washington said... "

"I AM MR. WASHINGTON! Look around! It's my face up there! And on that poster! And that sign!"

Big Al had pointed to the massive interior wall of the showroom, projecting the greatest hits of commercials that he'd starred in over the years. The video, which he hadn't taken the time to properly watch in who knows how long, provoked a sense of pride. *I sold a million cars because of those commercials.*

And then, Big Al remembered why he hadn't taken the time to re-watch those commercials that made him famous: he felt like a fraud every time he saw them. The truth was that he stole the idea for the "My 'dog' Teddy" commercials decades ago from a struggling Kansas City TV salesman named Bob Lambert, after flipping through channels at a roadside motel on a late winter's night. The ad featured Bob, in a cowboy hat, and his cat named Jack inside his small TV repair and resale shop. As Bob highlighted his low prices on TVs, Jack – who was, in reality, a racoon – wreaked havoc on the store. The commercial even ended with the same "If You're Happy And You Know It" jingle, only with altered lyrics: "If you want a better picture, go see Bob; for the lowest money down, go see Bob – go see Bob, go see Bob." Years after he stole the concept and expanded his dealerships across the country, Big Al received a letter from Bob. The moment Big Al saw the Kansas City return address on the envelope, he knew that its contents would not be friendly. A split second later, the letter ended up in the waste bin, unopened.

Typically, Big Al did not dwell on the past; in fact, he had a go-to quip for that weakness: "Ifs, ands, and Peter Pans." However, without much of a future to look forward to, the past consumed him. First, the memory of his late wife's painful death and now, a reminder of his fraudulent beginnings plagued his thoughts.

"We have a problem," Larry interrupted.

Upon hearing that Chad, his finance officer, had embezzled hundreds of thousands of dollars, Big Al was forced to shift his focus to the present. But, before he could deal with the Chad situation, he'd reached into his inner jacket pocket for his flask full of whiskey. For the majority of Big Al's life, he was a self-described casual drinker – a glass or two of scotch on the weekend type guy. But recently, as his cancer spread and subsequent pain accelerated, drinking had become part of his daily routine.

Once inside his office, Big Al found Chad, with his contrasting-collar button-up disheveled, lying on the outdated carpet in the middle of the room, beaten to a bloody pulp.

"What have you done?" Big Al asked his grandson.

"What have *I* done? Why don't you ask Chad what *he* did?"

"Listen, Luke. I know what Chad did. But that doesn't mean you can just beat the living shit out of him. The face of the company doesn't get his hands dirty."

"But Grandpa, he stole hundreds of thousands of dollars. He can't get away with that!"

Big Al slowly moved closer to Chad to inspect his condition more thoroughly, taking extreme precautions not to step in the blood pooling on the carpet with his cowboy boots. He knelt, as best as he could for an eighty-five-year-old man dying of cancer, to discover Chad's face was nearly unrecognizable – oozing pus, swelling bruises, and open gashes. And yet, Chad was somehow still breathing. Big Al shifted his attention back to Luke. *He isn't the one, Al. You can't put him in charge after this mishap.*

"Now listen to me, Luke. You need to go home now. Don't worry about the commercial."

"The commercial? This man stole from us, and you're worried about a commercial?"

"See, Luke, this is why you'll never make it. A true leader is proactive, not reactive. You have zero vision, boy. I'm pulling the plug on your big promotion. It's over."

"What? I did this for you. I do everything for you."

"Just go home. I'll have Larry fix it."

With that, Big Al turned his back on Luke as he exited the office. In the hallway, Big Al felt a sharp pain in his chest, and grimaced as he attempted to catch his balance. *Fuck. Am I having a heart attack? Is this how it's going to end, Al? Everything you've built will be destroyed by the people you've entrusted with the most responsibility to save it.* His stumble inadvertently knocked a framed photo off the wall; it was the one of him riding a killer whale at SeaWorld, who doubled as his "dog" Teddy for one of his more popular commercials. But paralyzed by the pain, Big Al didn't even seem to notice the sound of the picture crashing to the floor, or the glass shattering.

Now standing awkwardly against the wall, Big Al closed his eyes and inhaled through his nose to calm his nerves. *You still have some time. There's always stories on the news about how people overcame the odds after the doctor gave them six months to live. Why can't that be me?* Just then, Big Al's eyes flared open as if he had just received a shot of adrenaline. When he regained his composure, he straightened his bolo tie and set off again toward the main showroom, where Larry immediately intercepted him.

"Are you okay, boss? You don't look so hot."

"I'm fine. Did you take care of the production crew?"

"Of course. And they are setting up the exterior shot as we speak."

"This was supposed to be a monumental day, Larry. Now, look at it."

"I'll clean it up. You and Eva should get out of here."

"Not yet. Luke is a complete disaster. He can't take over for me, Larry. I'm going to shoot the commercial myself."

"Are you sure, boss? I can reschedule."

"I'm sure. It's like riding a bike – or selling a car, in my case. You just take care of the Chad situation."

A glint came to Larry's eyes as he silently strategized and quickly formulated a plan for what to do with Chad. After confirming again that Big Al felt well enough to continue, Larry darted away to the back office, rather than bother Big Al with the details. Even in a moment of chaos, Big Al stopped for a moment to appreciate Larry's unquestioned loyalty.

Walking out of the showroom, Big Al felt a rush of blinding light penetrating his cataracts. He squinted to avoid the sunlight, catching a glimpse of his impatient wife sticking her head out the passenger window just fifteen yards in front of him.

Realizing he couldn't face Eva in his current state of distress, he'd enlisted Madison the receptionist to cause a distraction. As Madison engaged Eva in small talk, Big Al skipped toward the rows of cars, hoping that the television crew had enough time to set up the shot.

"All right. Let's shoot this thing!" Big Al shouted.

"What about the other guy?"

"He's out. It's just me now. Are you ready?"

The director shrugged her shoulders and signaled to her crew to get the camera rolling, as if to say, 'Whatever it takes to finish the shoot from Hell as soon as possible.' Big Al dismissed the makeup artist's attempt to freshen up his face. After a minute of prepping the camera, the operator signaled that he was ready to shoot, prompting the director to yell, "Action!"

"Hey friends, Big Al here, we've got acres and acres and acres, rows after rows after rows of cars and trucks on sale out here."

Big Al made a sweeping motion to the cars directly behind him.

"Here's a beautiful Ford Fusion, and here's a top safety rated Ford Escape. Drive it home today with zero money down!"

As Big Al glanced toward the inventory, he discovered that the cars in the shot didn't have sticker prices on them.

"Son of a bitch! Where are the prices?"

"That's a cut. Who has eyes on the sticker prices?"

"Forget it. Just take them from the other cars. I don't give a shit."

"Copy that."

Sweat began to bubble atop Big Al's forehead. In an attempt to regain his composure, he leaned against a Ford Fiesta, and fanned the bill of his hat in front of his face. By the time the production assistant corralled a stack of giant green stickers, Big Al felt stable enough to place them on the cars in the shot.

"Picture's up!"

"And action."

"Wait a damn minute. I'm not ready yet."

"No worries. Take your time. Whenever you're ready, Mr. Washington."

Big Al shook his head in disbelief, but he was a true professional and had overcome worse shoots before. *All right. Focus on the task at hand and then you'll figure out the rest. At least I don't have a snake trying to strangle me this time.* Big Al got in position, took a deep breath, and looked directly into the camera.

"Hey friends, Big Al here! We've got rows after acres – no, that's not right."

"No worries. We're still rolling. Go ahead."

"Hey friends, Big Al here! We've got acres and acres and acres, row after row after row of Ford trucks and cars."

Just then, Big Al felt a shortness of breath. The morning breeze vanished, and without a cloud in the sky, the sun relentlessly beat down on Big Al. *It will pass. Control your breathing, Al.* He felt compelled to continue.

"I ain't going no place, hell, I've been here for forty-six years, so come on down and tell them...tell them Big Al sent you."

"And cut. Are you feeling all right, Mr. Washington?"

"Yeah, I'm fine. I could use some water, that's all. This damn heatwave is getting to me."

"Can somebody get Mr. Washington some water?"

Big Al opened the door to the nearest car, which happened to be a black Ford Escape, and ducked into the driver's seat to catch his breath. As he watched the crew scramble for water, he hoped no one noticed as his entire body started shaking. *If – and that is a big if – I miraculously finish this commercial, then I'll be rushed to the ER, where I'll undoubtedly die in a hospital bed within a matter of days, if not hours. No, fuck that – I'm dying on my terms.*

He'd hatched his plan when Brenda, his executive assistant, found her boss weeping at his desk on a late summer evening, about a month back. After decades of building trust, they both readily confided in one another about their respective cancer diagnoses. For the first time since his fatal sentence, Big Al felt a sense of relief, finally able to talk to someone about the dark cloud hanging over him every moment of the day. And that evening, although she didn't realize it, Brenda shared a story that would determine Big Al's fate.

Brenda had an uncle who also battled prostate cancer and, like so many cancer journeys, he had fought the agonizing cycle for years: diagnosis, treatment, remission and then, a simple checkup that would start the exhausting process all over again.

"My Uncle Greg, a husband and father of two teenage boys, emptied his life's savings on his previous round of chemo, and he knew that if he went for another round of treatment, he would go into unmanageable debt. Shit out of luck, right? But, no Uncle Greg had a notion to take matters into his own hands. See, as a teacher, the school district granted him a half-million-dollar life insurance policy. Problem was that after his latest diagnosis, he couldn't work – and after his unpaid sick leave ended, the school district would terminate his employment."

Brenda continued, her tone solemn but matter-of-fact. "That's when he turned to a family friend – Dr. Chakrabarti, a professor and cancer researcher at the University of North Carolina at Charlotte. This doctor supplied my uncle with a drug commonly used to combat prostate cancer. A drug called Xofigo, right? But, like any drug, a concentrated dose will kill someone. So, a week before the school district was set to terminate my uncle, he started the new treatment that he couldn't afford. He went into the facility to get his intravenous injection. Then he went home, enjoyed one final ice-cold beer, before injecting himself with the lethal dose of the same drug, in the exact spot as earlier in the day. He died in his kitchen a few minutes later, with his medical debts erased and his family a half-million dollars richer."

A long pause ensued as Big Al digested the story.

"Was it painful?" Big Al asked.

Sitting in the Ford Escape, Big Al reached into his right cowboy boot for a small, amber-colored vial. When he'd first stuck it in his boot a couple weeks earlier, it reminded him of walking around with a pebble in a shoe, only slightly less aggravating – *a small price to pay to die with some dignity intact.*

A knock on the car window interrupted Big Al's train of thought. He jumped in his seat as he attempted to hide the vial from view. The same production assistant that had hand-delivered the price stickers offered him a bottle of water. Big Al waited until the production assistant had walked out of sight, then unscrewed the caps on both the water bottle and vial of poison. The moment that he mixed the two, his breathing became labored, almost asthmatic. Without thinking, Big Al chugged three-fourths of his concoction before removing the bottle from his lips. Scowling at the unrefreshing temperature and taste, he could barely finish the last gulp without spitting out its contents. Figuring he drank a sufficient amount, he discarded the water bottle and vial underneath his seat before leaning back for a moment of rest.

As thoughts of regret and panic set in, Big Al tried his damndest to remember the good times. Nonetheless, he was dismayed to find that the unpleasant memories endured. *You are a good man. You led a good life – no, that's bullshit, and you know it. I should call Alice. Why didn't I reconcile with her? Because you're a piece of shit, Al. That's why. You've always been a piece of shit. Worst of all, you lied to your dying wife, the love of your life, when she needed to hear the truth. Elizabeth never got the chance to come to terms with her death because of you.*

Now barely able to control his breathing, Big Al loosened his bolo tie and removed his cowboy hat from his head to collect a trail of sweat beneath his thinning hairline. Finally, he stood, unbuttoned the top of his shirt and returned his hat to its rightful home.

"All right. Third time's a charm."

"You heard the man. Roll camera. Roll sound."

"Camera speeds."

"Sound speeds."

The production assistant struck the clapperboard as Big Al stumbled to his mark.

"Washington Ford, take three."

"Whenever you're ready, Mr. Washington."

Big Al paused for a second to admire his lot. *Well, this is it; this is the only thing you have to show for your life, Al. No family by your side. Just a fucking building on a piece of concrete, and cars as far as your legally blind eyes can see.* With another deep breath, he temporarily regained his composure, until a familiar thought entered his mind. *It will get better. It always works out in the end.* Big Al grimaced at the mantra that he once told his dying wife, then fixed his gaze on the camera lens and managed a wan smile.

"Hey friends, Big Al here and boy, do I have a deal for you..."

At that exact moment, he experienced an agonizing jolt, a pain so violent that it sent shockwaves through his entire body. His towering frame bent at the knees and descended to the unforgiving pavement. Just as he landed, Big Al's head whipped back, striking the hard surface, which caused a stream of blood to gush from his skull.

Big Al Washington died by suicide at 11:26 a.m. on July 3, 2028.

THE END

About the Author

Collin Brantmeyer lives in Colorado with his wife and son.
Death of a Car Salesman is his first novel.
If it's also his last...well, then something went horribly wrong.
Send help.

CPSIA information can be obtained
at www.ICGtesting.com
Printed in the USA
BVHW081041071020
590511BV00007B/94/J